Elkan

C.J. Kline

Dedicated to our dad. You are missed.

Jesus Christ is the same yesterday, today, and forever.
– Hebrews 13:8

Chapter One

*No one needed to tell him about human nature, for he
knew what was in each person's heart. – John 2:25*

The mountains provided a spectacular backdrop to a
near perfect day. Syene sat on top of the grassy hill watching
below in the small valley. This place with its tranquil beauty
had been her haven, but also her nightmare. She glanced
toward the dense trees surrounding the canyon, and a cold
shiver ran over her body. Her mind raced back to the day she
had sat here watching everyone train for their first battle. She
had been so naïve then, not realizing the power of the evil
hunting her. That day seemed so long ago. Her mother was
alive then, and Syene's heart still ached for her.

*Two and a half years ago . . . that doesn't seem
possible.* She shook her head in disbelief.

Syene would give anything to have her mom here with
them, for her to see her beautiful grandchild. Syene smiled as
she watched him play and laugh. Ariel was chasing him
through the tall wild flowers with Wesley not far behind,
barking loudly. Elkan's squeals rang off the mountains as he
yelled in delight for Ariel to stop. He adored Syene's younger
sister and had her mischievous spirit. If he ever wasn't with
Syene, he could be found following Aunt Ariel around.

Ariel bent over to scoop him in her arms.

"Stop? What do you mean stop? You've been bugging
me all morning to play with you." She blew on his neck,

making his laughter blossom again, and then swung him high in her arms.

Syene felt a gentle touch on her shoulder. She turned her gaze upward to find Jamille standing behind her. Jamille's striking beauty always surprised Syene. After all this time she never grew tired of the angel's glory.

"Elkan is beautiful, Syene. I had no idea how much I would love him. He has touched everyone's heart and soul." Jamille knelt as tears stung Syene's eyes. "I feel your sorrow, Sacred. Please release your pain. You cannot live in the past. He is your future. He is our future."

Syene leaned into Jamille, feeling the comfort and warmth of her angelic protector.

"I know, I know. I can't help but miss my mom. I want her with me so badly. And I know we must leave here eventually. How am I going to keep our beautiful Elkan safe until he is able to take care of himself?"

"We are here, we will keep him safe." Jamille kissed her softly on her cheek.

"But what about today, Jamille? Everyone is blaming him for that man dying. He was out of his mind screaming at Elkan and me. I can't stop Elkan from doing what he has been sent to do. You heard about the reaction of everyone in the store. They were terrified. People are not ready for him."

Jamille didn't try to hide her concern. Syene had become much wiser than her age. Jamille hadn't been with them at the grocery store when the incident had occurred, but several of the other angels reported the same thing. The gasps and the terrified looks on everyone's face could easily be imagined.

"Yahweh will provide a way, Sacred."

Syene shook her head. "I'm not so sure." Her faith was sliding.

Elkan stopped playing with Ariel to look up the hill at his mother. Syene made eye contact, and her son spoke to her—without words. It could be unnerving when he did it. To have her two-year-old silently communicate with her on an almost-adult level could be too much sometimes. So far, it seemed to be only her he did this with, other than with the angels, of course. Syene was grateful he didn't do it often. She looked away, breaking the contact. The memory of his birth flooded back.

****

The phone slipped from her hand as the pain tore through her body. She felt her legs giving out beneath her as she fell forward. The cryptic text from Amy was forgotten. Father Cervini rushed to catch her, but Jamille beat him there. Syene collapsed into Jamille's arms as the angel scooped her up, leaving a pool of liquid on the floor where Syene had stood. Syene's water had broken. It was time. Jamille went into command mode.

"Lizzy, go make sure the bed is ready, and make sure we have plenty of clean towels and linens. The baby is coming."

Lizzy nodded with a look of shock on her face and dashed off. Ariel and Julie were by Jamille's side within seconds. Julie began barking orders along with Jamille,

"Get some fresh water in the glass bowls and bring them to the room." Everyone sprang into action. They had all planned and practiced for this moment, but now that the birth was here, the atmosphere was thick with urgency.

Dave and Daniel had gone into town for supplies. Samuel seemed to be stuck in his spot with a frightened look on his face. Ariel's voice brought him back to reality.

"Sam! Stop standing there like a statue. Move! Go alert the angels that the baby is coming. Shut all the curtains, and call Dave on his cell phone and tell him to get back here!" Ariel was one hundred percent in control. She wasn't going to let anything happen to her sister or the baby.

"I'm right here, Sy. You're going to be okay. Grandma is here too. Can you hear me?"

Syene wanted to answer, but she couldn't make the words come out. Her sister and everyone else sounded so far away. Like she was under water. The pain was awful, and the only thing she could hear clearly was Hebrew being spoken. It was exploding in her head. She didn't know if it was God or the

baby speaking. Or both. It was too much. She silently screamed
for them to be quiet. It was piercing her ears.

The pain, with racking waves of nausea, seared through
her body. She could feel her grandma holding her hair back as
she vomited. There was nothing beautiful about this experience,
and Syene wanted her mother. She must have screamed for her.
Ariel rushed to her side. Syene could only hear her muffled
voice.

"Mom's not here, Sy. Please, you must push. The baby
needs your help. I'm here with you. Push, Sy. Push"

The Hebrew only got louder. Syene couldn't take it
anymore. She wanted to die. She could feel herself slipping
away, losing consciousness. Maybe this was it. She could be
with her mom and dad. She wanted it to be over. A dozen
colors exploded in her head. She remembered nothing after
that.

****

A small hand touched her face. Syene looked down at
her beautiful Elkan. She gently smiled at her son and pulled
him onto her lap. She could see the worry in his innocent
sapphire eyes. Squeezing him tightly she gave him a kiss and
whispered softly, "Everything is going to be okay." Syene
wanted so badly to believe this herself. For Elkan this seemed
to be all he needed. He hugged her neck and dashed off to play
with two of the angels standing nearby. They welcomed him
with joyous laughter.

Ariel climbed up the hill to where Syene still sat with Jamille. She settled close, right next to her sister.

"It's going to be okay, Sy. That guy in the store deserved what Elkan did to him. He was crazy."

"It isn't that, Ariel. And why is everyone assuming Elkan is responsible? Isn't it possible there was something else responsible for what happened? You should have seen how everyone looked at Elkan. They were scared to death. I thought they were going to try to snatch him from my arms."

Ariel laughed and used her best southern accent to make Syene laugh. "Well, that'd have been such a sight. God's army descendin' on the local town folk. Ain't no one gonna snatch our Elkan."

Syene smiled. "Town folk, Ariel? That is a terrible attempt at an accent. I know you are trying to make me feel better, but what happened in the store was terrifying."

Ariel sighed. "I know you are scared, Sy, but Elkan is going to be okay. God is not going to let anyone snatch him from your arms. We need to leave here at some point. Too many sad memories. Too many things lurking in the forest. We need a change."

Jamille's voice came from behind. "She is right, Syene. This is the Creator's plan. Not yours or ours. We cannot keep Elkan hidden forever.

As if on cue, Michael appeared and walked toward them. His immense beauty and presence took Syene's breath away every time. The Archangels were especially magnificent, and Michael was their leader.

She held up her hand to him as she stood. "I know, I know. You don't have to tell me."

Michael did not look pleased. "What were you thinking by allowing this encounter to occur?"

"Me? You're blaming me for this?" The blood rushed to her cheeks with her anger. "How about we blame the rotten creep in the store!"

Michael softened slightly. "It doesn't matter now. It is done. The town is rippling with the gossip. Most don't believe it, but many do." He paused glancing over at Elkan. "He won't be safe here forever, Sacred."

Elkan caught Michael staring at him and ran for him at full speed. The giant angel swept the child into the air with genuine love. Elkan went flying, screaming with laughter. Michael flew up to catch him as he came down.

Syene's stomach dropped every time Michael did this. She yelled after them, "Michael, don't go that high with him!"

It was too late, they were off and soaring above the tree line. She could hear her child's voice echoing through the valley. Syene could only smile. She knew Elkan couldn't be safer than when he was with Michael.

****

On the side of the mountain range he stood watching, cloaked and hidden by the shadows of the setting sun. He would wait patiently before his next attack, and they would belong to him. Safety was only an illusion.

Chapter Two

Such things were written in the Scriptures long ago to teach us. And the Scriptures give us hope and encouragement as we wait patiently for God's promises to be fulfilled. – Romans 15:4

Egypt – Four Years Later – Present Day

Thomas Cain watched his boss, Dr. Robert Kaufman, look at archaeological samples intensely through his microscope. He had no idea why the doctor had picked this location. Of all the places they could be, why here in the western desert of Egypt? The window air-conditioning unit was struggling to keep the trailer cooled, but the heat did not seem to faze the doctor.

Thomas fanned himself with his notebook and was beginning to question his decision to work with Dr. Kaufman. He knew without a doubt the doctor was probably the most brilliant man he had ever known, a world-renowned scientist and expert on historical artifacts, but he thought the doctor's obsession with Biblical stories was somewhat insane. After all, Thomas had given up a decently paid research position in the United States, and now he wanted to document empirical evidence that mattered to history and not chase childhood fairytales. Thomas was not a believer in the Bible, he was a historian. And right now he wanted to get out of this hot, miserable, desolate location.

The only good thing about this place was Laura Wilson, a young college graduate who had been with Dr. Kaufman for two years. Thomas caught sight of her through the small, dirty glass window positioned over his cluttered workstation. She stood at the dig site, speaking to some locals they had hired to help. Even in the sweltering heat she managed to look beautiful, with a huge hat that hid her dark auburn hair and protected her fair skin from the harsh desert sun. She was motioning with her hand to a group for them to move to a new area where excavation had just begun. Laura made the days bearable for Thomas.

Dr. Kaufman must have heard the deep sigh come from his assistant, and he looked up from the microscope.

"What is it, Thomas?"

The doctor stood, stretching his back and removing his glasses. His dank silver hair was a mess, and it made him look the part of the mad scientist.

"You sound like an old furnace when you make those noises. It disrupts my thoughts."

Thomas fumbled over his words. "Sorry, Dr. Kaufman. I didn't realize I was doing it." He could feel Kaufman's grey eyes staring right through him.

"Well, speak up. It does not matter if you realize it, what matters is you do it. I cannot ignore the fact that something bothers you. This space is too small, and the days too long."

Thomas could not look at Dr. Kaufman directly, and his cheeks felt hot with embarrassment. "I just"—he sighed deeply again—"I just don't understand why we are here. This place is miserably hot, and I can't see that we have found anything of interest or merit."

Kaufman placed his glasses back on and rubbed his neck. "What makes you say that?"

Thomas scratched his head nervously. "I don't understand this obsession with the Bible when so much is out there. Real things to be discovered."

"Thomas, it is time to let you in on what my project truly is. I must do everything I can to protect what I have found, until it can be fully tested, verified, and then retested again. I can't release my findings yet; I would be a buffoon in the scientific community. But if I am right, then what I have found will change the world."

He stood and walked to the window to look at the site where it all began.

"I am usually decent at observing people, and I think it is safe to say that you do not believe in God. Am I correct?"

Thomas didn't hesitate this time when he answered. "Sir, you are correct. I'm sorry if that offends you, but I just can't buy into all of it. There is no solid proof."

Kaufman frowned. "There was a time in my life when I felt that exact way. But I started to wonder if there was something more. Maybe it was me approaching old age and worrying about my own eternal life. Maybe it was hearing my mother calling me from the past to believe in Yahweh. Nevertheless, I became fascinated with Christianity. I just could not believe one man, Jesus Christ, could cause a mass hallucination for thousands of people, nor could I accept He had never existed. Either conclusion seemed impossible with the fact His teachings are still in constant use today."

Kaufman began to slowly pace the narrow pathway in the trailer, the only space not cluttered with books and tagged items from their dig. "During my search for some type of truth, I came across an article that mentioned a study done based on the science of probability. It set out the odds of any one man in all of history fulfilling even eight of the prophecies written about a coming Messiah. There is a one in a trillion chance to fulfill eight of the Old Testament prophecies. Jesus Christ, if real, which you and many others argue against, managed to fulfill over three hundred of them. The mass hallucination theory almost seemed as equally unbelievable to me as the theory of nonexistence. So I set out on a quest. A quest to prove or disprove Jesus Christ existed and walked the earth as a man of flesh."

"Okay, but it still doesn't explain why we are here wasting our time. Nor does any of this prove Jesus was a man who walked among us. I hate to sound rude, but do you seriously believe in all this Bible garbage?" He stared at his mentor, hoping he hadn't upset the doctor, but he needed some answers. "I have meant no disrespect, sir." He pointed his finger toward the floor of the trailer. "But, why are we here, Dr. Kaufman? Right now, in this place where I am standing? I don't understand what we are searching for."

The doctor sat back down on his stool and looked at Thomas with honesty. "To answer your question, yes, I do believe in all this Bible garbage."

Thomas's cheeks burned, and this time he knew it wasn't from the desert heat.

Kaufman continued. "But I am a scientist, and if the truth be told, I began this journey more to disprove Jesus's existence. Instead I found only truth." He looked at Thomas intently. "What would you say if I told you, I have evidence Jesus Christ was here on Earth, and everything they wrote about him was true? What do you think the entire world would say about this?"

Thomas didn't bother to conceal his surprise and skepticism. "That it better be damn good proof to make a claim like that." He paused. "Do you have proof?"

Kaufman chuckled. "Yes, you would most certainly be right about that; I better have damn good proof. To respond to your next question, yes, I believe I do have evidence."

Thomas shook his head in disbelief. "I still don't understand. I haven't seen one thing we have found pointing to a Messiah, or anything Biblical for that matter. I just don't see how it is possible."

"That's because you haven't seen the whole picture." Kaufman motioned him over to the table where his laptop sat. Thomas joined him and stared at the screen. He stared at pictures of what looked like to be very old handwritten scrolls.

"What are they? Latin?"

Kaufman smiled. "Yes, Latin with a little Greek worked into it."

"I didn't do very well in my Latin classes, sir. You're going to have to give me some help."

The doctor grabbed the other stool and had Thomas sit next to him.

"You are looking at the writings of the Roman soldier, Cassius. He was living and breathing during the time of Jesus. Not only was he alive during this time, but he was physically there in Jerusalem before and during the trial of Jesus Christ. He was an officer to be exact, and he had a very brief but life-changing moment with the Messiah. What happened between Jesus and Cassius in this very short time frame changed this soldier's life. Enough for him to flee from everything and everyone he knew." Thomas could feel the doctor's fervor that he understand the importance of who Cassius was and how he risked his life to write these scrolls.

"Thomas, Cassius was a centurion, what would be considered a captain in today's army. He most likely had moved up in the ranks for his ability to read and write, plus, of course, his skills and bravery in combat. He had much to lose from these documents."

Thomas couldn't hide his shock. He shook his head. "That's not possible. Even I know there is no Roman evidence of Jesus. Not even the disciples' writings indicate there to be a sympathetic Roman officer during those final hours in the life of Jesus. If the Biblical writings are correct, the Roman officials could have cared less about Jesus, other than he was a nuisance to them."

Dr. Kaufman smiled. "You are partially correct in your statements, but what if a huge piece of the puzzle went missing?"

Thomas shrugged, uncertain what to think or say.

"Now let me tell you what I believe happened." Thomas scooted closer, enthralled with the story.

"Pontius Pilate and the Romans did care. Pilate recognized the frenzy within the city he was to have control over. He knew of the uproar when King Herod ordered the beheading of John the Baptist, and whether he believed it or not, Pilate knew there was something different about this man they were calling the Messiah." He now had Thomas's full attention. "Pilate wanted nothing to happen to Jesus on his watch or by his hands. Not without the . . ." He paused. "Let's say not without the blessing of the people. So, he called upon the best of the Roman army to watch over the city before and during the proceedings of Jesus."

15

Kaufman walked back to a shelf and grabbed a book, handing it to Thomas. "When the order came concerning Jesus—and we all know how it ended—Pilate knew the masses would rebel."

Thomas nodded, captured by Kaufman's words.

"It is theorized in this book, and by many theologians, that a direct order came from the Roman Empire to execute all Romans involved in the mess that was the trial of Jesus Christ. A rebellion of the people was exploding in Jerusalem, and those in power had some covering up to do." Kaufman waved toward the stack of books against the wall. "I poured over every piece of Roman history, Biblical and non-Biblical, I could find. I spent a year visiting some of the best and most well-respected professors of history and theology in the world, asking any question I could think of on how such a situation would have been handled by the Roman and Jewish officials, and if it would have been possible to erase such an important piece of history."

Thomas was listening intently when the doctor paused. "What did they tell you? Could the individuals involved be wiped out by their own leaders?"

Dr. Kaufman nodded his head. "All of the scholars agreed on that one thing, yes, it would have been possible to exterminate not only the individuals involved, but their families as well, and do it very easily." He swirled around on his stool and grabbed a book from the stack on the floor. "Of course, at the time, they had no idea they were about to perform a cover-up that would change the world. They were concealing the murder of the Son of God, and as we know from history, the cover-up did not work. His teachings still reached the masses, and they spread like wildfire."

"I still don't understand how all of that led you here."

The doctor handed him the book he grabbed from the stack, *Training of an Ancient Roman Soldier*. "I read this book fifteen times to find insight." Thomas creased his forehead in confusion. The doctor answered before he could ask. "The training of a military Roman officer was nonstop—intense physical and mental training. I kept thinking to myself how, if true, could all those highly trained soldiers be taken by surprise and murdered. Wouldn't at least one of them be smart enough to survive?

"And that is exactly what happened! Our man, Cassius, was smarter than the rest, and he had the warning from his personal one-on-one time with Jesus Christ. He documents all of it. Every moment and every word spoken to him by Christ. Cassius fled the city of Jerusalem and he hid. He hid here." The doctor pointed down. "Right here, in this very spot where you and I are sitting. Cassius fervently wrote pages upon pages of documentation, a task you and I both know was not easy. He would have been paying a high monetary price for someone to bring him ink and papyrus, risking his identity by doing so.

You can see the hurriedness in his writing, he was obviously in grave danger."

Thomas glanced at the writings that were still on the screen of the laptop and could see the handwriting did indeed look rushed, but to assume these were contemporaneous writings because of this was ridiculous. He could not dispute the facts of how difficult this would have been for a man in hiding, but he could dispute why a highly educated Roman officer would put his life in danger to document these claims. "I'm sorry, sir, my passion has always been digging up military artifacts. I am a historian, I never spent much time reading the Bible or anything I felt irrelevant. Only a select few of Roman soldiers could have accomplished this, since most were illiterate. These are more likely a hoax created by a fanatical Christian believer."

Kaufman nodded. "I too was once like you. I never believed in anything I couldn't prove. I needed proof of science."

Thomas nodded his head in agreement as the doctor continued. "Yes, I need proof, most people do. The Bible always seemed to me a book full of folklore and legends."

Kaufman smiled. "Many have theorized Jesus was a fictitious character, just as they have said many of the people in the Bible are fictitious, but nevertheless Jesus is in the writings of Cassius. The Roman soldier knew they were going to find him. He wrote of the cover-up and of his comrades being murdered. He was scared and rightfully so. He left an amazing tale behind. Better than anything anyone has ever seen. Details of Biblical history that have been lost and buried under the sand. Pieces of the puzzle that have been missing for thousands of years. He wrote of the fate of mankind and things to come. Things that had been shown to him by Jesus in only moments. Moments, Thomas. Jesus touched him and revealed entire truths. Cassius had been carefully selected."

Thomas couldn't believe any of it. He sat shaking his head. "This can't be possible. These writings would have been found centuries ago. It must be a fake. Why would Jesus share this information with a Roman of all people and not one of his followers?"

Kaufman shrugged. "I don't know the answer, but I know what I found is truth. I studied and discussed and analyzed with my historian friends. Trying to put myself in the mindset of a panicked soldier, who was also a smart and savvy commander. How far could he travel in a day? What areas would have been considered safer than others for travel? Would he have had a horse? Was he on foot? This is not the first place I looked, by any means. I went on a hunch, or I suppose some would call it divine intervention, but I found my Cassius. And currently I have a very select few and trusted forensic scientists testing pieces of the writings. And none of them can disprove the authenticity. They all come back with the same time frame. The time of Jesus. The writings are real, Thomas. And I am going to make sure the world sees them."

"Where are they?"

"Somewhere safe. Only one other person besides myself, of course, knows the location. And that is the way it will remain until I decide it is time."

Thomas felt shell-shocked. The implications of finding something like this would be like finding Noah's Ark or the coveted Ten Commandments. So huge his mind couldn't even comprehend it. Dr. Kaufman could possibly prove God was real? And then the obvious question came.

"But won't everyone just try to disprove these, just like they have the other Biblical writings?"

Kaufman nodded. "Yes, of course, but for some reason Christ chose Cassius to share prophetic information of the future instead of sharing it with his disciples. So, to maybe answer your earlier question, Jesus knew only a trained soldier would be able to protect the information with his life. Or maybe the disciples were too emotionally vested to be given this kind of information. I don't really know."

"What did Jesus tell Cassius?" Even though Thomas said he didn't believe, he couldn't help but hope there really was a Savior they called Jesus.

At that moment, Laura burst through the door, her face flushed from the heat.

"Doctor, the boy from town, Ishil, brought me some news. You said you wanted to hear of anything that was odd that had to do with a child. She held up a piece of paper. "

"What is it?" Kaufman could see her excitement.

Laura walked to the doctor's laptop. "May I?"

"Of course. Please."

Laura began typing in the information that she had written on the piece of paper. "Ishil set an automatic search on his computer to hit on any bizarre news stories related to a young boy." She glanced back at Kaufman and Thomas. "That kid's a genius, you should put him on your payroll." She laughed as she said it, but she was only partially teasing. "I really can't believe he found anything. He must have spent days looking through all the articles."

She stepped aside to let them see what appeared on the laptop. Kaufman and Thomas huddled around the screen to read the newspaper article with the headline:

UNEXPLAINABLE DEATH IN LOCAL GROCERY STORE

After reading the article, Dr. Robert Kaufman stood and looked at his two young assistants. The article was almost four years old, but he had a feeling and pulling at his core. He had to follow his inner voice.

"Pack your bags. We have a mother and child to find."

****

Jerusalem – One month before the crucifixion of Jesus

Cassius stepped into the courtyard, watching as his daughter played and his beautiful Alypia held their newborn son. Alypia was his love, his lifeline. He loved her the moment he saw her ten years prior. It had been her eyes that captivated him. Their piercing color reminded him of the sea, and his home in Caesarea. He missed their home, but Alypia and his daughter seemed to have adjusted well. Jerusalem would be their new home for now, while Cassius undertook special duties. His career had been one of honor. He worked his way through the ranks and was now a chief Centurion. He had done well, but he was not happy with his new assignment. Jerusalem was filled with mysteries and unrest.

"What is it, love?" Alypia's voice called him back from his thoughts. He smiled and walked to her.

"Nothing, my exquisite." He leaned down to kiss her and rub the head of his infant son.

"You're a bad liar, Cassius. I can see it on your face, you are worried. Tell me what troubles you."

"Do not fret over my worries, Alypia. I am only ready to finish this assignment and be back home."

Alypia touched his face. "I like it here. The culture fascinates me."

He laughed. "Of course, you do. Your desire for knowledge is going to get you in trouble or, most certainly, get me in trouble."

"Nothing you can't handle."

"We will see if Pilate feels differently."

"Sabina," he called to his daughter, "come give your father a hug before I leave." Sabina raced over and leapt into his arms. She kissed his cheek and immediately squirmed from his grasp. She had her mother's eyes and had stolen his heart. He thanked the gods for his family. He didn't know what he had done to please them, but he was grateful for their gifts.

"I shouldn't be long. The Passover for the Jews will begin soon, and Pilate doesn't want any problems."

She raised her face for one more kiss. "We shall be here waiting. Love to you." Alypia always said this each time he left. No matter where he was going.

He smiled, leaning over to kiss her gently. "Love to you."

Chapter Three

Only fools say in their hearts, "There is no God."
– Psalm 14:1

Town of Spring Oak – Present Day

FBI Special Agent John Freely sat in the interview room with the local police chief. Both stared at the surveillance video from the grocery store.

"You tell me what the hell those are?" Chief Harris pointed to the screen in front of them.

Freely leaned in closer. "I have no clue. They look like wings? It has to be something on the lens or a reflection." Freely couldn't make sense of anything he was seeing. But recent events had brought him here to this small town to investigate a four-year-old cold case.

The chief shrugged his shoulders. "Let's say it is a weird reflection. Not one person reported seeing men that size. Those are big men—look at them compared to their surroundings. Something weird happened with the lighting, that's all. And why are the Feds suddenly interested in a case four years later?"

Freely ignored the chief. He didn't feel like he owed him an explanation. Instead he questioned Chief Harris for probably the tenth time. "You are positive that none of the witnesses mentioned seeing anyone like this in the store?"

Harris looked at the young agent, his exasperation obvious. "I just said this to you. I think I would have known if someone told me they saw two giants in the store. We may be a small department, Agent Freely, but we aren't a bunch of idiots. Everything is in the file I sent to you."

Freely shrugged. "Sorry, just had to ask." He stared at the monitor, his forehead creased. He could care less about offending Chief Harris. "I didn't see a copy of the autopsy report?"

Harris walked over to an old metal filing cabinet. It squeaked loudly when he pulled open one of the drawers. He pulled a brown file and carried it over to Freely, dropping it on the small desk. "Everything is in there. All the reports and interviews. I went down to the medical examiner's office myself when it happened to look at the body and take some pictures." He opened the file and pulled the pictures out. "The body looked like it had been charred on the inside. But from the outside it was perfectly normal." Harris slapped the pictures down in front of Freely. "Look for yourself."

Freely went through the pictures one by one. The exterior of the body looked untouched, but the inside was completely burnt. Internal combustion was what it looked like.

"How could this happen?"

He wasn't asking the Chief for an answer but talking to himself out loud, as he often did when he was working through a difficult case.

"Well, Mr. Freely, I am guessing you really are not looking for nor want my input." The Chief was clearly upset about his being there.

Freely rubbed his temples as he went through the file. He didn't care how mad the local police chief was, he was still not going to give Chief Harris an answer. He read and reread the statements given by the four witnesses. They all said the same thing. The child, estimated to be two or three years old, was speaking a language none of them understood as he approached the now-deceased Phil Reese. Mr. Reese fell to the ground, screaming and crying. The surveillance video confirmed everything. Except the two figures in the background. Not one person claimed to have seen these individuals in the store at the time of the incident. And they only appeared for a second and then seemed to vanish from the video.

"Does anyone know who the mother is? If she is the mother." Freely was hoping they had found her, since he couldn't find any reports mentioning her name.

"A few people in town know her, but she doesn't come around very often." The chief thumbed through the file and pulled out a report. "Her name is Syene Harper, here is a copy of the interview we conducted with her."

Freely frowned. "I didn't see this in the documents you sent to our department."

Harris gave no apology. "Not much there. She said she had no idea about any of it and that her son only approached the man out of curiosity because he was yelling and screaming. She said she grabbed him up, and they left the store immediately." He pointed to the screen. "You can see in the video this is exactly what happened. The boy never touched Mr. Reese. We didn't have any reason to keep questioning her."

Freely felt very annoyed with the Chief. "Except you didn't find it strange witnesses stated a toddler spoke a language they had never heard?"

Harris laughed. "You obviously don't have children, Freely. My grandchildren sound like they are from another planet half the time. And people in a small town like ours enjoy excitement when it happens. This sometimes causes some slight exaggeration and good ol' gossip."

Freely stood abruptly, closing the file in front of him. He had what he needed. "Thank you for your time, Chief. I'll let you know if I need anything else."

****

Special Agent Freely had been in law enforcement for fifteen years. He had a good reputation for solving mysterious cases, and he knew he was smart. There was always a logical reason for everything. He could feel the eyes of the locals on him as he walked down the sidewalk and headed to the grocery store. He wanted to see the crime scene, if it was a crime scene, for himself.

A woman stepped into his path, blocking his way. Her hair was pulled into a bun, wearing glasses too big for her face and holding onto a pad of paper and a pen.

"Agent Freely?" He wasn't excited to be stopped by this person. He was in a hurry and had a job to do.

"Who's asking?" He was hoping to make it clear that he was not in the mood.

"Hi, Rebekah Fabinski." She stuck out her hand. Freely shook it reluctantly. "You can call me Rebekah." She flashed him a smile. "I'm the reporter for the paper here. Are you here investigating the incident at the grocery store?"

Freely sighed, not in the mood for this. He couldn't stand reporters. In his opinion, they always managed to get the facts wrong.

"What can I do for you, Ms. Fabinski, besides answer questions about the grocery store incident?" His annoyance should have been clear.

Rebekah smiled, and he knew she was not going to let herself be ignored.

"Oh, come on, this town is too small for me to not know why you are here. You might as well answer a few questions now, or I will just keep asking."

He sighed heavily, letting her know he was irritated. "I don't have answers to your questions. Good day, Ms. Fabinski."

He moved around her, and instead of staying put, she fell into step with him. Freely thought the look he gave her made it clear he didn't appreciate her company. But she didn't appear a bit fazed.

"Well then, I guess there is no harm if I walk with you."

They walked in silence for the ten minutes it took to arrive at the grocery store. Freely stopped to look at her.

"Ms. Fabinski, I have a job to do, and if you continue to follow me around, I will have you arrested."

She shrugged nonchalantly. "No problem, I have already talked to all the witnesses. Actually, I talked to all of them almost four years ago. You'll only find two of them still working here—Bob and Melanie." She gave him another sweet smile. "I'll wait for you out here." She sat on a park bench in front of the store. "And by the way, since Chief Harris is a close family friend, you will probably have a hard time getting me arrested."

Ms. Rebekah Fabinski was quickly becoming his least favorite person.

The store was quiet as Freely entered. It had the familiar smell of an old grocery store. Remnants of food, year after year, being stocked and sold on the old metal shelves. He liked it. The store was clean and well kept. The owner, Bob

Matliff, had been in the store at a cash register the day the incident happened with the child. Freely spotted him stacking some cans on the end of an aisle. He recognized him from the FBI files, robust and bald. Not much had changed. Mr. Matliff looked up as Freely approached.

"Mr. Matliff?" Freely extended his hand as he approached.

"Please, call me Bob. Mr. Matliff was my grandfather." The man wiped his own hands off on his grocer's apron and shook his hand.

"Nice to meet you, Bob. I am John Freely, with the FBI."

Bob smiled. "Oh, I know who you are. The whole town is talking about you being here to investigate what happened. I have had more people in this store in the last few weeks than I have had in here when it first happened." He paused. "Wish it was because they loved my store, instead of a man dying here, but I guess I shouldn't complain. The Lord works in mysterious ways, wouldn't you say, Agent Freely?" Freely gave him the courteous smile he gave everyone he interviewed, especially those who used his full title. "The Lord and I aren't on the friendliest terms, but I will take your word for it."

Bob Matliff let out a small chuckle. "Seems to be the way it is with a lot of folks these days. Can't pray in schools, don't put *In God We Trust* on anything, don't offend anybody."

He shrugged. "But I know you didn't come here to talk about my thoughts on religion. What can I do for you?"

Freely liked Bob Matliff and knew he was going to be a reliable witness. Freely had a gift—he sized people up the moment he met them, and he was usually spot-on.

"I would like to ask you a few questions, if you have a minute."

"Sure, let's go to the back. I have a small office where we can talk." Bob shouted to the female cashier, "Melanie, I'll just be in the back, call me on the intercom if you need me." The cashier gave him a wave.

Freely was going to have to talk to her next. He recognized her name from the reports he had seen from Chief Harris and from the annoying reporter waiting outside.

"You mind if I talk to Melanie after we are done?"

"Not at all. I'll watch the registers when we are finished. You can talk to her in my office."

"Thank you."

They walked through swinging double doors and into a tiny office. Barely enough room for a desk, two chairs, and a filing cabinet.

Bob motioned to the chair on the other side of his desk. "Please, have a seat."

Freely sat and pulled a small voice recorder from his pocket. "I would like to record this if that's all right with you." Bob nodded.

Freely noticed pictures of a middle-aged woman, adult children, and what looked to be grandchildren. "Nice looking family."

Bob smiled. "Thank you. I lost my wife Donna to cancer almost six years ago. We had been married for forty-seven years."

"I'm sorry to hear that."

"Oh, it gets a little easier every year, but I still think about her every day. Drank a lot that first year, but the grandkids have definitely helped with the pain of missing her." He shook himself out of the memory and laughed. "I think I have fallen back a few steps again. My personal life is not what you came here to see me about either."

"I don't mind at all." Freely honestly didn't mind waiting a few minutes. People were better witnesses when they were relaxed.

Bob Matliff gave him a nod. "I'm ready when you are."

Freely pressed the record button. "I would really just like for you to tell me what you saw that day. I know it has been awhile, but anything and everything you can remember."

Bob repeated, almost word-for-word, what Freely had read in the police report. He had clearly told the story many times over the years.

There were a few customers in the store, along with the young woman and the child. The child walked up to Mr. Reese and began speaking an unknown language. Mr.

Reese began screaming at the woman and the child and then fell to the ground. He began convulsing and foaming at the mouth. Mr. Matliff immediately called 911, and by the time the fire department and police arrived, Mr. Reese was dead, and the woman and child were gone.

"What was Mr. Reese yelling at the woman and child? Do you remember?"

Bob nodded. "Oh, I remember, and a few of the words I am not going to repeat. He mainly kept telling the young woman to keep her bastard child away from him. The little boy just kept getting closer and closer to him. The mom kept yelling to hush him, but the little boy wouldn't stop. He sure was a beautiful little boy. Curly hair and blue eyes. He didn't seem scary to me at all. Not sure what Phil was freaking out about."

"So, you knew Mr. Reese?"

"Oh yeah. I knew his father, Jack, very well. Family never had much, but most were real hard workers. Not sure what happened with Phil. I heard through gossip that he got into drugs and maybe a little devil worship. But that part could be just made up to make the story better. You got to learn to take everything with a grain of salt when people start wagging their tongues."

Freely smiled. "Second time I have heard that today."

"But I do know the drug part was true, as were some physical abuse incidents with a couple of his girlfriends over

33

the years. He had been arrested more than once for those things."

These were all things that Freely already knew. Phil Reese was bad news, and from what they had found in his trailer, the devil worship rumors were not just wagging tongues.

"Bob, you said the mother was calling out to the little boy. Do you remember what she was saying?"

"She was calling his name. The boy's name is Elkan. She was trying to get him to come back to her."

"Elkan? That's an unusual name. Had you seen them in the store before."

"Oh sure, a few times before that happened. They were usually here with several different people. A lot of different people seemed to visit the pastor's vacation home about twenty miles outside of town in the mountains. Not so much now."

"So they are still here? I didn't see the address in the police file from Chief Harris."

Bob shrugged. "Yes sir, I've watched Elkan grow into a young boy. They come in here often, and he and Syene, his mom, have even been to my daughter's house for a barbeque. She's a sweet young lady."

Freely felt annoyed with Harris and knew the Chief was playing a payback game with Freely, but he was very excited to hear they were still in this area. "If you don't mind, I would like the address and directions to their home, and a phone number if you have it. Who did you say they are living with?"

"Pastor Dave and his wife Susan own the house. They have owned it for years."

He couldn't help but think back to Chief Harris's statement that *they weren't a bunch of idiots*. Freely thought differently.

"And you are sure you didn't see anyone with them that day? Two men, two very tall men?"

Bob shook his head. "No sir, I remember everyone that comes into the store. Especially the strangers. James was in the store with her and Elkan that day. She usually comes in with him or with Father Tony."

Freely frowned. There was nothing about this James or a Father Tony in the police reports.

"Father Tony and James?"

Bob nodded, "Father Cervini, he's a priest. He lives with them, along with James, Julie, Ariel, and their grandmother, Lois. Not sure what her last name is." He said it as if it was a well-known fact, but John Freely was dumbfounded. None of this was in the reports. It was starting to sound like a religious commune he was looking for instead of only a mother and child. His frustration was growing with the local police department.

"Have they always lived with this many people? This large a group?"

Bob Matliff laughed, "Used to be more. They have thinned out over the past few years. But they all seem like good people. I have never had trouble with any of them."

Freely jotted down all the names Matliff gave him. This was becoming weirder by the minute.

"You have been extremely helpful, Bob. Is there anything else you can think of that I might need to know?"

Bob stared for a few minutes lost in his own thoughts.

"No sir, but if it is Elkan and Syene you are interested in then you should probably talk to Karen Caldwell. I can tell you where she lives. Karen has lived here her whole life and is a cancer survivor."

"Why do I need to speak with her?"

"Well, a couple of years ago she says Elkan and Syene were here in the store, and when she reached out and touched the boy she felt a jolt of electricity run through her entire body and her cancer was gone." Bob shrugged. "I sure wish Elkan had been around when my Donna was sick. I've never known Karen to be a liar."

Freely wrote down her name and address. "I will definitely talk to Karen Caldwell. Thank you for the information."

Bob stood up. "Let me go get Melanie for you, if you still want to talk to her?"

The interview with Melanie was much of the same as Mr. Matliff's interview. Not quite as informative, because she was more interested in finding out why a FBI agent was here asking questions.

He couldn't help but notice Melanie smelled like cheap body spray and popped her gum while she talked.

"Is it true he was burned up on the inside? That's what the rumor always was, but no one knew for sure."

"I'm not allowed to discuss the details of the case." Freely's nerves were shot, and the gum-popping was striking on every nerve. He gave Melanie a noncommittal smile.

She shrugged her shoulders. "My cousin works in city hall, and he said Phil was completely burnt on the inside and his outside was completely normal."

Freely stared blankly, thinking to himself how glad he was he didn't live in a small community. "Well, I appreciate your time, Melanie. Is there anything else you can think of I might need to know?"

Her gum popped sharply. "My friend, Kelly, said Elkan saved her dog. Said her dog got hit by a car out on the road heading up to the mountains when they were hiking. Elkan and his mom saw it happen and stopped to help. Kelly said her dog's back leg had almost been ripped off, and he was bleeding badly. She said Elkan came up to her while she was crying and holding her dog's head. He put his hands on the dog and BOOM, his leg was back together. He was up and running and barking like nothing had happened."

Freely had had enough of this hocus-pocus garbage. It seemed to him the people in this town needed to find something to do instead of dreaming up stories about miraculous healings. He stood without even acknowledging the ridiculous tale.

"Well, I don't want to keep you. Thank you for the information."

As he turned to exit he heard a voice, but it wasn't Melanie's voice.

"I'm coming for you."

A cold chill ran over his body. Freely turned to look her. "What did you say?"

Melanie stared at him blankly, still popping her gum. "Huh?"

Clearly, she had not said anything or heard the voice. Freely rubbed his eyes. It had been a long couple of days of travel. He needed to get some sleep.

"Nothing, thanks again." The cold chill stayed with him. He was grateful as he stepped out of the store into some needed sunshine.

****

The reporter was still waiting on the bench. She stood up when she saw him. The too big eyeglasses where pushed on top of her head. Freely thought she looked much better without the glasses.

"Get what you needed?" She gave him a big smile.

"Ms. Fabinski, I have already told you I cannot talk to you about the investigation."

She gave him a shrug. "You going to talk to Karen Caldwell?"

Freely shook his head and couldn't keep from smiling. "I'm guessing you already knew about her?"

Her smile got bigger. "Follow me."

Chapter Four

There are "friends who destroy each other, but a real friend sticks closer than a brother." – Proverbs 18:24

"Syene?"

She looked up from her thoughts to find James standing with a cup of coffee in his hand as an offering. She smiled and took the coffee. He sat next to her, and they both stared out the large windows as the dark clouds moved. Syene glanced at James and could see the worry sketched in his dark, handsome face. Who would have thought the man who had murdered her father would be sitting next to her, one of her biggest confidantes and allies?

Syene smiled, thinking of the miraculous things the Creator had shown her. She felt ashamed for the constant feelings of anger and doubt. Syene was guilty of being mad at God, and she wasn't sure how to fix it. She and James sat in silence, and it was a welcome quietness. She sighed deeply, closing her eyes, letting her head fall gently on James's shoulder. She was forever thankful for the unlikely friendship. Syene's mind drifted to the day he showed up at the mountain home to see her.

****

"How are you feeling today, Syene?"

Pastor Dave was standing in the doorway of the living room. "You up for a visitor? Someone new has come to join us and would like to speak to you." He looked nervous as he spoke.

"Who is it? She was holding Elkan in her arms as he slept. Her wondrous boy was almost eight months old. He already had beautiful curls framing his perfect face. Syene could never grow tired of staring at him.

Dave reached out for the baby. "May I?"

Syene smiled as she lifted him to Dave. Everyone instantly fell in love with Elkan. He possessed the ability to capture people immediately.

Dave motioned his head toward the kitchen. "Our new guest is waiting to see you." She couldn't help but think Dave was acting strangely, and she was curious now. In the back of her mind she was hoping it might be Farrel. She knew it wouldn't be, but she still hoped he might come to see her child, whom he had so valiantly protected. It seemed the pain of missing him never faded.

Syene rose from the couch and strolled from the living room into the kitchen, trying to not get her hopes up. Foolish desires only made things harder. As she walked in, the sun broke through the dark clouds for a moment and shone brightly into the kitchen windows, casting an iridescent sparkle on the two people at the table. Sitting with Susan was a black man, probably in his early thirties. He stood when he saw Syene. She stopped walking. She knew immediately who it was.

"Syene, I am Jam . . ."

"I know who you are." Her voice was tight and guarded. The man who had murdered her father was standing face to face with her.

Susan stood from the table and walked toward Syene. She reached out and gently touched her arm.

"Syene, you need to have an open mind and listen to what James has to say. Your mom forgave him, and you need to, as well."

Syene couldn't believe Dave and Susan had allowed this person into their home. She knew her mother stayed in touch with James and his family, but Syene had refused to be a part of it.

James spoke again, a plea in his voice.

"Syene, I understand how you must feel right now. Seeing me standing in front of you. But I found you because of your mother. She asked me to come here."

Syene's eyes hardened. *"My mother is dead."*

James looked down at the floor. *"Yes, I know."*

Syene noticed the tears in his eyes when he looked back up. *"She was a wonderful lady. I can't begin to tell you how sorry I am."*

She didn't want to hear any of his sympathy. He was the reason she didn't have her father. She cut him off quickly.

"What do you want, and how did you find us?" Her guard was up.

Syene looked him over as she waited for a response. She could see faded tattoos on his forearms, probably remnants of his past. He stood well over six feet tall, and he should have felt like a menacing presence. Despite herself, she didn't feel threatened at all. James had a very kind and handsome face, and his eyes told the whole story. He was not here to harm her or Elkan. Sy knew this without a doubt.

He rummaged through a bag on the kitchen floor and pulled a folded letter out. "Your mom wrote to me before she died. I have the letter." His hand was trembling as he held it out for Syene.

Syene took it and sat at the kitchen table. As she unfolded the paper, she immediately recognized her mom's handwriting. A sharp pain tore at her heart. That familiar longing for her mother, never far from the surface, came pouring through. She did her best to fight back the tears as she read the words.

Dear James,

I hope life has found you in a happy place, and you continue your public speaking with the youth. Your mother sent me a recording of you in action. You have a real gift and a beautiful message to share. I have tried to reach out to you by phone but have not been able to make a connection. I began wondering if I had the right number. That is why I am writing to you. I know your mom will make sure you get my letter.

I believe I am going to need you, James, and I don't know for what purpose or even why I feel this way. I need to warn you of coming danger. I have so much to explain, and it is hard to express in a letter without making myself sound like I am crazy.

Here it goes, for whatever it is worth. My older daughter, Syene, has received a divine calling from our Creator, and we are currently living – but really hiding – at a home in the mountains. Hiding from society but also from an evil you cannot imagine. I do not want you to think this a completely terrible situation; as I write this letter to you, I am looking at a beautiful mountain range and five angels standing nearby. No, I am not insane, and no, you did not read that wrong. Real live angels. God's warriors to be exact. They are protecting Syene. Protecting her from a horror I would wish on no one.

I know, without a doubt, you are one of God's warriors here on earth. I am asking you to call me as soon as you get this letter. Your mom has my number. I can explain so much more over the phone. Please have faith in what I am writing. I know this sounds ludicrous and doesn't make sense, but please call. God will reveal all to you.

Your friend in faith,

Carol

A tear rolled off Syene's chin and hit the paper. She quickly wiped her face. She looked up at the man her mother had reached out to for help.

"When did you receive this?" Her voice had lost its previous edge.

James sat next to her at the table. "I got it about four months ago. But she mailed it long before that." He pointed to the postmark on the envelope. "She mailed it to my mom's house. I travel a lot for my speaking engagements, and I just didn't get it in time. I tried to call her as soon as I opened the letter, but it went to her voicemail every time. I was sick with worry." Syene could hear the genuine pain in his voice. "I am so sorry that I didn't get the letter in time. Maybe I could have prevented her . . ." His voice trailed off.

Syene reached out and placed her hand on top of his. It looked very small and pale against his dark skin. He placed his other hand over hers, and Syene immediately felt safer. James would be a much-needed ally. Syene's tension and anger left her as quickly as it had come.

"I'm sorry for the way I acted." She gave him a small smile. "It was quite a shock to see you right in front of me."

James flashed a beautiful and nearly perfect smile and chuckled. "Please don't apologize, I was actually expecting a possible attack on my body."

"I can't say the thought didn't cross my mind."

James laughed out loud. *"You have your mother's honesty. I loved that about her."*

Syene's forehead creased in thought. *"So, I am curious now. How did you find us?"* She looked across the table at Susan and could see the slight smile on her face. She turned to look at James again. *"Well?"*

James began telling his story. *"I had a speaking engagement, at a high school in Michigan about two months ago. When I was done, a young man approached me and asked if I had a few minutes. I thought he was part of the teaching staff at first, but I couldn't have been more wrong. What I thought was going to be a ten-minute chat ended up being a five-hour conversation in my car. He told me everything. He showed me everything. I can't even begin to explain what I saw."* James shook his head thinking back to the whole event. *"All I can say is that I immediately went back home, broke the lease on my rented house, cancelled the remaining speaking engagements on my schedule, got my finances in order for my mom, and came to find you."*

Syene was stunned. *"You left everything to come find us? But why? Who was the man you talked to?"*

James shook his head. *"I'm not completely sure, but he said his name was Farrel. He told me he had once been a great warrior for Yahweh. An angel of God. He knew my life story, and he knew I received a letter from your mom. I believed everything he told me, yet the things he showed me cannot be explained. I even saw you, your sister, and your child."*

Syene could feel her heart racing, "Farrel? Are you sure that was his name? And he was human?"

"As human as you and I."

She couldn't wrap her mind around any of it. Why had Farrel not come to see her? And why was he in human form again? None of it made sense. She knew the tricks of Lucifer and began wondering immediately if James had been lured here as a trap. She stood up, the comfortable feeling she had before slowly leaving.

"How do I know this isn't a trick?"

James looked confused. "A trick?"

"How were the visions revealed to you?"

"I'm really not sure. Farrel began speaking a language I have never heard, and for some reason I could understand everything he was saying." She could see James struggling to explain the glorious things he had seen. Syene knew immediately it was Farrel. Only the Creator could provide a pure vision. Her moment of worry was instantly gone.

"I believe you, James, and yes, I know Farrel. I know him very well." She couldn't believe Farrel was in human form again and had not come back to the mountains. She was angry and thrilled all at the same time. But more importantly, she had a new friend. Syene knew she could trust James because her

mom had, and now James confirmed Farrel was out there
protecting she and Elkan from a distance.

****

James's voice brought her back to the present day.

"Where is Elkan?"

"Ariel took him berry-picking. They have schemed up a way to make a pie and make it seem healthy to me." James laughed, but she could see he had something on his mind. Syene put her cup down and looked directly at her friend.

"What is it, James?"

He smiled. "You know me too well."

"I can see the worry all over your face."

He let out a deep sigh. "Julie and I were in town earlier, and there are a lot of people talking again. Apparently, some FBI agent is in town asking a bunch of questions about what happened in the store."

Syene sighed as well. "Well, I guess the calm couldn't last forever. We are preparing to leave anyway, and you guys have been trying to get me off the mountain for several years."

"Syene, I'm just afraid you aren't prepared for any of this. You have been hiding here since his birth, and now the FBI is here asking questions. This only proves we can't protect him from every little thing."

She felt immediately defensive. "It sounds like you aren't on Team Elkan. You have no idea what I'm prepared for, or how I need to protect him."

James shook his head. "Team Elkan? Are you kidding me? There are no teams here. I understand you want to protect him. I know every motherly instinct in your body is screaming right now, but you are being irrational." He paused, as though choosing his words carefully. "Elkan's safety is what all of us care about."

Syene could feel the tears brimming her eyes. She looked away. Julie came in and sat on the couch next to James, a look of worry on her face. Their hands intertwined. James had not only been sent for Syene; his endearing smile and spiritual heart had captured Julie. And Julie needed him. Losing Tim, in the same battle Syene had lost her mother, had almost destroyed her. James and Julie had become inseparable and were very much in love.

Julie spoke softly. "Syene, you know we love you and Elkan. You must listen to what we are saying. We have all watched you become very angry. The older Elkan gets, the angrier you get."

Sy knew they were right, but she refused to listen. She wanted so badly for Elkan to be able to have a normal childhood, at least while he was this young. She couldn't expect any of them to understand what she felt as his mother.

She really wanted to scream at God: *You couldn't have at least given me a few years of normality?* But she remained very quiet instead. Syene couldn't seem to release all the anger she was feeling. She was angry both her parents were dead, angry Farrel had disappeared and never returned, and angry people were going to fear her beautiful child.

She turned to look at the couple who stared up at her with genuine concern, but she felt nothing but resentment.

"I can't possibly expect either of you to understand."

She knew they could hear the tense anger in her voice, the kind of anger that could destroy a person's soul. She didn't care. She got up and walked away. James and Julie said nothing.

She went to her room, upset everyone seemed to hang over her, watching her. Telling her how she needed to be feeling. It seemed everyone wanted to minimize her feelings. She already blamed herself for her mother's death and for Tim's. She had encouraged everyone to train and fight in the battle against Lucifer's warriors, and because of her actions, she lost her mom, and Julie lost her husband. Now she was going to have the entire world after her child. Her beautiful boy was going to be a terrifying oddity to most people. The thought of all of it overwhelmed her. Not even her grandma, Ariel, or Jamille were able to bring her comfort. She felt as if they were all against her. Her own doubts constantly nagged at her. Tortured her.

She spoke quietly to the Creator. "God, I am the one this happened to, I am the one You chose to be the mother to Elkan, yet I am the one who feels You the least. Do You even hear me?"

Her head was pounding. Syene rubbed her temples. The headaches were there constantly since she had given birth. She was starting to think she was losing her mind. Maybe she would wake up and realize all of this had been some horrible dream, she would feel her mom gently rousing her from the nightmare. Syene wanted nothing more than to feel her mom's touch one more time. She relived the moment her mom was killed over and over in her mind. She fell back onto the pillow as tears rolled off her cheeks.

Her bedroom window was open, and the laughter of Elkan and Ariel penetrated her thoughts. She should have been with them enjoying the day instead of crying in her room, but she couldn't pull herself out of the darkness. Syene felt so lost and alone. Sleep seemed to be the only place she could find peace.

****

Syene woke to a soft knock on her door. The setting sun filtered through her room. She got up to answer it and pulled on the handle, but it seemed to be stuck.

"Sy, you're going to have to pull, while I push. The door is stuck." She recognized Jamille's voice and was filled with joy. Jamille, her protector, had been gone for several days, and she couldn't wait to see her. The door budged, but it only opened a few inches.

"Jamille, what is going on with this stupid door? Can't you use some angel power and get it open?" She laughed as she said it and peeked through the opening to see what was causing the door to not open, but it wasn't Jamille standing there. Her heart began pounding like crazy. He was there, staring at her only inches away, a horrid smile on his face. Syene began pushing on the door trying to get it shut, but it wouldn't close. The serpent tongue lapped through the slit, almost touching her face.

His voice washed over her like a smothering liquid. "Open the door for me, my sweet. I want to see your beautiful face."

His voice made her dizzy, and she thought she was going to faint. The booming in her chest was deafening. *Where was everyone? Why was no one helping her? Had he killed everyone? Was she alone? All she could think about was saving Elkan.* Syene watched in horror as his hand came through the opening, wrapping around the doorframe. She was frantic, looking for anyway to get out of the room. Through the open window she could see two angels in the distance by the tree line.

The window slammed closed just as she reached it. She frantically tried to open it, but it wouldn't budge. Syene began banging on it and screaming. She could hear him behind her scratching at the door. She was too terrified to turn around but knew she had to. He was now in the room. Elkan was her priority, and she had to get to him. She slowly tuned to face Lucifer. Was it possible for him to be even more horrifying than the last time she was in his presence? He was only inches away, his breath on her face.

"I have missed you, my sweet."

He reached out to stroke her hair. Syene slid down the wall, her legs failing to hold her.

"We will be together soon, my beautiful Sacred, I'm coming for you."

Syene closed her eyes and began praying, saying any scripture she could remember. She could feel his presence as he leaned in and inhaled, smelling her skin. Then he was gone.

Syene's eyes flew open as she sat up in bed, drenched in sweat. She stood quickly, scanning the room. The window was still open with no sign of anyone being there.

She plopped on the bed. "A dream? A damn dream."

Her heart was still pounding, and she swore she could still feel the coldness from when he had touched her. She shivered. She got up and walked to the door, quickly pulling on the handle. Ariel was standing in the doorway, and Syene gave out a startled yell.

Ariel laughed and held her hands up. "Chill. I know I'm scary without makeup, but I'm not that bad."

Syene burst into tears and grabbed her sister, holding her tightly. "He is coming for me, Ariel. He's coming."

Ariel's smile quickly faded as she clung to her sister.

Chapter Five

You are the God of great wonders! You demonstrate your awesome power among the nations. – Psalm 77:14

Dave and Susan had heard about Syene's reactions to both her friends trying to talk to her and about her nightmare. They were all extremely worried about her mental state. Susan decided to make an elaborate picnic lunch the next day, so they could get Syene outside to enjoy some fresh air and sunshine. Jamille had returned, and she, Ariel, and Sam played with Elkan at the bottom of the hill. His laughter rang against the mountains. Wesley was barking and chasing Elkan as he ran through the grass. Syene put her head on her grandmother's shoulder and sighed.

"Ariel is really going to miss Sam when he leaves." Syene was so grateful to Sam and his parents. They brought so much love and laughter with them on their visits, and she was happy each time she got to see them. It seemed he and Ariel became closer and closer every time they were here.

Her grandma nodded in agreement. "Young love is wonderful, and he certainly has grown into a handsome young man."

It amazed Syene every time she thought back to the day of the battle and realized how young Sam and Ariel had been. And now he and his parents were working hard in their home state to minister to people and get them to hear their Creator's word. After living through what they had on that dreadful day, they didn't want anyone to miss the love available to them.

Sy whispered quietly, "Don't leave me anytime soon, Grandma."

Her grandma kissed the top of her head. "I will do my best."

She glanced up at her. "I know you miss Mom too. I'm sorry I keep forgetting that."

"Honey, there is nothing more painful than losing your child. But having you and Ariel has helped me carry on." As if on cue, Wesley ran up and licked her grandmother's face. She pushed him away, "Oh yuck, don't lick me." She rubbed his head. "Yes, you helped me too, Wesley." He sat next to her, panting happily.

Syene could see Father Cervini in the distance making his way up the hill to where she and her grandma were relaxing. She sat up and smiled. Father Cervini exhaled, exhausted from the climb. "I think I need to exercise a lot more. That hill seems to be getting higher and harder."

Syene sighed trying to sound happy. "You won't have to worry about it much longer, since we have to leave."

He sat wrapping his arm around her shoulders.

"Isn't that what life is all about? Moving on to better things? It is time for all of us to begin the journey God has called us to be on."

Syene was quiet. She knew that she should feel that same way. *Especially her! She was Elkan's mother.* But instead she felt a complete disconnect. She felt abandoned and angry with God.

"I wish I had your faith and closeness to God. I just don't." She could feel her throat tightening and did her best to keep back the tears. She was so sick of being upset. Her grandma reached out to brush back her hair.

"It will come, Syene. God is surrounding you. Just look at what is around you." She waved her arm at the scene before them—filled with people who loved her and Elkan and, of course, the angels.

Syene made eye contact with her son. He stopped playing and stared at his mother in his unnerving way. It was always when he knew she was doubting and angry. Syene diverted her eyes, the guilt of her lack of faith was overwhelming. She shrugged.

"Mother Mary I'm not. I honestly don't know what God was thinking by picking me."

The priest chuckled. "No one expects you to be our beloved Mary. Different purpose, different plan. God will find you in that hardened heart of yours." He smiled and gave her a little nudge with his shoulder. "'For I know the plans I have for you, says the LORD. They are plans for good and not for disaster, to give you a future and a hope.' God knew exactly what he was doing when you were chosen."

Syene only sighed deeper.

"Spend a little time in the scripture, Sy. You will find what you are searching for."

She wanted to spout off something hateful, *like how the scripture saved my mom,* but she kept her mouth shut. She could feel Elkan's stare still upon her and forced herself to look in his direction.

Her child spoke to her using his mind. *"The Lord your God is with you wherever you go."*

Syene's head began to pound with another headache.

****

Special Agent Freely stared blankly across the kitchen table at Karen Caldwell. Her two children were fighting over something in the living room, and she yelled for them to *please be quiet while there is a guest in the house.*

Rebekah sat quietly sipping her iced tea. Freely could see the light smirk on her face at his annoyance.

Mrs. Caldwell finally turned to face him again. "I'm so sorry, teenagers can be impossible sometimes." She paused. "Where was I?"

Rebekah spoke up encouragingly. "You and your husband had just gotten back from the doctor." Freely was certain she had heard this story more than once.

Karen took a drink of water. "Yes, Chuck and I had just left the doctor's office." Tears brimmed her eyes. "I had had my last round of chemo several weeks before, and the PET scan results were not good. The cancer was spreading like wildfire, my husband and I decided for hospice care and no more treatments. We were on our way home to talk to the kids."

She got very quiet, and Freely could see this was a very painful memory for her to be rehashing for them.

Her voice cracked as she continued.

"We were getting close, and I told my husband to stop at the store." She smiled. "This will probably sound silly to you, but any time one of us has something bad happen or we spend too much time feeling sorry for ourselves, I bake a cake, decorate the kitchen with balloons, like it is a birthday party." She laughed. "And then we light the candles on the cake, and all of us sing 'Happy Pity Party' instead of 'Happy Birthday'."

She looked at Rebekah, "I know it seems silly, but it works. And then whatever we are feeling bad about never seems so bad after that. We end up laughing, eating the cake, and forgetting about what was so awful." Mrs. Caldwell looked at him. "It is like blowing out those candles is blowing away the problems." She shrugged a little. "I wanted a cake for the kids that day when we told them the horrible news, and I wanted to decorate. I didn't want any of us sitting around and feeling sorry for ourselves."

He didn't think it was silly at all. He wished many times in his life he could have had a signing off for pain. "Nothing wrong with wanting to help your kids through something painful."

Karen gave him a half smile. "When we pulled up to the store I saw the little boy and his mom walking in, I remember I commented to my husband what a beautiful child he was. Chuck was going to run in and get everything for me since I was so sick. At that point, all the chemo had taken its toll, and of course, so had the cancer. But I had insisted I wanted to do it with him. I could barely walk, and I had lost almost forty pounds. I basically looked like a living skeleton. I had to use a wheelchair to get around."

She held up a finger why she thought of something. "I have a picture, hang on." Freely watched as she walked out of the kitchen and looked over at Rebekah Fabinski, shaking his head.

Rebekah spoke quietly. "Just wait. I know you are a cynic, but I have known Karen and Chuck for a very long time, and I know she had cancer."

Karen came back with the picture and placed it on the table in front of him. "That picture was taken the day of my last chemo treatment. Not quite a month before the day we were in the store with Syene and Elkan. I don't know why, but Chuck insisted on telling me how beautiful I was, and he wanted to take pictures all the time." She paused. "Now I'm glad he did."

Freely picked up the picture, Karen was sitting in a recliner with the IVs administering chemo going into her arm, her husband and children surrounded her. It was a selfie-style picture taken by her husband; all four were smiling, but you could clearly see death was near for Mrs. Caldwell. He honestly couldn't believe the same woman was sitting across the table from him. In the picture she looked emaciated, and everything about her looked sick; her hair was gone, skin grey, and eyes dark.

Without being too obvious he began looking for any signs of photoshopping. The investigator in him was always looking for the lie and the angle. He wasn't certain how this was the same person sitting across from him. He was very familiar with cancer and its toll on the body. His own father passed away from colon cancer, so he recognized death when he saw it.

He looked directly at her. "How long ago was this taken?"

"About three years ago. I have my medical records, which you are welcome to look at, but sometimes a picture can speak a thousand words, right?"

He placed the picture back on the table, uncertain what to think but feeling very skeptical. "This is true. Please continue."

"Anyway, we were on the aisle with the boxed cake mixes when I saw the little boy and his mom pass our aisle. I guess Elkan must have been around three years old at the time. There was something radiant about him. Don't get me wrong, I think my children are the prettiest creatures on this planet, but there was something special about him. He stopped at the end of the aisle and smiled at me. I gave him a small wave, and he pulled away from his mom and came toward me. His mom came after him immediately, but I held up my hand and told her it was okay. A lot of kids would be curious about the wheelchair or me not having hair, so I was used to innocent curiosity. I asked his mom what his name was, and she told me Elkan. Syene was very sweet and lovely, also."

Freely stopped her. "Elkan? That's an odd name."

Karen smiled. "That's what I said to her. I even looked it up the next day. She told me his father had named him after I commented about it and said it was a Hebrew name." Karen paused for a moment Freely could see her becoming more animated as the story went on.

"The little boy came right up to me, and I reached my hand out to stroke his hair. He had these wonderful curls, I couldn't help myself. And in that instant, I saw a flash of a million colors, it felt like a thunderbolt jarred my body. But not in a painful way. I can't explain it to anybody."

She looked at Rebekah, who had heard the story many times. "I know I have told this before to you, but I just don't know how to explain it. It was like lightning made of a rainbow." Tears were now freely running down her face as she tried to explain it. "My husband, who hadn't been paying attention to any of it, said he felt the chair bump him. I must have jerked when I touched the boy. He said all he saw was the look of terror on Syene's face."

Karen looked directly at Freely. "Syene ran to grab him and pulled him away, she kept apologizing. And I couldn't speak. Finally, after a few minutes with Chuck beginning to get worried, I told him we weren't going to need the cake. I was ready to go home. I just knew. I don't know how I knew, but I knew immediately the cancer was gone. Syene and Elkan disappeared from the store."

Freely soaked all the information in, trying hard to not show the doubt on his face. The poor woman obviously believed what she was saying.

"Agent Freely, I can see you are having a hard time believing all this, but I am telling you I was on my deathbed. I was heading to my home to tell my two children their mom was tired of fighting and it was my time to go. And in one instant with the touch of a little boy, I was cured of cancer. How can anyone explain that?"

Freely thought it was a great story, but he was not a believer of miracles and knew there had to be a medical explanation.

"What have the doctors told you? Maybe the scans and diagnoses were wrong. Things like that happen."

Karen shook her head. "I understand this is very hard to believe, but you don't look at a Stage IV cancer patient and tell her that the scans were wrong. You know when you are dying from cancer. You can feel it taking over every part of your body and thriving on your blood supply. So please don't insult me by telling me the scans were wrong. You saw the picture, did I look like they were wrong?"

Freely felt like a complete ass, but he still couldn't believe any of this. "I apologize. I didn't mean to offend you. You have to understand, this is all very hard to believe."

"But *you* need to understand that I don't care what anyone believes, because I am healed of cancer. It is one hundred percent gone, and the doctors have no explanation for it. None. But I do. I know Elkan healed me when I touched him. I have all the current scans and documents from the doctors. They have it as unexplained remission. But I know the truth. It is called healed, one hundred percent healed by the hand of God."

Freely's black-and-white logic wasn't going to let him get wrapped up in this. It was a great story, but he seriously doubted God was at the front of it all. There was a medical explanation out there somewhere.

"So, you obviously found out who they were. What did his mom say about all of this?"

Karen shrugged. "Syene asked us to not tell people. She told me she needed to keep Elkan protected."

Freely looked puzzled. "Protected from what? Didn't that seem strange to you? If a child has healing powers like you have claimed, wouldn't she want people to know? Wouldn't she want him to help people like you all the time? Why would that need to be a secret?"

She shook her head and smiled. "I guess to keep him from being hunted by people like you." She paused. "You are hunting him, right?"

Freely couldn't help but laugh. "Touché."

He didn't want to seem rude, but he just wasn't interested in magic and miracles. He had all the information he needed. He stood, and Rebekah stood with him. "Thank you for your time, Mrs. Caldwell. You have been a great help. I am very happy for your change in diagnosis."

Karen shook his hand and gave Rebekah a hug. She walked them both to the front door. Just as they were about to leave he turned to ask her one more question.

"One more thing. You said you looked up the meaning of the little boy's name the day you first met him. Did you find anything?"

Karen Caldwell flashed him a huge smile. "Elkan means *Belonging to God.*"

Chapter Six

For no prophecy was ever produced by the will of man, but men spoke from God as they were carried along by the Holy Spirit. – 2 Peter 1:21

The three of them walked hurriedly to the rental car terminal after getting off the plane. Laura was certain they looked like vagabonds just off safari. They barely had time to pack their essentials, and by essentials she meant mainly laptops and documents. Dr. Kaufman wasn't much on the real necessities of life, like clothes, toothbrushes, deodorant.

Laura smiled thinking of his quirkiness. He was like a crazy old grandpa you couldn't help but adore. She was going to have to make a pit stop somewhere to pick up the items she had forgotten in the rush or simply didn't have time to pack. She didn't even have time to shower before they were on a plane heading back to the States. Laura wasn't going to complain though; being on this quest with the doctor was the greatest thing she had ever done in her life. She was twenty-three and living an adventure that could be straight out of a movie. Not many people could say they were on the hunt for God. *A real, live, hold-it-in-your-hands hunt.* Her heart was beating hard in her chest. What if Dr. Kaufman was right? What if this child was a child of God? The implications of how this would change the world were too overwhelming to think about. Almost impossible to believe. Almost.

She could see the pure excitement on Kaufman's face. Thomas looked dazed. She gave him a big grin. *Poor guy had no idea what he had signed up for.* He looked a little petrified. She reached out and pulled on his arm, encouraging him to keep up. Thirty hours in cars, on planes, and through airports was taking its toll.

Laura nudged him gently. "Not too much longer. And you can sleep in the car. I think it's only about a two-hour drive." Thomas did his best at a smile. All of them were exhausted, but she and the doctor were running on pure adrenaline. She knew Thomas hadn't quite grasped the magnitude of what they were searching for, but he would understand soon enough. If they were right, then all their lives would be changed forever.

Twenty minutes later they were loaded into their rented SUV and headed for small-town America. Thomas was asleep within ten minutes. Laura oversaw navigation while the doctor drove.

She couldn't help but share the observation with her mentor. "Poor guy has no clue. He must think we are crazy."

Dr. Kaufman chuckled, keeping his concentration on the two-lane blacktop. "Maybe we are crazy, but I am willing to bet my soul we aren't." He smiled. "Imagine the wonder he is going to experience when he realizes the truth."

"I can't wait to see the little boy. I know you are going on seventy-five percent hunch, Dr. Kaufman, but you are about to prove the existence of God! I don't think I can begin to truly wrap my head around it. God! It seems so surreal."

Kaufman frowned. "I don't think it's going to be that easy. I doubt the boy's parents are going to just hand him over for scientific study. But just to be around him, if it is him, will at least prove everything to me. My Cassius will be liberated. His sacrifice will finally come to light. And maybe I can share Cassius with the world."

Laura was appalled at the thought of not being able to examine the little boy. "But we have to have the boy to prove everything? Surely his parents are going to understand that."

"One moment at a time, Laura. Let us see if the boy is really who we think he is. *If* he is, then we will tell his parents of the warnings from Cassius." He paused for a moment and chuckled. "Or maybe they already know. Surely God is speaking to them in some way, and we are only a small part of the big picture."

Laura let out a sigh as she settled into her seat, her eyes heavy from the travel. She mumbled as she drifted to sleep, "It's him, I have a good feeling."

His words were the last thing she heard. "I wish I had your faith, Laura. Mine has faltered too many times over the years. The scientist in me struggles. It is almost too much to believe the child really exists in our lifetime, and the prophecy I discovered is true."

****

A little over two hours and the car slowed. The different rhythm woke Laura. She sleepily rubbed her eyes. "Are we there?"

Dr. Kaufman looked tired, and for once she could really see his age.

"You need to sleep."

Kaufman nodded in agreement. "I thought the adrenaline would keep me going, but it has failed this old body." He slowed the car. "The motel should be just ahead, and then we are finally here, one step closer to answers."

It was one o'clock in the morning, and they all needed some sleep in a real bed. Even if it was a small roadside motel. They pulled into the parking lot with the vacancy sign flashing. Kaufman let out a sigh of relief. He parked and got out to go get them all rooms.

He returned quickly, and Laura opened her door to get out of the car. Thomas spoke from the backseat, his voice still coated with exhaustion. "We there?"

Laura stretched and took in the cool mountain air deeply into her lungs.

"Yes, we are at the motel to get some sleep. The main town is half a mile more." Thomas stepped out of the car to stretch.

"Brrrr, we are going to freeze." His teeth were chattering.

Laura nodded in agreement. "I hope they have a store close by so we can get a few warmer things to wear."

The doctor handed them each a room key. "I have wake-up calls for all of us at seven in the morning. The clerk said there is a small store in town where we should be able to pick up some items we need."

That was the best news Thomas and Laura had heard in the last thirty-four hours, based on their shared smiles. They dispersed, and each went to the assigned room. With hot showers and a bed, sleep would find them quickly. Except for the doctor. Sleep eluded him, and he lay staring at the ceiling. The flashing of the vacancy sign every few seconds could be seen through the crack in his curtain.

What if he was wrong? What if he was crazy like so many people thought? What if he had brought these two young kids across the world on a wild goose chase, a fantasy in his head? All his credibility was on the line. The reality that his entire career was riding on one small boy felt like a house sitting on his chest.

"Yahweh, I know You haven't heard from me in quite some time, but I am pleading with You. Please, don't let this be a hoax. I need some proof of Your existence right now."

The room was silent. Silent as he always remembered growing up and praying to the God his parents so fervently believed in. He had done everything he could as a young scientist to disprove God's existence, and now here he was chasing after a mystic child to prove God was real. He finally drifted off into a restless sleep.

****

Jerusalem – Three weeks before the crucifixion of Jesus

Cassius rode through the city atop his powerful stallion. The medallions, earned for his acts of bravery, clanged against his breastplate. He made his way to the palace to meet with Pilate. The culture his Alypia admired so much eyed him with disdain and suspicion. He did not share her love of this place. As he approached the palace entrance, the gate opened.

Cassius was greeted with respect by the Roman guards as they took the horse's reins from him in the courtyard. He dismounted and made his way up the stairs to meet with Pilate.

Pilate was seated at a table surrounded by several of his advisors. A leader of the Pharisees was engaged in a heated conversation with an advisor.

Pilate stood up from the table. "Enough! I have heard enough!"

The Jewish leader was silenced. He gave Pilate a respectful nod. "Then I will excuse myself. I meant no disrespect. Good day, Prefect." He exited, eyeing Cassius with disgust.

Pilate waved Cassius over. "Cassius, come in. I apologize for the disorder."

"What was that concerning?"

"A nonsense rumor about a man they call Yeshua of Nazareth, a Galilean, arriving in Jerusalem to start a rebellion in the city." Pilate dismissed it with a wave of his hand. "It is rubbish. They are complaining of Jewish laws being broken. These things do not concern me."

Cassius remembered hearing of this man. "I heard of this Jesus. A comrade stated his servant was healed of an illness simply by this man speaking it so."

Pilate snorted. "Like I said, rubbish. A healer, a man of magic, is not going to start a rebellion against the Roman Empire. The Jewish leaders can deal with it. He is their problem, not mine. I only need your assistance during their Passover. We need to pacify their overt hatred for us."

Cassius asked the obvious question. "Then why have I been called here, only to be a peacekeeper? I am confused." Cassius was a warrior, not a mediator for these people.

Pilate smiled. Cassius wasn't sure if the forced smile was to reassure him or Pilate himself. "Only as a precaution. This man has struck fear in the Pharisees, I can hear it in their voices when they come to speak to me. They pretend they are trying to protect Caesar, but they are really protecting themselves, and you and I both know fear is what will cause problems."

Cassius nodded in agreement. Fear could be a dangerous fuel in a battle.

"Then tell me what I can do for you while I am here?"

"Keep your ears and eyes open. If you hear of this Jesus coming, let me know. If he makes it into the city, keep the calm by any means necessary. I will not tolerate bad news making it back to Caesar." He looked directly at the Centurion. "Understood?"

Cassius understood perfectly. "Understood."

****

Laura woke slowly, her eyes still felt heavy. She could see the sunshine peeking through the curtain. The alarm clock beside the bed read *9:05.*

"Nine? I can't believe I slept this late!" She obviously slept through the wakeup call. She quickly jumped from the bed and went to the window to pull back the curtain. The scenery was beautiful, breathtaking. She could see Dr. Kaufman across the parking lot talking to an older gentleman and knew she better kick it in gear. Once he was ready to go, they all better be ready to go. She was surprised he hadn't been banging on their doors yet. Laura quickly brushed her teeth, washed her face, and pulled back her hair. She found the warmest thing she had to throw on and went to meet the boss.

The morning air was cold; she was going to need to find some clothing. She wrapped her arms around her stomach to keep her hands warm. The thin flannel she had was not going to be enough. She was regretting not packing the few warmer items she owned.

She mumbled aloud, "That's what you get for letting excitement rule the brain." The frost from her breath hung in the air.

The doctor waved as she approached him. "Good morning, Laura. How did you sleep?"

"Obviously too well, it is past nine o'clock. I'm sorry for oversleeping."

Kaufman smiled. "No worries, I haven't seen our young Thomas either. It was a long trip, so I thought I would let you both sleep in."

"But you quite clearly didn't sleep in."

Kaufman shrugged. "What can I say, I am an old man. Old men don't sleep in."

Laura shook her head and smiled. "Who was the man you were talking to?"

"That was a wealth of information, is who that was. His name is Frank, and he manages the maintenance for this motel, along with several other properties. He was very familiar with the young boy and told me of some crazy rumors blazing through the town over the last few years. He also told me an agent from the FBI is in town investigating the incident from the grocery store."

She was surprised. "Really? What a coincidence."

Kaufman smiled. "There are no coincidences, my dear, only fate-driven collisions." They began walking to the motel lobby. "And the best news of all, he said the mother and boy are still in the area."

Laura couldn't hide her excitement. "So he knows where they are?"

Kaufman smiled at her enthusiasm. "Oh, most definitely. I have full directions and a bag full of small-town gossip."

"I can't wait to hear it! I'm going to bang on Thomas's door, so we can get moving."

He waved his hand dramatically. "Please, lead the way. We will make a quick stop for breakfast and fuel, and we will be off to see the Wizard."

"I love that movie."

Thirty minutes later, the trio was heading toward the town of Spring Oak for a bite to eat and to discuss strategy. The morning chill was long forgotten, replaced by apprehension and nervous excitement.

Chapter Seven

And it was not Adam who was deceived by Satan. The woman was deceived, and sin was the result.
– 1 Timothy 2:14

Enzril followed Menti up the steep corridor to Master's quarters. There was a new air about Menti. The little idiot thought he was some type of royalty. Obviously, his recent closeness to Master had gone to his head. Enzril wanted to toss him down the dark stairwell—he was nothing but a demonic cockroach. Menti must have felt the dark tension. He glanced nervously behind him and sped up slightly. When they reached the top, his arrogance returned, as he tried to make Enzril wait outside the massive archway.

Enzril wasn't having it. "Out of my way, you leach."

Menti hissed at the dark warrior as Enzril walked ahead.

Enzril heard Lucifer's voice from within the darkness of the room.

"Enzril, what has kept you away so long?" The voice was harsh and accusing. It was clear Master was not asking to make pleasantries.

Enzril was cautious with his answer. "You know I despise these cockroaches." He glanced in Menti's direction as he said it. "I knew if you needed me I would be summoned."

Master rose from his chair and faced Enzril. "Indeed."

He strolled closely. "I do have to question your loyalty at times, when you choose to not personally report to me." He was only inches from Enzril's face. "Possibly, I have allowed you to stay away too long. I am unsure if you have forgotten who serves whom."

"I have not forgotten. My loyalty remains with you."

Master circled him slowly, and Enzril could feel his breath on the back of his neck. "Your loyalty may be with me, but why do I have the uneasy feeling you do not serve me?"

Enzril remained silent. Master was not a fool, and he would not attempt to make him one. Lucifer leaned in closely and whispered, "I would hate to think it would be necessary to hunt you down just as I did Lantz." He paused. "It would be such a pity to lose the top General of my army."

"I am not Lantz, Master. I have no need for game playing."

"No, you're not like Lantz, Enzril. I have no doubt it would take you much longer to succumb to the tortures of the pit." Master turned to face the stone fireplace. The shadow of the flames bounced across his distorted figure. "I have great plans for you. Lantz was weak, begging like a whiney child. He is a fool, who let his own perversions drive him to rebellion."

Enzril couldn't help but think to himself, *not unlike you did*. It was if Master was reading his thoughts, and Enzril diverted his eyes.

"He was not unlike myself. However, I am not a weak sniveling idiot. My reign prevails."

Enzril had heard of Lantz's capture from his soldiers. He had not been surprised to hear it had not ended well for him or his two minions. Lantz was a lustful fool, blinded by his own desires.

Enzril was no fool. He nodded his agreement. "How may I be of service, Master. I am assuming you have summoned me for a reason?"

Master chuckled. "Straight to business. That is what I enjoy so much about you, Enzril."

Enzril waited patiently.

"As you know, Amy has been released from my, shall we say, *care*. I am, of course, watching her carefully, but I need your assistance. I need someone I can trust. She is easily manipulated, and I don't need her being influenced by anyone or anything. Do you understand?"

Enzril nodded. "Yes. No contact with Yahweh, his warriors, or human threat."

Lucifer turned to face him. "At least until I say it is time. She will be used until my plans are accomplished."

"And what are your plans, Master? I have been confused by the lack of action."

Lucifer raised his hand to silence Enzril. "I am going to obtain the Sacred and the child for my own." A lustful smile twisted his face.

Enzril spoke before he could stop. "It won't be possible."

Lucifer came closer, rage in his eyes. "How long have I ruled this world, Enzril? Have I ever failed at anything I have desired? Nothing is impossible." He sneered. "Isn't that what the great Yahweh has always taught?"

Enzril bowed his head. "I misspoke."

Lucifer's laughter rang against the stone walls, and Enzril thought Master was going mad. "You just don't have enough faith, Enzril. Faith is what the humans rely on, and you need a little. You could learn something from the ones you despise so greatly." He stared into the fire glowing in the hearth. "It is freewill, Enzril, and the Sacred will come to me willingly. This I promise. And my delicious little Amy is part of the plan. You will keep her safe."

Enzril nodded. Master waved him away. "We are finished." Menti reappeared to lead Enzril out.

Master spoke as Enzril reached the door. "Oh, one more thing, Enzril."

Enzril turned to look at his Master. "Do you have any idea how Jamille was able to escape from Lantz when she had been so badly wounded? I find it curious how she survived."

Enzril still kept his voice guarded. "No clue." He knew the Master was toying with him, but to admit the truth would be a fool's mistake.

Lucifer stared at Enzril. "Hmmm. Interesting, she should survive twice now from battles with my warrior and myself." Master paused, and Enzril said nothing.

"That is all." With a wave of his hand Enzril was released.

Menti opened the door for the dark warrior and began to follow him down the stairwell. "I know my way out." He shoved Menti to the side as he reached the corridor opening, caring little for Menti's furious glare and fervent threats.

****

Enzril flew hard. He was not looking forward to his new assignment. Babysitting a foolish girl was ridiculous. She wasn't going anywhere. Lucifer had used all the pleasures of the world to entice her. He had provided well for her. She fully belonged to the Master.

Enzril was frustrated, and he almost envied Lantz. At least the memories of anything were gone. His mind couldn't stop thinking of Jamille. He had been a fool to save her from Lantz in the last battle. She would never love him again. The only thing she cared about was protecting the Sacred. He was a fool for thinking about her. He ached for her, and he hated himself for it. It may have been idiotic to have saved Jamille that day, but he would never be sorry for it. It would be the second time he risked everything to keep her protected. She would never know of the first time; only the Creator and Michael knew the truth, and she had always assumed it had been Michael who saved her from Master's pit.

****

Amy was settled into her new condo. She had everything a person could want or desire. A successful career, money, great place to live, beautiful clothes, and a sleek new sports car. No more drugs, she was healthy again. She felt as normal as possible under her circumstances. Sometimes she wondered if she would wake up from a nightmare. Who in the world came face to face with Satan and lived to tell about it?

It baffled her to this day how people were so blind to the world surrounding them. How had she been so blind? Her life in college with Syene and Lizzy seemed like a million years ago. She often questioned if she was even alive. She was always a little surprised when a real person spoke to her. *Oh, they can see me.*

She missed her friends but knew there was no going back. They would think she was crazy if she told them the truth. She could only imagine how the conversation would go.

"Oh, hi, Syene and Lizzy, sorry I haven't called in so long, but I have been in Hell with the devil. All that stuff you read in the Bible, well, it's true."

She looked at her reflection in the mirror. "Well, most of it is true."

God didn't save her. Her Master saved her. She needed him.

"Selling your soul to the devil wasn't that bad, right?" Her reflection didn't respond. What choice did she have? She chose to forget the things she had had to do and the torture she had succumbed to for survival. It was easier to forget. Things were good—for now.

The young woman in the mirror wasn't the same person her friends once knew. This Amy looked very well kept, with great style. The scar of her suicide attempt was still faintly visible. She subconsciously touched the marks on her wrist. A constant reminder from where she came. Fury boiled in her when she saw it. It made her think of Lantz.

"I'm glad you suffered, you bastard. This is all your fault." Hatred ran through her veins. She lost everything because of him, and she hated him. Her friends, her family, her past life was gone.

Master did allow her to call her mom a few weeks ago.

Her mom cried for the first fifteen minutes, praising Jesus the whole time. Amy couldn't help herself when she spouted off. "Jesus is the last person you need to be thanking for this call." Her mom pretended she didn't hear her say it. Oh well, some things never changed, and her mom was one of them. Amy was shocked to hear her dad had stepped down as pastor of the church and was no longer attending any church. He took a sales job at a local computer store and wasn't at home when Amy called.

"Tell him I called, and tell him I'm sorry. I can't believe he isn't going to church." Amy felt sad about it but

didn't know why. Who cares if he didn't believe anymore? What was the point anyway?

She could hear the sadness in her mom's voice. "I'm heartbroken but praying he will find his way back home. Same prayer I say for you, honey. Maybe if we could see you it would help. Can you come home?"

Amy sighed. "Not right now, Mom, maybe you and Dad can come here to see me. Let's see, okay? I only wanted you to know I was okay. I know you have been worried."

The disappointment was obvious. "Oh, yes. I will come any time, just let me know. Please stay in touch with me. A part of me has been missing with you gone. I love you, Amy."

Tears were stinging Amy's eyes. Ridiculous. She wiped them away quickly. "I'll call soon." She hung up. There was no room for weakness and emotions in her life.

Amy quickly was brought back from her memory. Enzril was in the reflection of the mirror staring at her from her bedroom doorway.

"Don't you know how to knock?"

She was irritated with the popping in and out by whoever Master saw fit. She had no privacy.

"What are you doing here?"

Enzril chuckled. "You sure have a brazen attitude for a servant."

Amy whirled around to face him. "Servant? Look who is talking? You are no better than I am."

Enzril moved close. "Be careful what you say. I am not one of Master's minions to be manipulated."

Amy wasn't going to let him know she was a wreck on the inside.

"Whatever." She shoved him out of the way as she walked into the living room. "You didn't answer my question. What are you doing here?"

Amy walked to the kitchen to get a glass of wine, her hands shaking as she poured the needed liquid. Her hands were always shaking these days. Always waiting for Master to pop in on her. She would never let Enzril know, but she was glad it was him and not another dark warrior. He always unnerved her, but he somehow felt like an annoying older brother. She knew she was supposed to fear him, but she never did. For some reason she felt safer when he showed up. She gulped half the glass with her back turned to him. She almost enjoyed their sparring.

Enzril roamed the living room, not paying attention to anything she did. "What I'm doing is none of your concern."

Amy turned around to look at him. "Let me guess? Making sure I behave myself. Your duties sure have been dumbed down. Fearless dark angel now a useless babysitter. He must be really upset with you."

Enzril smiled. "That's right, a babysitter. I like the new title. Keeping an eye on a worthless human will be a much-needed break. Just remember I despise everything about humanity, so if you decide to do anything stupid, it will be my pleasure to take care of the problem."

"Thanks for the head's up." Her voice dripped with sarcasm.

She knew Enzril couldn't have cared less about any insults she threw his way. He opened the French doors that led to her balcony, the night breeze flooding her living room.

"Be smart, Amy, and you will stay alive. Master won't like his play-toy misbehaving." Then he was gone.

Amy's hands still shook as she sloshed more wine into her glass. She was living in a world most didn't believe existed. Her heart sank at the realization she would never be free. Amy knew Master was using her for something—she just didn't know what it was. Her only job right now was to stay alive.

****

Farrel watched as Enzril flew into the darkness. It was curious Lucifer would be using his best warrior for such a meaningless task. Farrel was beginning to think Amy wasn't a person to ignore. There was a reason Lucifer was keeping such a close eye on her. He was planning something for her. No human had ever survived his world of darkness with their soul intact.

His mission was to find out exactly what Lucifer was planning. He saw Amy step onto the balcony. Her head was down, and he could see she was wiping at her eyes. Farrel knew immediately what he needed to do. He was going to

85

befriend Amy, protect her. He watched her walk back into her condo. Farrel had no doubt this was exactly where his Creator had led him. He didn't know how Amy would help complete his plans, but he was certain she had always been a part of it.

He felt the presence behind him immediately and turned to find Michael.

Farrel smiled and went to hug his old friend. "So good to see you, Michael."

"And you, Farrel. You are greatly missed."

Farrel motioned to a small alleyway where they could talk.

"Maybe best if we step in here. I can't risk someone calling in because a crazy man is talking to himself on the sidewalk."

Michael chuckled. "Of course." They stepped into the safety of the darkness.

"How is she? How is Elkan?" Those were the two things he wanted to know the most. He missed Syene with every ounce of himself.

Michael answered honestly, "Sacred is in turmoil and misses both you and her mother very deeply. And Elkan, he is amazing. Everything about him brightens life."

Farrel ached to see both but knew he couldn't. "Well, I know you didn't seek me out to make small talk. Why have you come?"

Michael's tone changed. "There was an incident involving Elkan several years ago. It has now come up again and brought unwanted attention."

"Are he and Syene okay? What can I do to help?"

"They are both fine, but they have no choice but to leave Spring Oak. They are going to be on the move."

Farrel knew the danger they were going to be in leaving the safety of the mountains. Not only being hunted by Lucifer, but at risk of being known too soon by the humans. Both situations posed serious threats.

Michael placed his hand on Farrel's shoulder. "I have come to ask you for your help. I need you to return to her when they arrive at their new destination."

Farrel shook his head. "Michael, I cannot. I left so I could be more reasonable while protecting her. My feelings clouded my judgment. I wasn't even able to protect her mother during the battle, so how can I possibly keep her and Elkan safe?"

"Farrel, you know better than most souls, you cannot control freewill and you can return home any time. Yahweh will always welcome you."

"My soul is not ready. I cannot serve our Creator like I did before."

"Understood. But please reconsider your duty of protecting her and Elkan as they begin their new move. You are needed."

Farrel's heart wanted nothing more than to see Syene again, but he knew with certainty the Creator was calling him to Amy right now. He didn't know how, but he knew he had to save her.

Chapter Eight

Behold, I send an angel before you to guard you on the way and to bring you to the place that I have prepared.
– Exodus 23:20

Special Agent Freely and Rebekah were winding through the mountainous road toward the young mother and her child. Freely didn't know why he had allowed Rebekah to come along, but for whatever reason he liked her and thought it might seem less intimidating if she were there.

She broke the silence. "So, what are you expecting to find when we get there."

He chuckled. "A mother, her son, and nothing more."

"Nothing more? Really? Even after the conducting interviews, watching the tapes, and reading your reports?" The last words were said with a bit of resentment. He hadn't given up any information on why he was here to investigate a death that happened four years ago. He knew she desperately wanted to know what really happened.

"I'm not giving you the reports to read, period. Nor am I telling you why I was asked to come reopen the case." He smiled at her persistence. "You are already on the Godly child bandwagon, and I don't need any more people feeding the frenzy."

Rebekah frowned at him.

"Don't look at me like that, you know I am right. This little boy is not some mystical being, and there will be a full medical explanation to what happened to the poor sucker in the store. Besides, I read Mr. Reese's past rap sheet. The world is a better place without him."

Rebekah gave him a fake smile. "Special Agent Freely! I am shocked at your hateful view of a man you didn't even know."

Freely shook his head. "Whatever. Just don't get wrapped up in gossip. You don't need to be buying into the small-town talk of a child from God healing people of cancer and resurrecting dead dogs. Do you realize how crazy all these people sound?"

She sighed. "Oh, so Melanie from the store told you the dog story."

"Yeah, she told me, and I think it's all a bunch of crap. I think people like a feel-good story, and things get embellished."

"Well for the record, the dog was not resurrected. Elkan only healed his injury." It was hard to keep the sarcasm out of her tone. "If you're going to be a cynic, you need to get the facts correct."

Freely knew he had offended her, and that was not his intent. He could not tell her the FBI was already aware of these stories—an unknown source had sent copies of ancient writings about the prophesy of a child along with the information about Elkan. Freely was here to investigate and put a stop to the nonsense, but he didn't want to hurt Rebekah. She had quickly become his ally, and he liked her.

"Listen, I'm sorry if I have upset you, but do you have any idea how crazy all of this sounds? I mean really, this is ridiculous to be having this conversation. A boy sent from Heaven? Give me a break."

She turned in her seat to look at him, "Yes, I do know it sounds crazy. But wouldn't it be great if it were true? A child sent by God in our time? The little boy could change this crappy world. So excuse me for choosing to believe in something wonderful."

Freely decided he wasn't going to win this argument and was not going to discuss it further. "Let's just stay focused on the task ahead. I want to talk to the mother and wipe it off the to-do list."

They rode in silence the rest of the way. Freely hated to extinguish her excitement with his matter-of-fact mentality, but he wasn't going to be sucked into the delusions of others.

****

Syene sat on the back deck with her legs stretched out. Elkan sat quietly with her, reading a book. His intelligence scared her sometimes. She did everything she could to give him normality and make sure he still did six-year-old boy things, like play catch, go fishing, hide and seek, and chase with Ariel and Sam. She smiled at her beautiful child and thought how strange it was he could seem like a typical boy, and in another moment be speaking Hebrew to her like the wisest of souls. She spoke his name quietly.

"Elkan."

He looked up at her, putting the book down. His cheeks were flushed with the colder air. She stroked his hair. He never lost his beautiful curls from when he was young, and she may have been guilty of not cutting his hair often enough because she was afraid they would disappear.

"I love you, I will always protect you." And she meant it with every part of her body and soul. She had no idea she could love another person as much as she loved him. Her heart ached every time she thought of his possible fate. How was the world going to treat him? She knew they were going to try to tear him apart, treat him as a scientific oddity, hate him for the messages he was to bring, and try to take him from her. Tears sprang to her eyes thinking of all the *what ifs*. She hid her face, so he wouldn't see her sadness. His fingers touched her cheek, and she turned to look at him giving her bravest smile.

"I love you, Mommy. God loves you. 'And which of you by being anxious can add a single hour to his span of life?'" He was speaking to her in Hebrew again with his mind and of course quoting Scripture. She tried to encourage him to use his words, but he seemed to prefer this method.

"Elkan, I have asked you so many times to use your voice."

He shrugged. "I have my whole life to use my voice."

Syene could only smile at his simple answer. She pulled away to look at him.

"You're too smart for your own good."

He kissed her cheek and picked up his book to read again.

James stepped out onto the deck. "You have visitors."

Syene could see the worry on his face. "Visitors?"

"An investigator with the FBI and a young woman are here to see you. Ariel answered the door, she's with them now. They want to speak with you." Syene stood, looking at Elkan.

"I'll stay with him. They are waiting on the front porch." Elkan adored James and immediately put his book down.

James tousled his hair. "Let's grab the gloves and play some catch." Elkan ran inside to get the gloves, and Syene followed.

She found Ariel sitting on the couch flipping through a magazine.

"Ariel, really, James said you were with them?"

Her sister shrugged. "They can wait outside by themselves. They are only here to nose around about the creep in the grocery store. That's old news, so I didn't see a reason to stand out there and answer any questions."

Sy shook her head in exasperation. "Seriously?"

Ariel only shrugged again.

Syene walked to the front door and opened it slowly, dreading what was coming next.

"Can I help you?" Syene stepped onto the porch and thought they would for sure be able to hear the nervousness in her voice.

The agent forward. "Syene Harper?"

"Yes."

He stuck out his hand. "Special Agent John Freely." His hand was ignored. She, like Ariel, was not interested in answering questions from an incident four years ago. She had already been through this with the local police.

"What can I do for you, Agent Freely?" She said the words while looking at Rebekah, who began to blush at the intense stare she was receiving. Syene was putting up her walls. Rebekah smiled. Syene did not return the smile. She was not in the mood for questioning about Elkan.

"Hi, I'm Rebekah Fabinski." The woman apparently learned from her companion's mistake and didn't offer her hand.

Syene's eyes went back to Freely, her arms crossed across her chest. She was doing her best to make it clear she did not want them here.

Freely slightly cleared his throat. Syene was making this awkward, and she found it slightly amusing. He pulled out a pad of paper and began reciting information.

"I would like to ask you a few questions about an incident at the local grocery store you may have been witness to? It involved a man by the name of Phil Reese."

Syene stood her ground.

"I'm aware. Whatever happened to Mr. Reese, happened a long time ago. I answered a dozen questions for the police back when it happened, so why am I being questioned again?"

Freely nodded and abruptly answered, "Yes, I read the report, but unfortunately, the FBI has decided to review the case a little more closely, and I have to interview all available witnesses." He showed her his identification and waited patiently.

The FBI? This was getting worse by the moment, and Syene realized her abrupt attitude was not going to help. Freely was clearly growing tired of her rudeness, and his tone became sterner.

"Ms. Harper, I would like to talk to you about the incident and exactly what happened that day."

Syene glanced behind him and Rebekah, where several of the warrior angels lingered close by. Freely turned around to see what had captured her attention. He quite obviously saw nothing. He was not a believer and would not be granted the gift of sight. She could see her nervousness was making them nervous.

He spoke again. "Are we boring you already, Ms. Harper?"

Syene snapped her eyes forward again. Rebekah kept glancing behind them.

"What is it you need, Mr. Freely?" Syene couldn't keep the coldness out of her tone.

Syene's mind was running a million miles a minute. *What was she going to say? Why was this coming back up?*

Right then, the front door opened, causing a startled Freely to take a step back.

Ariel stood in the doorway.

"Syene?" She could hear the concern in Ariel's voice. Everyone was too jumpy, so this was not going well. Sy knew she was going to cast more suspicion on the situation if she didn't do something. The holstered gun on his right hip did not go unnoticed. She normally had all the good faith in the world for law enforcement, but right now Elkan was the only thing that mattered. She shouldn't have been so rude and immediately softened her tone and stance.

"Agent Freely, I apologize for my abruptness. Our father was a police officer, and I have nothing but respect for what you do. I just don't know what you want from me. All that happened so long ago, and we have already told the police everything we know."

Ariel stayed lurking in the doorway. Syene knew her sister was ready to become her warrior if necessary. In her most cheerful voice, Syene introduced Ariel. "I believe you met my younger sister, Ariel, earlier. I apologize for her rudeness, as well."

Ariel stuck out her hand this time. "Hello again."

Freely shook her hand. "Special Agent John Freely, and this is Ms. Fabinski."

Rebekah smiled and shook her hand. "Please call me Rebekah. Ms. Fabinski sounds like a schoolteacher." Syene felt a good energy from Rebekah and felt guilty for being rude to her.

Ariel smiled sweetly. "What exactly is this about, Agent . . . Freely, was it?" Ariel was always a much better charmer than her older sister. Syene was grateful for the intervention, since her mind was not functioning fast enough.

"Yes, it's Freely." Sy could see him physically relax a little. "I was just telling your sister I wanted to talk to her about the incident at the grocery store several years ago concerning Mr. Phil Reese. She and your nephew were on the surveillance video, and I was hoping she could shed some light on what happened that day."

Ariel glanced at Syene "Sy, do you feel up to talking about what you saw that day?" Syene could see her sister urging her with her eyes to say something, but she was frozen in time. *No, she didn't want to talk to them*, but she could almost hear Ariel screaming at her *SAY SOMETHING, YOU DUMMY. YOU ARE MAKING IT WORSE!*

Syene got the message, and she gave in peacefully. "Of course, please come in."

They followed Syene and Ariel inside. Syene scanned the room quickly and outside in the back for Elkan. She didn't see him. Ariel answered her question without her asking. "Elkan went to his room to play, since he decided it was too cold outside for catch." Sy gave her a smile.

Ms. Fabinski picked up a frame holding a picture of Elkan and Syene. Elkan was laughing as Syene was attempting to give him a bear hug.

"Is this Elkan? He's beautiful. I'm surprised I have never run into either of you in town."

Syene smiled. "We don't go into town too much. And Elkan is homeschooled, so we rarely have a reason to be there unless we are just in the mood for an outing."

She motioned to the living area. "Please, come sit."

She watched as Freely made a quick glance around and how he positioned himself near a chair with a good vantage point for entries into the living room. He was clearly not comfortable and could feel something in the air.

The agent began his inquiry. "Is this your home?"

Syene shook her head. "No, it belongs to Pastor Dave Rose and his wife, Susan. Dave and Susan were friends of my parents." She glanced at Ariel. "We lost our mother six years ago, and Dave and Susan have been kind enough to let us stick around. They really took us under their wings when we needed them the most."

Freely looked around. "Are they here?"

"No. I am not sure where they are. They said they were going to town to run errands."

"And your father? Where is he, if you don't mind me asking? You mentioned he was a police officer."

"He died years ago when I was little. Ariel was only a baby." She paused. "He was killed in the line of duty."

"I'm sorry to hear that." Sy could hear the genuineness in his voice and knew he meant it.

"Does anyone else stay here with you?"

Syene nodded. "People from the church always come to visit." Freely pulled a pen out and began writing in his small pocket notebook.

"Anyone visiting right now?"

Syene cautiously answered his questions. "James is here. He is a close friend of the family." Syene thought it best to not mention he was the man who murdered her father. Freely already seemed suspicious enough of the situation. She watched as the angels moved within the living room surrounding them. She was grateful Freely was looking at his notebook and not at her, but she could see Rebekah looking behind her to see what had caught Syene's eye. Of course, she saw nothing, but Sy could tell she was feeling uneasy.

Freely kept pushing. "Anyone else?"

"Yes, Julie stays here and helps with Elkan a lot. She is a widow and a dear friend of ours. Our grandmother is visiting, but she is out shopping with Julie. And Ariel's friend Sam was here visiting for a few weeks, but he just left to go back home. Oh, and Father Cervini lives here."

When Syene said the words out loud it was very awkward, and she realized how bizarre everything sounded. She honestly couldn't blame either of them for the strange looks they had on their faces.

"A priest lives here?"

Syene shrugged her shoulders. She was speechless at this point and didn't know what to say. How in the world was she supposed to explain why these odds and ends all lived in the same house? She looked to Ariel for some help and got zilch. From the look on Ariel's face it looked like she was having the same thoughts as she was. *We sound like a bunch of whack-jobs living together.*

Like magic, as if he knew he was needed, James appeared in the doorway. Syene couldn't hide her relief, and the agent turned to see what had caused the smile on her face.

Syene saw the look of surprise on Freely's and Rebekah's faces.

"James Viney, it's nice to meet you." James shook both of their hands with his normal, open friendliness. Syene could see Freely looking at the gang tattoos riddled over James's arms. Tattoos from a previous and long-forgotten life.

Unfortunately, this was only adding to the oddity and suspicion of her situation.

Rebekah was smiling sweetly, but she too could not keep the look of surprise from her face. Syene knew they made a very unlikely pair to be close friends. It became very apparent how superficial people could be. She felt pained for the prejudice James had to suffer throughout his life, not only because of his race but also the life choices he had made when young. She was firmly realizing what a true overcomer he was. She was proud to call him her friend.

The looks of shock did not go unrecognized by James, and she saw the all too familiar smirk her dear friend got on his face when he was amused. Syene knew without a doubt, from the stories James had told her, Agent Freely was aware of what the tattoos represented. But she also knew this was nothing new to James, that he had learned long ago to not let it bother him.

"What brings you here today?" James sat next to Syene on the couch.

"I have some questions about what happened with Mr. Reese in the grocery store several years ago."

James nodded. "It was all very bizarre."

Freely shook his head. "Bizarre is putting it mildly. So you were there when the events occurred?"

"I was, sir. I didn't witness him collapsing, but I was at the store with Syene and Elkan."

Freely, again began writing in his notepad. "Can you tell me what you did see?"

James shrugged his shoulders. "Well, I honestly didn't see much. I wasn't at the front of the store with Syene. But I did hear some shouting, and by the time I made it there, Mr. Reese had already collapsed. He was foaming from his mouth and looked as if he was having a seizure." James waited for Freely to finish writing. "Other than that, I can't really tell you much."

"Did you hear what he was yelling?"

James shook his head. "No sir, I didn't."

Freely seemed disinterested in James's well-rehearsed story and turned his attention to her. "Ms. Harper, surveillance video shows what appears to be your son approaching Mr. Reese before he collapsed. Witnesses have stated that he was yelling at Elkan loudly. And that your son seemed to be speaking a different language. Can you confirm any of this?"

She did her best to sound nonchalant. "Agent Freely, Elkan was two years old when this happened, so the only language he would have been speaking was toddler gibberish. And as far as Mr. Reese goes, he seemed deranged. He kept yelling for Elkan to stay away from him. The man seemed terrified. Of what, I don't know. All I wanted was to get Elkan out of there." Syene prayed her face wasn't showing how nervous she felt inside. She could feel her palms becoming sweaty.

"Do you have any idea why he was yelling at your son to stay away from him?"

"No, of course not."

James spoke up. "Agent Freely, let's be honest here. I know the tattoos have not gone unnoticed by you, so I know it won't come as a surprise to you I know some things about drug addiction."

Freely stopped writing to look up at James. Syene could see Rebekah's cheeks flushing again with embarrassment.

"From what I read in the paper, Mr. Reese had a long criminal history involving drug abuse." James continued, "I can speak personally about this. When you are high, you see things that are not there. They are drug-induced hallucinations, as I am sure you are very aware. So I must question what any of this has to do with Syene or Elkan? Mr. Reese obviously died as a consequence of his own addictions."

Freely looked directly at James. "I would, in most cases, agree with what you are saying. However, the video shows Elkan reaching out to touch Mr. Reese."

Syene shook her head. "And? I picked him up before he touched anyone. And why would that matter anyway? You think my two-year-old son caused that man to die?"

"Of course not, I am only here to gather information on a suspicious death." Syene could hear a hint of hostility in his voice. "A drug-induced heart attack may be what the newspaper assumed was the cause of death, but the truth is, Mr. Reese was burned to death from the inside out."

Syene knew the look of shock on her face was visible. And James was clearly having the same reaction. She couldn't speak. Thank God James was there.

"What? How is that even possible?" James's voice rang with the same shock Syene was feeling.

"That is exactly why I am here, Mr. Viney. I have no idea how it is possible, nor do I understand why this wasn't investigated further. All I know is I am here now to do just that, find out how."

Syene found her voice. "I still don't understand what this has to do with Elkan? By your tone, it sounds like you think my son, or I, had something to do with this?"

"Ms. Harper, I am only here to find out what you observed that day? I am not making any accusations."

"Okay, let me tell you exactly what I observed that day. I saw a man out of his mind, screaming obscenities at me and my son and God only knows who else. I grabbed my son to get him away from the situation, and the man collapsed. That is all I can tell you, and that is all I remember. Elkan was too young at the time to remember any of it. Is there anything else you need?"

"Any idea what he was screaming?"

"No, I already told you I didn't understand a word of it." That was a lie of course, she knew exactly what he had been saying. He was speaking in a mixture of Latin and Greek, and Syene understood every word. He was screaming at them to stay away and a warning his Master was coming for Elkan.

"I'm really not comfortable answering any more of your questions." Syene found her strength quickly. She stood to indicate the questioning was over, and it was time for them to go.

Freely stood, and Rebekah followed his lead.

He reached into his pocket and pulled out a business card, handing it to Syene "My contact information, in case you think of anything else you might have forgot." Syene took it, relieved they were leaving without a hassle.

She and James walked them to the door. Freely casually turned around. "Oh, just one more question. I know this may sound strange, but did either of you happen to see two extremely tall men in the store that day? Some strange images showed up on surveillance video."

James asked the obvious. "Strange how?"

Freely laughed. "Well, I feel silly even saying it, but it looks like the men have wings."

Syene knew her face was giving it all away. "Ummm, excuse me?"

Freely already had his answer from her face. She was not good at hiding her emotions.

"Oh, never mind. I'm sure it was nothing. Some type of trick on the eye because of the lighting. Thank you both for your time."

James closed the door behind them. Syene was reeling from the information she just heard. Burned on the inside? She had never heard any of this.

****

Rebekah looked over at Freely as soon as the car door shut. "What the hell was all that about?"

He started the car and began driving.

"Syene Harper is hiding something. She is fully aware of what we saw on the surveillance video. After all these years as a law enforcement agent, I know when someone is lying."

Rebekah continued with her questioning as if he hadn't spoken. "Were you serious with all that? He was burned from the inside out? Figures with wings? What is going on?" Her reporter's mind was going a hundred miles per hour.

"I expect you to keep everything you have heard confidential. You are only here because you know the area and the local people. Is that understood? If one bit of this ends up in your newspaper article, I will make sure you and the newspaper is sued for leaking classified information."

Rebekah glared at him. "I'm not an idiot. You don't need to speak to me like I am. But I am involved now, and I would like some answers."

"Fair enough." He began filling her in on some of the details of the case as they drove back to town, obviously leaving out anything that might be classified. She listened carefully, without saying a word, as any good reporter did when being fed information.

Rebekah went over everything in her mind. What appeared, on the surface, to be an odd relationship between Syene Harper and James Viney. Syene's defensiveness. Their interview with Karen Caldwell. What did the young woman keep looking at behind them when they were sitting in the living room? Something felt very strange in the room. Rebekah's mind was racing. She felt as if something bigger than anything imaginable was about to happen. She felt energized.

Freely's voice brought her back to the car and out of her own head. His voice was stone cold. "I don't know what the hell is going on in that house, but I am damn sure going to find out."

She could tell he was not feeling her same excitement and decided to keep her thoughts to herself. Rebekah agreed without a doubt something big was happening, and she also knew Special Agent Freely was keeping information from her. She planned on finding out exactly what it was he was hiding.

Chapter Nine

Jesus went through the towns and villages, teaching as he went, always pressing on toward Jerusalem. – Luke 13:22

The bell over the door chimed at the local café. Father Cervini glanced past Dave and Susan, seated across from him, to see three people walk in and find a table. The older gentleman made eye contact with the priest and gave him a friendly nod, while his two younger companions headed straight to a booth. Cervini smiled at the man and brought his attention back to the couple sitting across from him. They both looked worried.

"Tony, I just don't know how we are going to move Syene and Elkan safely." Father Cervini watched as Susan put her hand on her husband's and squeezed. He could see how stressed they both were.

"Worrying is keeping Dave up, and lack of sleep isn't helping anything. It's the reason I asked you to come with us, so we could talk alone. I don't want to upset Syene more than she already is. We just need some guidance. Any guidance."

Tony reached across the table and patted both of their hands.

"Dave, look at me."

Dave reluctantly looked at the priest, the dark circles from sleep deprivation obvious.

"Hasn't God proven himself to you? Has He not shown His great power and love? A love you can touch and feel and hear? How much more does He need to reveal until you stop trying to rush ahead and take control of His plans? Wasn't it our wondrous Savior who said, 'Don't worry about tomorrow. It will take care of itself. You have enough to worry about today.' You of all people know this. You've preached it to your congregations."

"Tony, I know you are right. I hear you, but I am struggling. I don't know what's wrong. I feel a darkness over me. I respect and admire you as a priest and a friend, but I just don't have your faith right now. This is bigger than all of us. How does God expect people like us to protect Elkan and Syene? Susan and I have to return to our home and our church. Our friends Darla and Charles have agreed to take them in, but how can we possibly prepare them for what they are about to be exposed to? We are dragging yet another couple into a situation we have no control over."

Tony was fully aware of struggles in faith and worry; he himself had dealt with it more than once. And the tasks ahead of them were overwhelming.

"Dave, I do understand. I wonder the very same things. Why me, God? Why us? I have no idea how we are going to keep him safe, but I know we were chosen for a reason. God has always chosen for a reason. I must have faith. If not, I have nothing. Without faith there is no hope. And I believe, because of Elkan being here with us, this entire world has hope again."

Susan spoke up. "You have to tell Tony about the dreams. They are only getting worse. And now Syene is having nightmares again. Lucifer is after our peace."

Dave had night terrors almost every night. Nightmares about the battle they had fought. The dark angels, the death of the people that day. Syene giving birth, in such excruciating pain, crying out for her mother. It was torturous. And Satan was always there. Laughing and dragging Elkan and Syene away from all of them.

Father Cervini looked directly at Dave. "Tell me."

"It's . . ." He paused. "It's just not getting enough sleep, I'm sure."

The priest nodded. "Perhaps, but why don't you go ahead and tell me."

Susan urged him. "Please honey, tell him."

Dave sighed deeply. "It's Satan, I know it is. He is entering my dreams. I see him as a dragon and the monster he is, or at least the monster I imagine him to be. He always manages to get Elkan and Syene away from our protection. The Creator's warriors are slaughtered, and he is always standing there with a blood-dripped grimace. Laughing. Thousands of people standing behind him cheering. Cheering like idiots. But they don't see what I see. When he turns toward them he is a beautiful figure they trust. I feel like Lucifer is disguising himself as someone good, and we are all going to be fooled. It terrifies me." Dave tried to smile. "Stupid, right?" He looked to the priest for reassurance.

Cervini now realized the depths of his friend's sorrow and understood the reason for Susan's concern. She was frightened, not only for her husband, but for all of them. He wasn't sure how he missed the deterioration of his friend's physical appearance. Cervini remembered his own frightening nightmares in the beginning, dreaming of the dragon emerging from the ocean and devouring innocent souls. The dreams that led him to Syene. He understood how terrifying they were, and he also understood it was very possible for Satan to be in human form. He was the *Deus Deceptor* after all.

"Not stupid at all. You must protect yourself. I believe we have all become complacent while surrounded by the Creator's warriors. We have forgotten we must restore our faith daily. But you must stop with the nonsense of doubt. Do you not see you are letting Satan manipulate your mind and soul? Deception is his greatest gift. He built an army based on his lies. I can only imagine turning God's own angels against their Creator was not a small feat. Manipulating a few simpleminded humans such as us is nothing to him."

Dave nodded his understanding. "That is my point exactly. He was able to deceive God's angels, why couldn't all of this be a trick too? Of all the years of training and experience I have had as a pastor, I never thought I would be the one having these doubts. What if we are wrong? What if all this is a trick by Satan to deceive the world? Wouldn't this be a perfectly executed plan?"

The priest shook his head. "Dave, that's nonsense, and you know it. His skill of deception is where it all went wrong. He thought himself to be greater than his own Creator. He was boastful and arrogant. He even believed he had enough power to turn God's Son against the Creator. You must stop with the questioning. You have seen God's warriors fight by your side. Lucifer might be a master of deception, but he cannot duplicate the love you have felt while on this journey. He cannot duplicate the angels, the love of the angels, the love of the strangers who have come on faith alone, the love of Syene and Elkan."

He took Dave's hand. "Do you understand what I'm telling you? What you are saying is not possible. Lucifer is not capable of all those things that you have experienced. And let me tell you the simple reason why. Because he does not understand one thing about love. Certainly he is capable of manipulation, using our own weaknesses. He can cause worry, discontent, and disbelief. But he is the one who is weak. He has no power over his Creator. He has no power over you."

Dave smiled, a real smile this time, and Tony could see some of the worry dissipate from his eyes. "You are right, I have allowed him to prey on my weaknesses."

The priest shrugged. "Take it as a compliment, he goes after the strong. When we fight for God, the real spiritual warfare begins. We all face moments of weakness. You just need to polish up the armor you have worn so well, for so long." He smiled at Dave and Susan, hoping he brought them some peace. He had his own worries and concerns, but doubt was not one of them. He knew he was exactly where God needed him to be.

"We all could do a little polishing. I almost feel as if being with the angels for this amount of time and being with Elkan every day has dulled the experience. We must never forget the incredible journey we are on. What a beautiful gift we have been given. We should never lose the awestruck wander every time we are in the presence of one of our Creator's holy creations. And as far as your friends Charles and Darla are concerned, I will be there to consult and guide them. God has already laid out the plan for them. I have a feeling they are not going to be as shocked as you think when they find out the truth."

****

Dr. Kaufman strangely felt some sense of relief a priest was in the restaurant eating when they walked in. He chuckled to himself at the thought of a Jewish man finding comfort in a priest. Kaufman felt as if he was being watched by someone when they were outside. It was not a good feeling. He saw the priest as a sign of protection. A sign from God perhaps. Silly, he knew, but it helped him reason through this irrational path his life had taken.

What if he was wrong? What if the Cassius writings were a hoax? He would be a fool who had wasted much of his time and resources. Not to mention dragging his two young comrades along with him. Dragging them across the world in search of a child who might not exist.

Laura and Thomas were oblivious to anyone and to the worried look on the doctor's face. The only thing on their minds was the food in front of them.

"I didn't realize how much I missed American food." Laura looked down at her half-eaten plate. "It's good to be back." She took a big gulp of orange juice, feeling happy and excited for the day ahead. "So, what's the plan for today? I can't wait to hear what you've found out."

Thomas slowed down on the pancakes to give his attention to Kaufman.

"Well, according to our friend at the motel, there has been a lot of activity happening again in town surrounding the death of the man in the newspaper article. He told me some of the rumors in town about how the child was speaking a different language in the grocery store, causing Mr. Reese to collapse and die and . . ." Kaufman sipped his coffee looking back at the priest, who made eye contact again.

Laura brought him back. "And?"

Kaufman smiled. "Patience, young Laura, patience."

"Sorry. I'm just so excited about all of it. I honestly feel like we are about to find something so wonderful and amazing."

"I think you are right. Our gossipy gentlemen told about a woman in town healed from cancer because of the little boy. He said it was all kept very secret, but the rumor was out there. And the child's name is Elkan."

"*Elkan?*" Thomas stopped the doctor. "What kind of name is *Elkan?*"

Kaufman smiled knowingly. "The Hebrew kind. The name means belonging to God."

"What?" Laura couldn't believe it. "You can't be serious. Cassius's writings said the child's name would be *belonging to God*. This is unbelievable! We have found him, Dr. Kaufman. We have found him!"

Thomas seemed confused. Laura looked at him exasperated. "Did you not read any of the writings?" Thomas blushed. He obviously had not. He was still not a believer.

"Thomas! Cassius called the boy to be born as belonging to God! Are you kidding me? How could you not know any of this?" She looked at the doctor. "This is not a coincidence. We have found him. It has to be him!"

Kaufman calmed her. He wasn't ready to announce all of this to the entire café.

"One moment at a time, Laura. We must be sure. We must make sure this is real. We cannot assume."

Laura sighed and lowered her voice. "I understand, and I'm sorry. I'm just so excited."

"I know, young Laura, I know. Let us finish our breakfast and go meet our Elkan."

****

Jerusalem – Less than a week before the crucifixion of Jesus

Cassius pulled off his armor and placed it near the door. It had been a long few weeks. News of the Galilean coming to Jerusalem was causing exuberant behavior within the city's walls. Pilate had warned the Pharisees they better deal with their problem, but Cassius and his men were still dealing with uproar associated with this man Jesus.

"You look tired, my love." His Alypia was the best part of his day. She walked to him and kissed him gently. He kissed her back, thankful she was his.

"Come." She pulled him into the triclinium where she had prepared a beautiful dinner.

"Where are the children?"

She looked at him with her seductive eyes.

"Asleep. I needed time with my husband." She poured his wine and sat on the luxurious pillows she had set out for their dinner.

"You, my beautiful Alypia, are the reason I live."

She kissed him again and smiled.

"Eat and drink your wine. Tell me of all the adventures you had today, and I will tell you of the rumors I have heard in the market."

Cassius couldn't help but laugh. "I can hardly describe my days here as adventures. But if you want me to bore you with details, then very well."

She settled in closely to him and prepared his plate, excited to share everything she had been hearing and to compare their stories.

He obliged her with the stories of the last few weeks, trying to add some color to his tales. The Jewish community was gathering in large crowds, demanding answers from the Pharisees. Was Jesus their new King or a fraud? He told her of the angry comments and actions against the Romans.

"You must be careful right now going out to the market. They are angry about our presence here. Some of them believe this man is going to free them from their poverty and create a new kingdom here on earth."

"You are holding back, Cassius. There is something you are not telling me."

"You know me too well." He sighed heavily. "I know Pilate is hiding something from me, I can sense it. He is worried about this man, and I feel as if I am on a collision course with disaster."

She held his hand tightly. "You must pray to the gods, Cassius. They will protect you."

Cassius shook his head in agreement only to appease his wife. He knew the gods would not help him this time.

Alypia was not afraid; she had never been received with anything but kindness by the people here. She spoke quietly. "I have heard them talk of him in the market. They say he heals the sick and raises the dead. The blind can see now because of him. Is all this true?"

Cassius shrugged. "I have heard the same, but I know of no man that can do such things." He touched her perfect nose as she looked at him. "You need to stop listening to the rumors of the local women. They only want to believe in their religious prophecies."

"I would be bored if I didn't have their stories. Their traditions fascinate me."

He knew he wouldn't convince her to stop her market trips for good. "Can you please send the servants to the market until their Passover is finished. Please, for me."

"Very well, my love. I will stay away until the trouble passes. You have my word. Now finish your dinner so I may have my way with you."

"My dinner can wait."

He pulled her tightly into his arms, unable to resist her any longer.

Chapter Ten

***The woman approached him, seductively dressed and sly
of heart. – Proverbs 7:10***

Jamille walked into the room as Ariel sat with Syene
talking about the upcoming move and their visit from Special
Agent Freely. Syene ran to her as soon as she saw her.

"Jamille, I am so glad you are back." Jamille hugged
her tightly.

"I hear you had some visitors in my absence."

Syene told her everything and all the questions they
asked. "I just don't understand why all this is coming back up?
And now we are moving, which is going to cast even more
suspicion on Elkan."

Jamille did her best to reassure her. "I believe answers
will be revealed to us soon as to why there is a focus on Elkan.
We will get through this together."

Syene clung to Jamille. She loved everything about her.
Her smell, her strength. She made her feel closer to her mother.
She felt protected when she was near.

She whispered, "Did you see my mom?"

Jamille squeezed her tightly. "Yes, I saw your mom and
your dad. They told me to tell you and Ariel how much they
love you. They are always with you."

"I know. I just wish I could see her and talk with her
one more time."

Jamille pulled back. "One day, Sacred. One day. You have got to stay focused on Elkan right now. He needs you now more than ever."

"You're right. I'm stuck in this selfish cycle of sadness, and I can't seem to pull myself out." Syene looked to her protector for answers. "What's wrong with me, Jamille?"

"Nothing is wrong with you. You are in pain, and you have gone through more things than the human mind can handle. This will pass, Syene. Unfortunately, pain is an unavoidable part of life. No matter who you are. You can either let it take you to a place of darkness or grow from it and fulfill your Creator's purpose for your life."

Jamille gently pulled Syene's chin up so she would look at her in the eyes.

"Elkan was not your only purpose. You have a choice to make. You must always make the best of this life you have been given. Although unimaginable grace and beauty awaits you with the Creator, it is always about fulfilling your purpose here."

Syene knew she was right. The logical part of her knew everything being said was true, but the emotional part would not allow her heart to heal. She felt as if she had to trade people she loved so she could protect her son. She hated the thoughts invading her head. He was everything to her, yet she sometimes resented his birth. When those thoughts took over she could hardly bear what she had become.

"Syene . . ."

She looked at Jamille.

"Perhaps you need to remember to place the Creator at the center and not all the thoughts haunting you."

The bitterness did not subside, but Syene managed to keep her thoughts to herself.

Not one person understands what I am going through. Not even Jamille.

She had never felt so alone.

She was allowing her own inner battles to dilute her life in the here and now. She was allowing Lucifer to enter her dreams and attack her insecurities. She was allowing him to win.

****

Enzril stood on the mountain range watching the house. He was aware of Jamille's presence without seeing her. He knew she had returned; he could feel her. The numbers of the Creator's warriors were increasing. Something was about to happen. The demons were hiding among the trees surrounding the house. They wouldn't dare get close while so many warriors protected the child and his mother, but should an opportunity arise, they could attack. The irritating roaches scattered and kept their distance whenever Enzril arrived, but he could still hear the hisses from the forest.

The sun was setting and shone its last rays onto the house. Then she appeared on the back deck. The glow from the last light of the day shimmered off her raven hair. She was so breathtaking, making his heart beat loudly. Jamille looked up into the mountains as if she knew he was there watching. He would give anything to touch her again, to speak to her. But her love for the humans made it impossible. Or was it his hatred of them? Things didn't seem as clear as they once had.

****

"Beautiful, isn't she?"

Enzril turned around, startled. Kefira, one of Master's warriors, stood behind him.

"Kefira, I didn't hear you. Your skills are becoming stronger."

She smiled.

"Well, I have been trained by you, Enzril, and you are the best. Although you did seem preoccupied. So is it my skills or your fascination with her that kept me unnoticed?" She glanced back at Jamille.

He didn't respond to her questioning. "What brings you here, Kefira?"

Kefira had become Enzril's project by orders of Lucifer. He was to train her to become a commander. She was one of the few females to be given this position, and she knew Enzril was proud of her progress. She was strong and smart.

The warrior pushed her blonde hair out of her face and smiled at her commander seductively. "Master has asked for me to stay with you until he further orders. The demons have told him of the recent activity surrounding the child, and he wants my training to continue.

Enzril nodded. "Very well." He turned his attention back to the house.

She wanted to scream on the inside. *Very well*? That was it? No signs of excitement at all. Why wouldn't he look at her the way he had been staring at Jamille? She hated the Creator's angels, and she was going to make sure Enzril forgot about her. Kefira may have been sent by Master to stand by her commander, but she had her own agenda. Enzril would be hers, whether Jamille was alive or dead. And the latter was preferred. She stared at her General possessively and smiled to herself. She would win his affection . . . she never lost anything she went after.

Not too much longer, and it would be *Jamille who?* Although she did have to admit it was taking much more effort than her previous targets. If she were being honest, the chase only made it more enticing.

Kefira looked at her dark commander. His rebellious attitude toward Master made him sexier than ever. She wanted to have some fun with him before he was caught and tortured. And he would be caught, there was no doubt. Males and their egos could be quite dangerous to themselves.

She touched his arm and kept it there a little too long. "Come, let's go. There is nothing here for you. You know I am right. It is time to move on."

Chapter Eleven

God looks down from heaven on the entire human race;
he looks to see if anyone is truly wise, if anyone seeks
God. – Psalm 53:2

Syene and Ariel were trying to pack up Elkan's belongings, with him making it almost impossible by taking everything out of the boxes as soon as they could put them in.

"Elkan! Please, we have to pack." She gently pulled his hands out of the box.

He ignored her request and moved to another box.

Syene was on edge, and she raised her voice. "Elkan, what are you doing? Stop!" She instantly saw the hurt on his face. It was rare she ever lost her temper with him. She sighed deeply, feeling guilty.

"Come here." She held out her arms.

He shook his head. "I'm too old for that."

"Please. You may be too old, but I'm not." She spread her arms even wider. He walked over, climbing into her lap and resting his head on her chest. "I'm sorry, honey. I'm just tired." He squeezed her back tightly.

"I just wanted to find Muffin. I don't want to lose him." Muffin was his stuffed toy dog he had since he was a baby. Her mom bought it for him while Syene was pregnant, and Elkan slept with him every night.

She looked at her sister, tears in her eyes and exhaustion all over her face. Everything was taking its toll on Syene.

Ariel gave her a reassuring smile. "I put Muffin in your backpack, Elkie, safe and sound. I thought you would want him with you."

He released Syene and jumped to his feet. "Thanks, Aunt Ariel!" He kissed her on the cheek, happily running out of the room.

Syene fell back on the floor, rubbing her head.

"What a creep I am. I forget too often he's only six."

Ariel lay next to her, and they both stared at the ceiling. "Remember when we would lie on the trampoline in our backyard for hours naming all the different things we would see in the clouds?"

Syene did remember. "That seems so long ago doesn't it? I sometimes can't believe I am going to be twenty-six."

Ariel leaned up on her elbow. "Ewww, you *are* old."

Sy laughed out loud. "You're right! I am." She sat up and looked around at the disaster they created while packing.

"How are we going to do all this without Grandma's expert organizational skills?"

Their grandmother had gone back home to finalize all the financial situations. She and Ariel had finally decided to sell the home they had grown up in, and Grandma had agreed to take care of everything for them. It would have been too hard emotionally for them to go back and see it.

Syene glanced at her sister. She had been so self-absorbed, she wasn't considering how hard everything had been on Ariel. Her little sister must be feeling heartbroken since Sam had left. She was almost nineteen now, and Sy knew she and Sam had grown very close.

"How is Sam? Have you heard from him since he left?" The few times he visited a year never seemed enough time for any of them and especially Ariel.

"He pretty much calls every day. And we text." She shrugged. "He wants to move with us, but I told him to stay and finish school. He will lose his scholarships if he changes schools."

Sy felt deeply sad for Ariel. She had given up everything because of Elkan. "Well, maybe we can get you enrolled in college when we get to our new place. If Sam still wants to be a veterinarian, he can apply to a program closer to you."

Ariel sighed. "I know. I just miss him."

Syene gave Ariel a tight hug. She didn't know what she would do without her, and she couldn't manage to shake off the feeling of warning overtaking her every thought.

****

Father Cervini stood in the doorway watching Syene as she stared out the window. Wesley lay at her feet and jumped up to greet the priest happily.

"Anything I can help with?" He motioned toward the scattered boxes. Today and most days he could see the sadness and worry on her face. The view of the mountains and trees brought no enjoyment.

Syene let out a deep sigh.

"No. Just wondering what our new home will be like. I know it seems weird, especially after losing my mom and the others here, but the mountains and forest surrounding the house made me feel safe."

Tony walked over to where she stood and looked out across the forest where most of the battle had taken place.

"Not weird. Maybe it comforts you to know you are close to where you lost your mom. I don't find it strange you want to stay near to where you think she might be."

Syene remained silent.

"Sy, you know she is with the Creator now. She left the moment it happened, but she is always with you no matter where you are."

"I know."

He wrapped his arm around her shoulders. "Besides the ocean air will be good for you. Good for all of us." Tony watched as the tears rolled down her cheeks.

"I just want to keep Elkan protected from everyone as long as possible. Is it sad to say the fear of what humans will do to him scares me as much as Lucifer?"

"Not at all. We live in a violent, deceptive world. It seems people are consumed with their own desires, hatred, love of self and idols. It is a shame they can't see how close God is. If they would only reach out."

Syene nodded. "I can hardly bear to watch the news anymore. It's always bad news. Murders, shootings, racial and political turmoil. I find it hard to believe this is how God has it planned. Giving freewill was a horrible idea."

"But then God allows us to have a glimmer of something wonderful. The birth of a child, an act of kindness, a renewal of faith in a struggling soul. In those brief moments I understand why God loves us so much, and I know how desperately He desires for us to succeed in this life."

He looked at Syene. "Now you need to tell me why I found you staring out the window lost in your thoughts instead of packing up the rest of this war zone." He finally got a smile out of her. It really did look like a bomb went off.

"Did you hear that an agent with the FBI showed up at the house?"

"Yes, James told me."

"Did James also tell you what happened to that man? Mr. Reese?"

The priest nodded his head. "He told me. The man was demon-possessed. Elkan had nothing to do with it. He was trying to help him, not harm him. I am convinced of that."

Syene said nothing.

Father Cervini pulled her face so she would look at him. "I have seen some terrible things done in Satan's name during my years of priesthood, and I can tell you with certainty Elkan did not do that to Mr. Reese. Nothing of God would have done such a thing. It is the *Deus Deceptor* and his trickery working on you. He is causing you to doubt God, Elkan, and yourself. You must stop this nonsense."

"I know you're right. My thoughts are awful, but I can't make them stop."

"What else do you need from God, Syene? What else can He possibly do to prove Himself to you? You do understand that it is not His job to make you a believer? It is *your* job to prove you believe. You are standing among the angels, His most glorious creations, and yet you still doubt? Why?"

Syene sat on the end of the bed, put her hands to her face, and sobbed. Wesley jumped up trying to lick here face and bring her some comfort. She pushed him away. "Wesley, stop!" He settled back down, dejected.

Father Cervini sat next to her.

"I'm not saying these things to hurt you, Syene. You must know this. But you have walked around in a world of depression for far too long. When will it be enough?"

He knew she didn't have the answer, didn't know how to pull herself out of the darkness.

"I want to give you something, Syene." He reached into his pocket and pulled out a rosary made of wooden beads. He took her hand and placed the beads there, closing her fingers around them tightly.

She looked at him, confused. "What am I supposed to do with these?"

"Do some research and then come talk to me when you are ready." He kissed her forehead gently and got up to leave. Wesley jumped up to follow.

"I think you need what the rosary has to offer. Answers you are seeking."

****

They drove up a winding road for seven miles and missed the gravel driveway on their left. Laura was driving and trying to concentrate. Dr. Kaufman was not the best copilot. She found a place to turn around and backtracked a half mile. They turned onto a narrow, tree-lined, gravel drive, and in another two hundred feet they came into clearing with a beautiful house and the mountains as a backdrop. The mixture of tension and excitement was heavy in the air.

Laura parked the car, "Okay, what is the plan? I guess we should have decided that a few miles back."

The doctor couldn't help but laugh. "That couldn't be a truer statement. I hadn't thought this far in advance. I was too excited we very possibly found the child our Cassius wrote about."

They were all three silent.

Thomas, being the least believing and therefore most at ease, spoke up.

"I say we just go up there and wing it."

Laura and the doctor laughed. Kaufman agreed.

"Winging it is what we shall do, Thomas. Good decision."

He grabbed his briefcase with his documentation and opened the car door. Laura and Thomas followed. He had no idea what he was going to say, but if this really was who he was looking for then the conversation would not be a hard one.

As they walked to the front steps the front door opened, and a handsome black man walked on to the porch.

"Can I help you?" His voice was friendly enough but guarded.

The doctor glanced at his notes. He had written down the name of the couple he was told owned the house.

"Mr. Rose?"

The man shook his head, "No, Dave is inside. Let me get him for you. Can I tell him your name, please, and what this might be about?"

Kaufman had been told by their friendly town gossip that several people lived in the home with the pastoral couple, so he was expecting to meet more than Dave and Susan.

"Dr. Robert Kaufman." He walked up the steps extending his hand. "And these are my two assistants, Ms. Laura Wilson and Mr. Thomas Wright."

"How do you do, I'm James." He shook all their hands, and Dr. Kaufman handed him a business card.

James took it, examining the card. "Impressive credentials. If you would like to wait inside, I will get Dave for you."

Kaufman graciously nodded. "Please tell Mr. Rose we apologize for the abrupt visit, but we have traveled all the way from Egypt on simple hope and a prayer that what we are seeking might be here."

James smiled politely, obviously noncommittal. He led the trio inside.

"Have a seat, I'll get Dave for you."

They all three sat, anxiously waiting.

****

James went to the kitchen where Dave and Susan were sitting discussing the plans of their move.

"Dave, there are a few people waiting in the living room. They asked for you. I pray this isn't trouble." He handed him Kaufman's business card. "There are two assistants with him, both young, probably around college age. He said they traveled from Egypt to come find you."

"What? To come find us? For what?"

Susan and Dave both stood from the table. Susan glanced out the back window. "I'm glad Syene is outside with everyone. She's had enough surprises after that FBI agent showed up."

Susan could see two of God's warriors already standing around the threesome in the living room, unbeknown to the guests. One of the angels gave Dave and Susan a reassuring smile. She felt immediate relief.

The trio all stood up when their hosts entered, and Dr. Kaufman stepped forward to greet them.

"Hello, my name is Dr. Robert Kaufman, these are my assistants, Laura and Thomas."

Dave examined the business card he had been handed. Susan could tell he wasn't quite ready to get overfriendly. "What can I do for you, Dr. Kaufman? I hear you have traveled a long way to come see us."

"Yes, you and others hopefully."

Susan put out her hand. "I am Susan Rose, it's nice to meet all of you. I apologize for my husband's abrasiveness, we just don't have many surprise visitors."

"I saw you both in town," Dr. Kaufman said with a smile.

Dave and Susan both looked confused.

"With a priest at the restaurant? We were there as well, having breakfast."

"Oh yes. We were there with our friend, Father Cervini. You must have a knack for faces."

"A gift of a photographic memory." He chuckled "Came in very useful when I was a young man in college."

Susan liked him. She knew there was no danger with him, and she could see her husband relax, but he did get right to the point.

"What exactly brings you here? James said you traveled from Egypt."

"Well, please don't think I am crazy, but I believe God has led me to you. At least this is my hope."

Susan and Dave both looked at each other and smiled.

"We are certain nothing you could say to us will make you seem crazy. Please continue."

Kaufman appeared happy to hear this as he pulled out his briefcase and began his story.

Chapter Twelve

For I hold you by your right hand—I, the Lord your God.
And I say to you, "Don't be afraid. I am here to help
you." – Isaiah 41:13

Farrel approached Amy as she dined alone at a small local restaurant. She was seated outside and looked preoccupied. He knew the demons wouldn't recognize him in human form. They were mindless imbeciles, and he hadn't seen any of them or the dark warriors lurking around. He saw his chance, and he was going to grab it.

"Hello." Amy looked up startled.

"Hel-lo." She fumbled over the greeting. She wasn't used to strangers just coming up to speak to her. Most fans didn't recognize her without makeup and her hair pulled into a hat. Master had her under constant supervision, although the reins had been loosened some, as of late. She was playing her game correctly, and she didn't need anything screwing it up. Her tone immediately went icy.

"Whatever you are selling, pawning, or giving away I am not interested."

Farrel laughed. "None of the above." He immediately recognized the vibrant, tough personality Syene had described about her friend.

She took her sunglasses off to look him directly in the eyes. "Then what do you want? And if it's a date, I'm not interested in that either." Truth be told, Amy wasn't allowed any friends. Male or female.

Farrel gave her a dazzling smile. "Not that either, I'm afraid." He motioned toward the chair across from her. "May I?"

She glared at him. "If you must." She knew the minute Master's little beasts saw her they would go back to report anything out of the ordinary and her little bit of freedom would be snatched away. She looked around nervously.

Farrel watched her looking around. He spoke to her quietly.

"Don't worry, they aren't around." Amy's head whipped back to look at him. Her eyes narrowed.

"Who are you?"

"A friend of Syene's."

Amy's face softened for a moment. Then it was gone.

"I don't know who you are talking about."

Farrel could only imagine what this poor girl had been through. He wasn't here to play games, and he wasn't going to add to her stress. He was afraid she was about to bolt from the table.

He slid a piece of paper over to her with his number.

"My name is Farrel, you can call me anytime. I am here to help you." He got up and left quickly.

Amy's heart pounded. She stared at the note lying on the table. She knew what would happen if she was caught. She put her napkin over it and slid it closer.

****

Enzril watched the scene unfold; Farrel's senses had obviously dulled in his wretched human form. He hadn't even noticed Enzril and Kefira watching. They were both lucky the cockroaches weren't crawling nearby, or Amy would be in for a horrific session with Master. He saw Farrel slip her a piece of paper, and the little fool grabbed it from under her napkin. Both were idiots.

"What is he up to?" Kefira's voice brought him from his own thoughts.

"Not sure, but it won't take long to find out."

Kefira stood very close to him, almost too close. She stirred a desire in him, and he wanted no part of it. He put distance between them. He knew she noticed his attempt to move away when she smiled slightly. She was getting to him and she knew it. Her seductiveness had power, and she was obviously going to use every bit of it to capture his attention.

"Are you going to tell Master his stupid little human is messing with one of the *good guys*." She laughed.

Enzril shook his head. "Not just yet. No need to put her through mindless torture when nothing has transpired. I will watch her and Farrel. Not necessary for you to be involved."

"Whatever you say," she replied sweetly, "but I really don't know why you care if a worthless human is tortured or not."

Enzril did not feel the need to respond. Kefira was young in her years as a warrior and had much to learn.

****

Amy didn't see the dark angels make their exit. Her heart was pounding wildly, and she wanted to run somewhere as fast as she could to call the stranger. Could he really be there to help her? She didn't dare get her hopes up. It was also possible this was just a cruel trick by her Master to test her loyalty. She was going to have to be careful. Amy stood and slipped the number into her front pocket.

Chapter Thirteen

This is the Lord's doing, and it is wonderful to see.
— Psalm 118:23

Syene watched as Susan walked across the grass to where she reclined, enjoying the sight of Ariel romping with Elkan.

She sat next to Syene. "How are you?"

Elkan laughed as Ariel and Julie chased him through the tall grass and wild flowers. Wesley bounded after them barking. Father Cervini was throwing a ball for Wesley, but the pet found Elkan and Ariel more interesting. His antics stirred up what seemed like hundreds of butterflies, floating around them like small blessings.

"Sad we are leaving here. I can't tell you enough how much I appreciate everything you and Dave have done for us."

Susan reached over and took Syene into her arms for a warm hug. "We love you, you know this. Please stop thanking us."

Sy loved Susan for everything she had done and who she was as a person. She always saw the positive in everything. Her faith never faltered, and Syene truly admired her for it. She was heartbroken the Roses weren't coming with them to their new home.

"I can't believe we are going to be without you guys. It's not going to be the same."

Susan held her hand tightly. "Us too, Syene. But we need to get home. You know we are only a phone call away, and of course we will come visit. You are going to love Charles and Darla. They said you can stay as long as you need to until you find your own place."

Syene nodded. "I pray we love it there. Nothing feels okay anymore."

Susan picked up the wooden rosary beads lying next to Syene on the grass. "You giving up on us Baptists and becoming Catholic?"

"Not sure what I am supposed to do with them." She waved in the direction of Father Cervini. "Tony gave them to me and told me to do some research."

She watched as Susan ran the beads through her hand. "Well, isn't that just typical. Our friend the priest always trying to convert another one?" She gave Syene a wink.

Syene smiled slightly. "Well, I'm not sure religion really matters at this point." She looked at her beautiful boy still running and laughing through the flowers.

Susan followed her gaze. "I think you're right." She looked back down at the beads in her hands. "I bet Tony had a much deeper purpose when he gave you the rosary. I would start with Mother Mary in your research."

Syene chuckled. "Oh great, that's all I need, more confirmation of how poorly I am doing this mother thing."

Susan didn't laugh. "You are a wonderful mother. Your mom would be so proud of you."

Sy didn't say anything. She was struggling with her own emotions and abilities. Susan handed her back the rosary.

"You ready for another surprise?"

"Oh no." Syene groaned. "What now?"

"We have a few more guests here to see you."

Syene thought she might burst into tears. She couldn't take one more piece of bad news today.

"Who is it?'

Susan put her hand on Sy's arm, reassuring her. "I think you are going to enjoy talking to these folks. But I don't want to steal their thunder. Come up when you are ready."

Sy watched as Susan walked back to the house. Julie met her at the top of the hill, and Wesley gave up on chasing the butterflies and bounded after the duo. Undoubtedly, he knew he would be getting fed treats when he made it back to the house. Father Cervini came and sat silently with her just as Jamille appeared.

Syene looked up at her protector. "More guests, but I guess you already knew they were here long before I did."

Jamille smiled. "I knew, but it's nothing to dread." She playfully touched Sy's nose. "And by the way, I don't know everything. Only the Creator has the ability to see all. I am just allowed from time to time to have special insight."

"Well, I sure wish I could get some warning every now and then." For just a moment she wished for a normal life and immediately felt guilty.

Jamille brushed Syene's hair from her face. "I know you are tired and afraid, Sacred, but the Creator never allows pain without a purpose. And you have had to face a lot of pain. Be strong and trust in the Creator's timing." Syene pulled her legs in closer and put her forehead on her knees.

"Everyone keeps telling me that. I feel guilty for my anger and doubt."

"Your Creator knows your heart. You can't hide the hurt and confusion. Time will heal you. You are loved no matter what doubts you have." She felt Jamille's loving touch, and it settled her.

Tony stood and pulled Syene to her feet.

"Come, let us go meet our guests. I look forward to hearing what they have to say."

Syene felt a twinge of excitement about who was here. She called to Elkan and Ariel to come on in. A beautiful purple and blue butterfly landed on her arm as she waited for them to make their way up the hill. She smiled, thinking it might be her mom coming to say hello. She closed her eyes. *"I love you, Mom. I miss you more than I can express."* She opened her eyes and watched the butterfly drift away on the wind.

A cold shiver ran over her as she looked to the mountains. She knew Lucifer's legions were watching, waiting for their chance to attack. Sy glanced toward the house and saw Michael land nearby. He knew it too; she could see him looking in the distance and Jamille become very tense. Syene yelled to Ariel and Elkan to hurry. The quicker they were inside the better.

****

Kaufman watched the young woman stand and wave the little boy and his female playmate to come on. He recognized the priest from the restaurant. Could this child really be him? He somehow had convinced himself he was chasing a fairytale. He would have never admitted it, but he had doubted he would ever be able to prove the writings were real. But now . . . now there was hope. He wanted to run outside himself and chase the butterflies with the boy. It was hard to wait patiently inside.

Susan came back to the house with her new female companion and a very large dog following her. He stepped away from the windows. They came through the back door simultaneously, the big dog almost knocking both women over, so he could meet the new people.

"Wesley!" Susan was clearly exasperated. "I am so sorry. This is Wesley."

The dog ran over to say hello everyone. Kaufman stuck out his hand and greeted the dog with a rub on the head, and laughter. "Well, hello, Mr. Wesley. It is very nice to see you."

Susan shook her head. "He needs definite work on his manners, but I am afraid he is too late in life for that."

Kaufman smiled as Wesley made his way over to Laura for more attention. "He is a welcome distraction."

Susan didn't look too convinced. "If you say so." She shrugged. "I let Syene know you were here. They will be up shortly. And this is our beautiful friend, Julie."

Kaufman politely introduced himself and his assistants to Julie. He could feel his hands sweating like a young schoolboy. The moment of truth was here. Either way, he and his two young colleagues' lives would be changed forever. Good or bad. The anticipation was heavy in the air.

Susan came back from the kitchen with water and tea on a tray. The doctor felt grateful. His throat felt like sandpaper. She handed everyone a glass.

"Thank you so much. You have been very kind." He let out a nervous laugh. "I feel very apprehensive." Dave and Susan gave him a knowing smile. Thomas and Laura seemed oblivious to what was about to happen. *Oh, to be young again and to just roll with whatever life brings you. What a gift young people have. What a gift he once had.*

James tried to lighten the mood with conversation. "Dr. Kaufman, you must have had some amazing adventures in your studies. I have always been fascinated with archeology. Such wonderful history to discover." He knew the young man was only trying to get his mind off meeting the young mother and child. He also knew every person in the room could see him glancing at the back door every ten seconds awaiting their arrival.

Dave approached him and gently touched his arm. He whispered, "You aren't going to be disappointed. I promise."

His heart was racing with excitement. The moment was finally at hand.

****

Jerusalem – Twilight on day of the crucifixion

Cassius was awoken in the middle of the night by the banging at his front entrance. He grabbed his sword and went to answer.

Three soldiers were waiting for him.

"Sir. We are sorry for disturbing you at this hour. Pilate needs you. The Jews have taken the Galilean into custody."

He nodded. "Very well. Wait for me." He closed the door, dreading the task ahead. He had heard of the commotion since the holy man had arrived in the city. Obviously, the Pharisees taking him into custody broke many of their laws. Cassius knew his suspicions had been correct. The Pharisees already had approached Pilate, long before the Galilean's arrival, about taking care of their unfortunate situation, known as Jesus. Pilate had most likely refused, and now they were going to force his hand to keep the peace among the people. Clever.

His beautiful Alypia sat up sleepily. "Why must you go at this hour? Can it not wait until at least the light of day?"

Cassius smiled and gently touched her face. He loved her so dearly. Their beautiful baby boy and small daughter lay peacefully next to their mother.

He spoke quietly as not to wake them. "I won't be long, I promise. I am sure it is only a matter of indulgence for Pilate. They have taken the Jew, Jesus, into custody. Enforcement will be needed; it is a minor matter." Cassius leaned over and kissed her. "Get some sleep, my love."

Alypia returned his kiss as her eyes were shutting. "Love to you."

She was back asleep before he could respond.

He dressed quickly in his armor and strapped his sword to his side. The three soldiers were waiting where he had left them. Two of the soldiers began walking with Cassius while one stayed behind at the front entrance of his home. Cassius stopped.

"Why are you not coming with us?"

"I have been ordered to stay behind, Commander, as protection for your family. Pilate believes there will be great unrest in the city soon."

Cassius stared at the soldier standing guard by his door. His unease was growing. "Very well." He motioned to the two other men. "Let's get moving." They mounted their horses. The foreboding was thick in the air.

Upon his arrival, he was informed Pilate was meeting with the Pharisees. Cassius was to make sure the Galilean was being properly guarded and to wait for Pilate to come get him. He made his way down the dark stone staircase following the soldiers. It was damp and cold where they kept the prisoners. The stench was a mixture of blood, feces, and death. *Disgusting.* Cassius took the cloth being handed to him by the soldier, so he could cover his nose and mouth. They walked past several prisoners, shackled to the walls, waiting for their inevitable death. The man causing so much trouble was being kept in a corner by himself. His hands and legs were shackled, connected to an iron collar, and chained to the wall.

His head was bent over, and he was mumbling. As Cassius got closer he realized the man was praying. Cassius shook his head. Praying would not save him now.

Jesus lifted his head as Cassius approached. His sapphire eyes were electrifying and clearly seen in the dim lighting. Their vibrancy unarmed Cassius. He could see the bruised face and dried blood of an earlier beating. He turned to the soldier in charge of the prisoners.

"Who did this? Who beat him?"

The young soldier stammered over his words. "I do not know, commander, he looked this way when he arrived." Cassius doubted all of this had been afflicted elsewhere.

Cassius was a man of war, but he did not advocate abuse of the underserving. "Get me some fresh water." The soldier rushed away, and Cassius stared at the man he had been hearing so much about. The soldier returned quickly with a pail of water. The commander waved his hand disgustedly.

"Leave us."

The soldier quietly slipped away into the darkness.

Cassius stepped closer to the shackled man.

"Would you like a drink of water?"

The sapphire eyes bore into him.

"Yes." The man's voice was hoarse with thirst.

Cassius unlocked the chains that bound him. He watched as Jesus drank from the pail of water.

"My name is Cassius, Centurion for the Roman Army."

"I know who you are."

The Roman shook his head. "That's not possible. I have never seen you."

He could see the Galilean smile. "Everything is possible."

"I am not in the mood for riddles. Who are you? And why are the Pharisees in such fear of you?"

"You have nothing to fear from me, Cassius."

He laughed. "I fear very little. I asked why *they* fear you?"

Jesus looked at him. "They fear their own hearts. I have exposed who they really are."

This man was unnerving, and Cassius did not enjoy the feeling of vulnerability.

Jesus kept his gaze on Cassius, not saying a word.

He asked again, "Who are you? Why are you here? They say you are a holy man."

Jesus calmly answered, "I am the Truth. I have brought the Truth."

Cassius was becoming annoyed with the labyrinth of words.

"What nonsense are you speaking? I want facts."

"I only speak facts. And now, Cassius, I need you to listen to me. I do not have much time. You have been chosen by the Father, and the truth will be revealed to you."

"Chosen? Why do you speak to me as if you have known me my entire life? I don't know you or this Father you speak of."

Jesus extended his hand to Cassius. "Please. Everything will be revealed to you. Take my hand."

Cassius did not know why, but he was compelled to do as he was asked. He reached out and instantly everything was changed.

Chapter Fourteen

Then they will come to their senses and escape from the devil's trap. For they have been held captive by him to do whatever he wants. – 2 Timothy 2:26

Amy fiddled with the piece of paper in her hand. She had been thinking of her encounter with Farrel for the last week. The handsome man didn't seem like one of Master's servants, and he said he was a friend of Syene. Tears came to her eyes at the thought of her friend. Amy missed the joy of friendship. Everything good had been taken from her. Her soul was empty.

She looked at the paper with the number scrawled on it. He had been careful to not put a name, and she had never been questioned about any of it by Master. Surely, he had been sent to help. Her heart fluttered with hope. Hope was something she hadn't felt in a very long time. Amy wanted to call him, but she knew Lucifer was the commander of treachery. It could all be a trick. A cold shiver ran over her at the thought of what would be done to her if she proved to be disloyal. She couldn't go back to his lair. Amy knew she wouldn't survive it again. She also knew if she betrayed him, he would go after her mom and dad. She couldn't let anything happen to them. She slid the paper under her jewelry box on the dresser.

"How are you, my sweet?"

Amy jumped, startled.

"Master, you surprised me." Her heart was racing. Had he seen her with the piece of paper? How long had he been standing there? She did her best to hide her fear.

He approached her slowly. Amy was grateful he had chosen human form to appear to her.

"Why so jumpy?" He reached out and stroked her face.

Amy laughed nervously. "No reason, Master, I was just startled. I wasn't expecting you." Her mind screamed. *Please don't let him have seen anything. Please.*

"Hmmm." He looked at her closely as his hand ran along the length of her bare arm. "You look stunning this evening. Blue is a good color for you."

"Thank you, Master, I'm glad it pleases you."

Amy kept her eyes diverted. He leaned in to smell her— she could feel his breath along her neck, followed by tremors throughout her body. She hated herself, hated him, for feeling desire. She knew this was why he was so successful at luring souls. Master was indeed the *Deus Deceptor*. He captured with the desires of the heart and entangled it with the feelings of pleasure, then he twisted and turned it until the desire consumed the soul and nothing good was left. You belonged to him before you were aware of what happened. Lost in the depths of whatever your weakness was.

He stepped away, and she felt grateful.

"Why so dressed up on this twilight?"

Amy did her best to smile. "A cocktail party to celebrate the new magazine cover, but I can cancel if I am needed."

"No, I will join you tonight. You know I enjoy on occasion interacting with my prey."

Master had given her a wealthy life. She was modeling and doing very well. He used the souls who had already sworn allegiance to him to make this successful. People in her circle thought he was her dark and mysterious manager. Amy couldn't count the number of women who begged her to introduce them to him. They were captivated by his dark sex appeal, and he was incredibly handsome in human form. Amy, of course, always ignored the requests. She would never bring anyone else into this never-ending darkness. They were indeed his prey being captivated by deceit.

"That would be wonderful." Her voice and face did not betray the real emotions of fear and dread coursing through her body. She had learned to play the game of survival well.

He moved closer. For a moment she caught a glimpse of his true ghastly form in the mirror, and then it was gone.

"But first, I think I might partake in pleasures with my beautiful toy."

Toy. That was exactly right. Nothing more than a toy. No one cared about her, no one missed her, no one loved her.

He pulled her to the bed. Amy mindlessly gave herself to her Master, uncertain how this life had become her normal.

Tears slipped down her cheeks. Despair and darkness enveloped her.

****

The party was in full swing. Amy watched as Master worked his way through the crowd, captivating men and women both. If they only knew the truth. The room was filled with his demons, following the humans unmercifully, attaching themselves to them, whispering to them. Amy couldn't believe no one felt them or saw them. But she too had once been blind. People were so focused on the here and now and what they viewed as reality. Worrying about pointless things: money, success, social media status, and their appearance. They missed the reality surrounding them. The real war of evil and good right in front of their eyes. She couldn't help but think, *we aren't very bright as humans*.

He caught her eye from across the room and raised his glass. She smiled. It was all she could do. She realized quickly in the beginning he could not hear her thoughts, and she was grateful for it. She used to pray to God, but the prayers stopped long ago. Apparently, those were never heard either, but why would God care about her when she had succumbed to evil so easily. Her mind immediately went to the man she met at the restaurant. *Or were her prayers heard?*

"Hello there, the star of the evening." Patsy Trumane stood inches from her. Patsy was a socialite. She had made a fortune going through wealthy husbands, and now she owned one of the top magazines in the world and had her last victim of marriage to thank for it.

"Patsy, how wonderful to see you." Amy air-kissed both of her cheeks, the smell of alcohol and cigarettes lingering on the magazine mogul. The world of superficial living was exhausting. Amy saw Patsy's gaze go across the room to Master.

"When exactly will I get a proper introduction to your business manager? What is his name?"
Amy heard the slur in Patsy's voice and knew she had too much to drink. She forced a smile. "Apollos Drake, and he's just so busy. I hardly see him myself."

"Apollos, sounds like a Greek god or something."

Amy let out a fake laugh. "Something like that, I guess."

Patsy was clearly enchanted with him. "Well, he looks like one at least. You can't tell me the two of you don't have something going on? I would eat him up if he were my manager."

Amy couldn't stand the gossip of society. She looked at Patsy sweetly.

"No, just business. He is always about business."

Patsy seemed happy to hear that piece of information. "Well, then I think I'll make my way over and introduce myself."

"Good luck." It was hard for Amy to keep the sarcasm out of her voice. People were stupid.

Patsy sat her empty wine glass down on a passing waiter's tray and gave Amy a once-over. "Luck has nothing to do with it, sweet little Amy. This is all skill and manipulation."

Amy watched as Patsy made her way over to Master. She shook her head and mumbled under her breath. "Manipulation is right, you idiot. Welcome to the Devil's den."

"Not a fan of humans, Amy?"

She turned quickly to find Enzril standing behind her. A woman was draped on his arm. Amy didn't know what surprised her more. Seeing him in human form or seeing him with a woman.

"Enzril, I would like to say it is nice to see you, but that would be a lie. I see you have been forced to slum with the humans. Sucks being a servant, doesn't it?"

She saw his eyes narrow. "You need to remember your place."

Amy was silent but knew he wasn't any better off. He was stuck just as much as she was.

The woman next to him intervened. "Now, now you two. Play nice with each other. None of us want to upset Master or cause a scene." Amy knew instantly she was a dark angel and not human.

"And you are?" She didn't know why, but she felt protective over Enzril. Not in a jealous lover way but like a sister. He was the only one who had shown sympathy for her during her stay with Master. He claimed he hated humans, but she sensed good in him still, and this new warrior was wrapping herself on him like he was her property. Amy instantly hated her.

"My, my, you do have quite an ego for such a lowly piece of scum. I am Kefira, warrior for Master, and you better step down from the tower you are living in." She moved in closer to Amy. "Understood?"

Amy glared and pulled away when Kefira stroked her arm seductively. She pressed her lips to Amy's ear and whispered, "Be careful, little toy, or I might share a secret about you meeting strangers at restaurants."

Amy stepped back. Yes, she absolutely hated her. She couldn't help herself before the words came out. "Well, it looks like I was wrong; Enzril was slumming way before he got here."

She could almost hear Kefira hiss at her. Before she could launch at Amy, Enzril pulled her back.

"Kefira, enough!" He spoke through clenched teeth.

Amy smirked sweetly. "So nice to meet you, Kefira, please don't be a stranger."

She could feel Kefira's eyes boring into her back as she walked away. It was a dangerous game she was playing, but for now the Master needed her and the dark angels couldn't touch her. Amy couldn't keep the smile of satisfaction off her face.

Chapter Fifteen

Praise the Lord, you angels, you mighty ones who carry out his plans, listening for each of his commands.
– Psalm 103:20

Jerusalem – Twilight on day of the crucifixion

Cassius firmly grasped the extended hand of Jesus. What he saw and felt was unexplainable. He saw everything, Jesus with God, the angels, His birth, His Holy mother, His journey with the disciples, the betrayal, His end, the reason He was here and what the future held. Cassius passed through every moment, given the gift of sight, truth, and prophesy. There was no questioning who this man was. Jesus released his hand, and Cassius fell to his knees weeping.

"My Lord, forgive us. What have we done?"

Jesus touched his shoulder. "Cassius, look at me."

Cassius shook his head. "I am too ashamed."

"Look at me." The Roman raised his head with contrition as he looked upon his King.

Jesus spoke gently, "I must tell you everything, and you must listen. All of this must be documented. You are the one chosen to do this task."

"Let me get you out of here, my Lord. I can take you with me. I will slaughter anyone who tries to stop me."

He could see the tears in Jesus's eyes. "Cassius, you cannot stop what the Father has put into motion. My fate is sealed with my own blood, and I welcome what I must do."

Cassius stood. "I will do whatever you ask of me." The commander in him would obey without fail.

Jesus looked upon him with sorrow in his eyes. "When I am done speaking, I will have delivered painful news for you. Please be strong and follow your Creator's purpose."

Cassius nodded, not knowing what was about to happen.

"You have already seen my purpose through vision. I am here to create a way to the Father. I have humanized our heavenly Creator and brought the truth of love for humanity. All humanity. I will die for your sins and all the sins of the world. Any soul, if desired, can be with me for eternity. I am taking on every act of evil unto myself, so my Father can forgive those who have acted against the Heavenly laws. This has to happen. I will not be saved."

Cassius listened with tears streaming down his face. He knew the horrific torture Jesus was going to face at the hands of his fellow Romans. He himself had performed torturous acts of war. His stomach now churned with nausea and disgust for his past and what Jesus was going to face.

"Cassius, my spoken words and stories of kindness and mercy will spread like fire throughout many different lands. No one will be able to stop it. The Holy Spirit will be upon you, just as it will be upon my own followers."

"I don't understand. What do I need to do?"

"You will write of the future I have shown you, Cassius. Long after I have ascended to my Father's home the male child will be born. A child belonging to God. He will be born of a spiritual birth like mine, but his purpose is much different. I will soon become the Savior of all, and he will be the last chance for many. A reminder of my sacrifice and God's love. Lucifer himself will come after the child to destroy him, along with many human souls. They will fear this child just as they feared me. The child must be protected, and he must fulfill the Creator's plan. As he comes of age, he will be the last messenger sent by the Father."

"How am I to do this? I am not educated to write of such things. I have not been educated in your ways. Who do I give this information? I cannot possibly do what you are asking of me."

Jesus touched his shoulder forcing him to look into the piercing eyes again.

"Cassius, the Father has chosen you. I will never leave you. Let the Spirit guide you. You will do this, and you will succeed."

Cassius could feel love and mercy coursing through his own body, simply from the touch of this man, who was hailed the King of the Jews.

"Now, my heart is heavy with great sorrow. You are in danger, Cassius, and must flee from here as soon as you can. When I am taken to my end, you must be gone before then. You cannot return home, you must leave. They will come after you."

Cassius shook his head. "I cannot. I must return home for my wife and children."

He saw the sadness overcome the man before him. Jesus shook his head. "They are gone, Cassius."

Cassius railed back. "NO! NO! It can't be true! He immediately thought of the soldier who stayed behind at his home.

Jesus stepped forward and wrapped him in a hug as sobs racked his body. "I have prayed for the Father's mercy on their souls. They will be in eternity with me, and with you when your time comes."

Cassius cried out, "Why?" The depth of his sadness was unbearable.

Jesus spoke with honesty and love. "I do not know why. The human heart was created by a loving and just Father. I cannot tell you why evil sears the soul, allowing Satan to take over. The flesh is weak."

"I will murder all of them for what they have done."

Jesus shook his head. "You cannot seek revenge, Cassius. It is not the way. You must leave here. Every person tangled with my trial and death will eventually be murdered.

Stay focused on your task. You have been chosen, and you have a Heavenly duty to perform. It is not the time for hatred. Remember what I have shown you, remember what you have felt, you will see them again. I promise. Remember me."

The door swung open, startling Cassius. Two soldiers stepped inside. "We are here for the prisoner. Pilate has ordered for you to stay until we bring him back."

He nodded, shielding his face so they could not see his anguish. As they grabbed Jesus, Cassius made eye contact with him one last time. He thought to draw his sword and murder the soldiers, but he saw the Savior slightly shake his head no. He heard the unspoken word.

Run.

He knew without a doubt any person involved with this travesty would be destroyed.

Cassius followed them up the stairwell. He watched as they led the Holy Galilean to His inevitable death. A sadness even greater than his pain for his family swept over him. He had no time to waste. He made his way out through a servant's entrance. When he was in the early morning darkness and out of sight, he ran. Cassius knew he shouldn't return home, but he had to see for himself. He couldn't just leave without seeing them. He had to say goodbye. Cassius mounted his horse and rode as fast as he could through the streets.

His home was quiet and dark. He knew all too well the familiar smell of fresh blood. He slowly entered his home with his sword drawn. The soldier was long gone. The body of their servant lay slain in the hallway. He made his way to the room where he shared his bed with his wife. Her lifeless body was draped over their children. She had been protecting them. Even in the darkness, Cassius could see the dark staining of blood surrounding their bodies.

He knew with certainty he had no time to mourn. Everything Jesus had told him was true. He had to run. There was no room for doubt. He leaned over and gently kissed his wife and children for the last time. "Forgive me, my love, for not protecting you. Forgive me for leaving you here like this." Tears of anger and sadness clouded his vision. Cassius quickly grabbed the money he had hidden and clothes that would not identify him as a Roman. He gave one last glance at his home as he rode away. This pain in his chest would surely never heal.

****

Kaufman stood from where he was seated on the couch as the back door opened. Thomas and Laura both stood and walked over next to him. Ariel entered first, followed by Syene, Elkan, and Father Cervini.

"Hello, I'm Ariel Harper." She was friendly and shook all their hands.

Syene held onto Elkan's hand. She was very reserved and didn't offer a handshake.

"I'm Syene Harper, and this is my son Elkan."

Kaufman smiled and completely understood her stand-off position.

"I can't begin to tell you how wonderful it is to meet you both finally."

Syene looked confused. "Finally?"

He turned to his assistants.

"Laura, please get me my files."

He watched as Laura rushed over to a table and picked up the file folders. He could see how nervous she was, pulsing with excitement. Her hands shook as she handed him the material. He smiled and patted her arm. Silently he encouraged her to calm down. Kaufman knew all too well the emotions she was feeling.

"May I?" Motioning toward the mother and son.

Syene nodded her acceptance. Kaufman stepped next to her and opened one of the files. They were photocopies of writings, very old writings.

"These are copies of original writings I uncovered in Egypt. Writings I believe to be about your son." He paused. "I pray to be about your son."

Syene looked perplexed but curious. She was not screaming at him to leave, and Kaufman took this as a good sign. She took the files and carried them to the couch, sitting down with Elkan close to her. Elkan gave the doctor an encouraging smile.

Kaufman followed cautiously; he did not want to do anything to alarm them.

"These are in Latin, I have them translated to English in the folder underneath.

The young mother stared at him. "I read Latin."

Kaufman did nothing to hide his surprise.

"Really? My apologies, there are not very many people I have met that are fluent in Latin, especially the young."

Syene looked at him blankly. "I read and understand many languages since my pregnancy with my son."

Kaufman felt his heart beat faster. If this were true, then her pregnancy had to have been something divine. Something of God. He didn't want to push, but he had so many questions. He knew he must be patient.

"That is quite curious. How many languages have you tested this on?" He was doing everything he could to sound calm.

She shrugged at him. "I'm not really sure. I got bored with it after around fifty."

Kaufman heard the priest chuckle behind him. Father Cervini introduced himself and added, "You'll have to excuse Syene, she doesn't get out much."

Kaufman smiled politely. He could care less about her brashness, he was just so happy to be here.

Syene spoke softly to the doctor. "Dr. Kaufman, if you will allow just a few moments so I may read this, I will answer whatever questions I can for you." He blushed and nodded. Dave gave him a wink from across the room, assuring him he was doing fine.

He watched as she read unable to read her expression. He did not know what this girl had been through but sensed she was not going to be shocked by the writings of Cassius. When she was done he was surprised to see tears begin to roll down her cheeks. She quickly wiped them away.

"Did you know?" She was speaking to someone behind him, and Kaufman turned to look but saw nothing. He was feeling very confused. Syene looked at the writings again. Her sister finally spoke up.

"What did they say, Syene?"

Syene gave her a small smile and let out a deep sigh. "He was planned. Elkan has always been planned. Jesus told this Cassius everything." Syene handed the English version to her sister so she could read it for herself. The boy didn't react to the news his mother shared. It was as if he already knew all of this.

"Dr. Kaufman, I can't tell you I am shocked by what I have read. Nothing takes me by surprise anymore, but I am comforted by learning Elkan was always known."

He could see she was sincerely grateful.

"I believe you were meant to find those writings and make sure the world knows Cassius. My soul hurts he lost his family and his own life to protect what he had been told, but now I must ask you to protect Elkan as well."

Kaufman immediately felt guilty. He had been so focused on the prize of finding the child he had failed to think about the pain Cassius must have been in when he lost his family. Dr. Kaufman had also suffered great loss in his life and now felt ashamed his tunnel vision had kept him from seeing everything. Laura and Thomas remained quiet. He knew they also had been only focused on finding the child. Especially Laura. The doctor glanced in their direction to find they both were looking at the ground feeling the same discomfort.

"Ms. Harper, I am ashamed to admit I have been so focused on the quest, I have forgotten the human side of the writings and, of course, how the secrecy of your son is crucial."

"Dr. Kaufman, I do believe the writings by Cassius have been compromised. An agent from the FBI came here to question us about something that happened several years ago, but now I think it had something to do with your findings."

Kaufman remained quiet. He had been certain they were kept secret but now questioned their security. It was possible he had trusted the wrong people and put Elkan in danger.

Syene continued. "I would like to share something with the three of you, but I don't want you to be afraid."

She sat quietly for a moment staring at the trio. She glanced at everyone else in the room, her family and friends who had been with her since the beginning. They all seemed to approve.

She quietly spoke to her son.

"Elkan, how do you feel about this?" He held onto her hand as he stood, shyly smiling at their guests.

Syene stood with him. "Laura, Thomas, if you would come join Dr. Kaufman on the couch, my son would like to share something with you."

They sat on either side of him, having no clue what was about to happen. All three stared at Elkan and Syene nervously. Kaufman thought his heart might pound through his chest.

Syene gave them an encouraging smile. "Please join hands. It will make things much easier. And please do not be afraid."

They did as they were told. Kaufman realized Laura was as nervous as he was. He could feel her clammy hand shaking in his. He squeezed her hand gently.

Elkan stepped forward, placing his small hands over theirs. Their lives were about to be changed forever.

****

Somewhere in Egypt – One year after the crucifixion of Jesus

Cassius sat by candlelight writing everything as fast as possible. He had to stay hidden both day and night. He was being relentlessly pursued by his own people and by the criminals hired by the Jewish leaders. On the day of the crucifixion, Cassius had stayed hidden in Jerusalem only long enough to try to warn several of his trusted comrades of their upcoming doom if they did not flee. He was too late. He found them and their families murdered, just as his own family had been slain. He would be next, for so Jesus had told him.

A year of hiding had taken its toll on him physically and mentally. He was done running and almost complete with his writings. He agreed to pay a young Egyptian boy to bring him ink and papyrus over the last several months. Cassius instructed the boy to take the writings and hide them among the caverns. Cassius knew God would lead the right person to their discovery when it was time. This would be his final letter.

Death is inevitable. They will stop at nothing to cover up their atrocity and it does not matter who must die, for they have all committed a crime. A crime that will be held as the greatest coverup known to man. They have murdered God in the flesh. They have made a horrible mistake. I write these things fervently. I must finish my purpose, I must finish my writings. I feel as if I will fail this task in my rush, but I will pray to the God I was shown, I will pray the writings will be found by a follower of Jesus. I pray whomever finds my words will understand the importance of what I was told.

Have I done enough? I do not know.

Have I written enough about the visions I was shown when I do not completely understand the depth of their meaning? I am not an eloquent man.

Will people understand there can be no doubt Jesus was exactly who He said He was? He was the true Savior. He was our gift from the Creator. And He was murdered. My mind struggles to understand at times.

Have I done enough to explain how it was to be in His presence? He was everything in one man—mercy, grace, kindness, courage, love.

I pray the child of the future will be welcomed as the messenger for Jesus and not persecuted by hatred. I pray ignorance and fear will not take over the hearts of men. I am ready to join my family in eternity. My light will soon be extinguished. God's will be done.

Cassius

****

They sat on the couch in silent. Everyone else in the room waited patiently. The truth was fully revealed, and they were now all intertwined minds and souls.

Father Cervini broke the silence. "How are you feeling?"

Kaufman looked at his young colleagues and could see their stunned expressions. He understood completely. He stared blankly at the priest, his heart pounding rapidly within his chest.

He finally found his voice. "Quite at a loss for words, to be honest. I am not sure what I expected." He looked at the young mother who waited quietly with her son.

"I feel I owe you a tremendous amount of gratitude. I cannot express this overwhelming sense of . . ." He stood, unable to explain any of what he was feeling.

Syene smiled at him and walked over, touching his arm.

"You don't need to say anything, and I don't want to overwhelm any of you, but I also don't want any unexpected surprises for you. Now that you have been given sight by Elkan, you are going to see things you never thought possible." She motioned with her head for them to turn around.

The three of them slowly turned in the direction she and everyone else was now looking. Thomas let out a startled yell and fell off the couch, crawling backward and away from what was standing before them.

Kaufman could not believe his eyes. He stood in awe, staring at two of the most amazing creatures he had ever seen. Angels. Real angels. The size and the magnificence of them was breathtaking. He reached for Laura's hand, who was now standing with one hand over her mouth and squeezing his hand with her other. Kaufman suddenly found himself laughing and crying at the same time.

He looked at Laura, who had tears running down her cheeks and a look of amazed disbelief in her eyes.

"This is real, Laura. Everything I read as a child. It's real!"

He looked to Syene for approval, as he nodded toward the angels.

"May I?"

Syene laughed. "Of course. You certainly don't need my permission. They have much more say in it then I do."

Kaufman cautiously walked around the couch and approached the winged giants standing before him.

Michael spoke. "I am Michael, Archangel, and General for our Creator's army. And this is Jamille, protector of Sacred."

Kaufman could find no words. He heard Laura behind him in an almost unrecognizable voice.

"Michael! As in Michael from the Bible? The Michael who battled Lucifer?"

Michael nodded, a slight smile on his face. "Yes, the same."

The doctor removed his eyeglasses, cleaning them on his shirt as if this would help confirm what he was seeing. He carefully placed them back on and blinked slowly.

Michael extended his hand. Kaufman took the it and instantly had a feeling that could only be explained as divine.

Jamille did the same. "I am Jamille, and it is very nice to meet you."

He shook her hand and respectfully asked, "May I touch the wings? I apologize, but at the end of the day I am still a scientist."

Jamille smiled. "Of course."

He reached out gently stroking the massive wings and looked back at Laura and Thomas with childlike delight.

"Come! Come!" He beckoned them excitedly "You must touch them!"

The young pair approached cautiously. Michael nodded, giving them permission to come closer, allowing them to run their hands across his wings.

****

It was shocking for Syene to realize how much she had taken for granted. To see the reaction of new believers was humbling and a needed reminder of her Creator's purpose for her. She couldn't help but think how wonderful it was to see the new wonder of sight for the first time. This was a breath of fresh air for her depleted soul. Elkan released a huge yawn. Syene couldn't help but laugh. *Well, one of us needed the reminder.*

She kissed his cheek and told him he was free to go. He happily ran up the stairs to his room where the few unpacked toys remained. The disappointed look on the doctor's face as he watched Elkan disappear out of sight was not missed by her. The phantom he was chasing for years was now a reality. Dr. Kaufman knew about Elkan before she did. She was looking forward to hearing the doctor's story in more detail.

"Don't worry, Dr. Kaufman. He isn't going far. He does still have the patience of a six-year-old boy, and it seems we have become very acclimated to the wonders around us." She gave him a wink to reassure him he would have time to spend with the child he had been searching for so long. He gave her a warm smile, and Syene knew without a doubt he had been sent as part of the plan. She sat down next to Father Cervini and watched the trio continue their childlike delight in the angels.

The priest took her hand in his. "This is what it is all about. Too see all of this through new eyes is a gift."

Sy let her head rest on his shoulder, smiling and not saying a word.

"Thank you, Syene, for allowing me to be a part of your life. For allowing me to join you on this journey. I can't tell you enough how blessed I am to be here."

She lifted her head, "Seriously? I am the one who is blessed you found me. I can't imagine my life without you in it. Your joy in everything has kept me going in all my continued moments of doubt."

Syene and Tony quietly listened as the trio bombarded Michael and Jamille with questions about Heaven, God, Jesus, Mary, and then finally Satan.

Kaufman asked first, "Is he real? Did one of God's angels really turn against his Creator?"

James was conversing with Thomas, and suddenly the room grew quiet. All eyes were on Michael. Everyone in the room had experienced Lucifer firsthand except for the newcomers and James, but interestingly James had never asked the question. Possibly the demons he had seen when he was a drug addict had been enough proof. But now he sat forward eager to listen to Michael's response.

Michael's face hardened. "Yes, it is true. Lucifer was a friend and comrade. His jealousy of the humans distorted his perceptions, and his reality became dark. He wanted the Creator to love him more than the humans were loved, and his lust for acceptance twisted his soul. When he saw he could influence several of the other angels, he craved power and set his fate into motion."

"What is he like?" Laura's question was innocent, but it was a reminder to everyone the horror Satan really was.

Michael shook his head. "It depends on what he chooses to be. He is the *Deus Deceptor*. He fools many by using different forms. Visions of what they perceive to be beautiful. But his true form has only been seen by very few human souls." He glanced toward Syene and Father Cervini.

Thomas, Laura, and Dr. Kaufman turned toward the pair sitting on the couch. You could see the fear in their eyes as they listened to Michael. Syene couldn't help but think to herself nothing would prepare them for the reality of Lucifer.

Michael continued. "It has typically been only warriors who have seen him. He has built an army and now sends his legions to do his battle. He is selective of who sees him."

Laura couldn't seem to help herself. "Why?"

"I don't have a good answer for that. Shame of what he has become? Arrogance because he is no longer the glorious angel he once was. Who knows."

It was Kaufman this time. "So what is he now? Horns? Tail?"

Michael shook his head. "Your worst nightmare. He can appear in many forms."

Kaufman looked to Syene and the priest. "You saw him?"

"I did." Her eyes filled with tears. "I still do."

The doctor immediately apologized for upsetting her and asking the question.

Syene held her hand up. "It is fine, I promise. I need to talk about it. You need to know what is ahead of you."

Tony could see her struggling, so he intervened on her behalf.

"All of you will see the demons and dark angels since you have been given the truth. You need to be prepared. When you separate from God's warriors, it will seem as if the demons are everywhere. They almost seem to attach themselves to the humans, and it will be alarming." He could see the startled panic he was causing in the three of them.

Father Cervini immediately added, "You will be armed with powerful scripture and I will teach you the principles of the rosary. Mother Mary's rosary is a sword in the armor of God. Please know you are always protected. Michael can be called upon any time you feel ultimate fear. He will be with you."

The threesome glanced at Michael, and this seemed to ease some of the strain on their faces as the priest continued.

"But I am not going to lie to you and say you won't feel fear when you see the demons or a dark angel for the first time, because you will. And I can only speak for myself on Lucifer, but it is the evil you feel in his presence more than his form. It is pure evil, and it drains your soul immediately when he is around. It was the darkest place of despair I could ever imagine."

Syene nodded in agreement. It was unexplainable.

They all three nodded their understanding. The air in the room was heavy.

Kaufman, trying to lighten the mood, smiled and asked the priest, "How soon can I get one of those rosaries?"

Thomas and Laura chimed in along with James.

"Yes, please, how soon?"

Father Cervini laughed.

"Now is the perfect time. I shall go to my room and get them."

Kaufman chuckled,. "A Jewish boy with a rosary. Who would ever believe me?"

Michael laughed loudly. "Oh, I know a few famous Jewish people who will believe you."

Sy smiled. She loved when Michael smiled and laughed—it warmed her soul.

The doctor shook his head in awe.

"I just can't believe Michael is standing before me. I can't believe I found the child. It is overwhelming."

Sy could see the emotion he was feeling. She walked to him and embraced him warmly. He hugged her tightly and whispered, "You have my promise I will do everything possible to protect the writings and keep Elkan safe. If I have compromised your safety I will do whatever is possible to fix it."

Syene could only pray silently for God to prepare all of them for what was coming.

Chapter Sixteen

The serpent said to the woman, "You surely will not die!"
– Genesis 3:4

Amy moved cautiously on the busy sidewalks. She was nervous and wanted to be certain she wasn't being followed. Master's little minions seemed to appear around her without warning. One of her recent photo shoots had given her a little extra in cash, and she had been able to buy a prepaid phone. Master was very careful Amy never had money he couldn't trace. She hid the cash for a week before purchasing the phone. She had to be certain he didn't know she was hiding anything from him. The phone, now in her front pocket, rubbed on her hip bone as she walked and it brought her some comfort. Amy knew without a doubt she would be dead if caught in any type of betrayal.

She didn't care—she already felt dead.

Amy had to talk to Farrel. There was something about him, and she knew she could trust him. He wasn't one of the dark souls. He was her last chance.

She slipped into the coffee shop she knew had another exit at the back of the store and made her way to the bathroom. She pulled the phone out of her pocket and called the number she had memorized.

He immediately answered, "Hello." Amy knew it was him from the English accent.

"It's Amy. Can you meet me in twenty minutes?"

"Of course. Where?"

"There is a small Italian restaurant on Santa Monica. Meet me there. Please wait ten minutes after you see me arrive." She paused, her voice shaking with fear. "I have to make sure I haven't been followed.

"I'll be there."

Amy hung up, glancing around the shop after leaving the restroom. No one was following her. Her heart pounding, she made her way to the back exit.

****

Farrel watched as she entered the restaurant. He could see from her body language how nervous she was. He knew the danger she was putting herself in by contacting him. He would do whatever he could to save her.

He pleaded silently, "My Lord, please be with me, I need your help." A tingling ran through his body confirming he was heard.

Farrel crossed the street and entered the restaurant cautiously. It took his eyes a moment to adjust to the low light. He scanned the tables quickly, spotting Amy in a corner peering nervously around. He approached her table and sat across from her. She looked terrified. His heart went out to her.

"Thank you for meeting me." Her voice was barely a whisper. Farrel couldn't stop himself. He reached across the table and took her trembling hand. Amy's eyes instantly filled with tears when she looked at him.

"It's going to be okay. I'm here to help you."

A tear ran down her cheek.

"Who are you?"

"A warrior for Yahweh and a friend of Syene." He thought he glimpsed a small smile at the mention of her friend.

"How is she?" The sadness quickly returned. "I miss her. I miss a lot of things."

The door to the restaurant opened, and she jumped. It was clear how tortured her life was, if he even dared call it a life.

"I am going to get you away from him. I promise."

Her eyes held his. "And who do you think he is?"

Farrel knew she still didn't comprehend. She had been surrounded by evil for so long she had forgotten good existed.

"Lucifer." He said it without hesitation.

Amy sighed with relief and sat back in her chair.

"You know. You really do know." She shook her head. "I don't understand if you say you are a warrior for God, then what does that mean? Are you a pastor?"

Farrel smiled, shaking his head.

"Not exactly. I am an angel . . . was an angel."

"Angel? You don't look like an angel. You don't even have wings."

"Amy, I am who I say. I have chosen to be in human form to help Syene and now you."

"Syene? What is wrong with Sy?"

"You don't know?"

Amy shook her head. "No. Is she okay?"

Farrel spent the next hour telling Amy everything. When he was finally done, Amy was silent for a moment.

"Why now? And honestly, before we go any further, I still can't believe this. I don't even know if I believe in God's goodness. I prayed and prayed, and He never came for me." She looked at Farrel, and he could see the anger and hurt in her eyes. "So, answer me, why now? What makes God any better than my Master."

Farrel's soul ached for her. He knew she would never fully understand she had assisted in her circumstances by her own actions. Freewill was always something hard for humans to comprehend when they cried out for God.

"Amy, I am here for you because of God. Every prayer has been heard. Not only your prayers but all the prayers from everyone who loves you. You have not been forgotten. Please take my help. Syene needs you."

Amy looked away. He could see she was thinking about everything he had said. Processing. Her voice was quiet.

"Lucifer is using me to get to her and Elkan. It all makes sense now. I prayed to die, I begged to die. Now I know the reasons he wouldn't end it." She spoke with urgency. "He won't stop until he obtains what he wants."

Farrel abruptly stood. He picked up the glass of water he had been drinking, turning and taking it with him.

"I'll find you."

He quickly disappeared. Amy started to call out to him but stopped immediately. The restaurant door opened, and there he stood. Her nightmare, her reality, her Master. She could feel her heart begin to pound wildly. He had found her. Did he know? She watched as he spotted her and made his way to her table. She could see his eyes rake over the table, checking to see if she had been alone. Farrel must have known and took his glass with him.

"I've been looking for you."

She could only pray he didn't see her fear.

"Well, you found me."

His eyes narrowed as he stared at her.

"And what are you doing here, my sweet? Sitting here all alone?" He took her hand. "You are alone, correct?"

She kept her cool. Inside she was shaking with fear, but her exterior was calm and cool.

"Of course I'm alone. I need quiet time from prying eyes."

He smiled his evil smile and kissed her hand.

"Good, because if you are lying to me, there will be consequences."

"Master, why would I lie to you?"

"You are correct. You know exactly what will happen to you if I find out you are being untruthful." The look he gave her said it all.

Amy felt the cold surround her and all hope fade.

Chapter Seventeen

No power in the sky above or in the earth below—indeed,
nothing in all creation will ever be able to separate us
from the love of God that is revealed in Christ Jesus our
Lord. – Romans 8:39

Syene lay awake in the early morning hour. It was still dark outside, and she could hear the distant whistle of a train. She had done it many times, lying awake listening to the train whistle echo through the mountains. It brought her a sense of normality hearing the train. Her world was anything but normal, and the remote sound of the locomotive on its journey reminded her there was a whole world out there of people living ordinary lives. They had no idea what surrounded them.

She frequently longed for normal and ordinary again. Elkan was next to her, having come to cuddle with her at bedtime and staying cozy for the night. She could hear his light breathing as he slept. A sudden twinge of guilt ran through her.

I wouldn't have Elkan if everything were normal again.

She quietly got up to look out the window. As she pulled the curtains back, the moonlight flooded the room. She was happy to have the light, the darkness scared her now. Syene left the curtains open as she carefully lay back down, so she didn't wake Elkan. She watched him as he slept. Her heart ached with how much she loved him. She prayed quietly.

"I don't know if you hear me, but please keep him safe. Please."

Her eyes closed as she drifted off to sleep.

The room filled with an energy she had felt before, and Syene knew instantly she wasn't alone. She rolled over slowly and could see Him standing by the window. He turned and smiled.

She quickly sat up, not really believing.

His voice brought an instant calm.

"You are struggling, Syene, so I came. Even when I am near, you don't listen. I know you need to see to believe."

She couldn't find her voice. And she suddenly felt more ashamed than she had her entire life.

"I'm sorry." Her guilt wouldn't allow her to look at Him.

He walked to her and held out his hand.

"Come."

She took His hand without hesitation, and instantly they were in a beautiful meadow with the sun warming her skin. He sat down in the middle of a patch of beautiful flowers. Something about them reminded Syene of her mom. He motioned for her to sit.

She sat cross-legged as close as possible to Him, everything about Him calling her closer. His eyes were the blue she remembered, but now they looked even more blue. She had a million questions running through her mind, but her tongue was tied in awe.

He smiled. "Well, I am here, so ask what you need to know."

Syene found herself crying as she poured out her soul. How scared she was and angry about her mom, her dad, all the people who had died because of her and Elkan. What about Elkan's life? Would he grow to be old? What was he to do, what was his true purpose? How could her son help all the bad in the world? Her confusion about her emotions. Her terror of Lucifer. Her guilt for doubting and not understanding. Her desperation to hear from God. Where was God? Where had He been?

When Sy was done it felt as if she had talked for hours. Jesus let her say everything without saying a word. She wiped her tears and felt Him take her hand.

"Syene, I can't provide you all the answers you are seeking, but you need to hear what I say."

She looked at Him, trusting everything He said and wishing she could hang on to this feeling always.

"The Father hears every cry, every prayer, and feels every emotion in a soul's life on earth. Both the beautiful and horrible moments. Do you really believe I was sent in flesh because the Father doesn't care? The urgency, the desire, is to have every single soul understand God is real, God wants to know every soul intimately. I was here to bring Heaven to all souls. To bring the Father to anyone who was in need."

He gently took both of her hands, and she could clearly see the cruel proof of His life on earth. The scars of torture glared at her. Syene couldn't stop herself and touched one of the healed wounds. She immediately retracted.

Jesus smiled gently. "Go ahead, touch them. I wanted them to stay as a constant reminder of the love and sacrifice for you. Every soul matters."

Sy could feel the power of the scars coursing through her body.

"God seems so far away, and You seem so real."

"Syene." His tone had changed, commanding her attention. "God is I, and I am God. We are here. Always. For all. We cannot stop the freewill of choices. Those choices are what make the human soul so incredibly beautiful. Destroying freewill takes away the reason of my sacrifice."

He looked saddened. "The Father listens to the sorrows, cries through the pain, celebrates the triumphs, and in the end rejoices when the soul returns home."

Syene couldn't help but think to herself, *if only Jesus would just come back and show everyone He is real, He is alive, let people be with Him and near Him, then they wouldn't need Elkan. No one could ever doubt with the proof right in front of them.*

"Proof is given every day, little one."

She felt her cheeks burn with embarrassment. Of course, He could hear her thoughts.

"There will always be those who won't believe, who refuse to believe. It is a choice. And my time of return has not yet come."

She smiled, a genuine smile, for the first time in a long time.

"They need Elkan."

He released her hands,

"Yes, they need him desperately. A reminder of their Creator. A great and powerful voice of this time. A connection to me." He stood, and Syene followed. Jesus wrapped her in a warm embrace. She wanted to have this indescribable feeling forever.

"Lucifer is toying with your mind, using your doubts against you. He preys on your insecurities and fears. Hold on to the truth, Syene. Pray for guidance and strength. Remember the Father is with all of you, always. He hears all prayers. Not a single prayer goes unheard."

She clung tightly to him, her face pressed into His chest. She could hear His heart beating. *Proof this had to be real and not just a dream.* They were suddenly standing back in the room, and Jesus released her. Jamille was there watching over Elkan. Syene watched as Jamille and Jesus embraced.

Jamille looked radiant at the sight of Him. Sy didn't think she had seen her look more beautiful than she did right now.

"My Lord, how wonderful to see You."

Jesus beamed at her beautiful protector.

"You as well, Jamille. Thank you for your love and loyalty. You humble me."

Jamille bowed her head graciously. "It is my honor to serve You. Always."

Jesus looked lovingly at Elkan sleeping and gently reached out to caress his curls.

"He will know what to do when the time comes, Sacred. Put all your fears aside and place them before me."

Syene was overwhelmed with emotion. If only everyone could experience this, and then she remembered this was the purpose, the purpose of Elkan. How could she had been so selfish? To deny anyone of having this feeling. Experiencing God. She felt her soul releasing the anger. The tears sprang to her eyes. She was beginning to fully understand.

He gave her one last smile.

"I must go."

Syene opened her eyes. Jamille was standing by the window, the moonlight reflected off her wings.

She whispered, "Jamille, it was real, right?"

Jamille smiled and nodded. Nothing else needed to be said.

****

Special Agent Freely rubbed his temple. His files were spread out across the hotel bed. A phone call to his boss earlier had proven useless. He wanted to know how the FBI obtained the Roman writings. He was told it was of the utmost security and he would not be given that information. The conversation was short and to the point.

"Do your job, Freely. Get the requested information, and report back. Nothing more."

Why was this bothering him so much? He couldn't stop thinking about Syene's reaction to the news of how Phil Reese died. He was certain she didn't know. And then the feeling he was being watched . . . was his own trusted organization having him followed? He picked up a folder and noticed a handwritten name scrawled on the inside. Strange he hadn't noticed it before.

"Apollos Drake?" Not a name he remembered seeing. Freely grabbed his computer and searched the name, clicking on the first article he found.

APOLLOS DRAKE TAKING THE SOCIAL MEDIA SCENE BY STORM WITH $500 MILLION PURCHASE

Below the article was a picture. Freely clicked the picture, staring at it in stunned silence. He had seen this guy before he left for Spring Oak and thought it strange. Once in his New York City neighborhood during his morning jog and then again at the airport. The guy put off a presence, and Freely remembered thinking how odd it made him feel. Now looking at Apollos Drake smiling at him from the photograph, Freely sat back a cold shiver running through his body. None of this made sense, but he was certain it was the same sinister man he had seen before.

Freely picked up his cell phone, dialing the number quickly and waiting until he heard the voice recorded greeting on the other end. He left a message, determined to get some answers.

"I want to know who Apollos Drake is, and I want to know why the hell I am really here. You need to call me."

****

John Freely sat in a restaurant with a beautiful ocean view, with Rebekah across from him. The sun was setting, and the view was breathtaking. The sun's last rays were streaking across her face and hair, and he thought she looked even better than the view. She turned to look at him to say something, but he couldn't hear her. He could see her mouth moving but couldn't make out the words. He was becoming very agitated. The restaurant seemed to have grown increasingly loud within seconds. He got up to move his chair closer to hers and glanced out to the water.

"What is that? Do you see that?"

He looked at Rebekah to see if she could see anything he was, but she only stared at him with a smile on her face. It seemed no one was experiencing what he was. The noise in the restaurant was deafening. He covered his ears and looked around. Only he was being bothered by the sound. He thought

192

it was the combination of the music and conversations, dishes clinking, but realized it was coming from the ocean. He stood, while Rebekah looked like a beautiful mannequin, stone still, not blinking, not talking, only smiling. He looked back to the water and saw the beast coming from its depths.

"What the hell is that? Is that a dragon?"

No one on the beach was running. They seemed to want it there. The dragon snarled and roared. Freely didn't want to take his hands off his ears. Blood dripped from its mouth, and its eyes were the darkest he had ever seen. Evil. Pure evil. He knew he needed to tell everyone to flee. He looked at Rebekah, screaming at her to get up and run. He couldn't hear himself. She couldn't hear him. She only sat smiling.

"REBEKAH, WE HAVE TO RUN!"

She didn't respond. He reached out to grab her, and suddenly it wasn't Rebekah. He fell back into the table behind him and onto the ground. He began crawling backward while keeping an eye on what was before him. It was black and slimy-looking. Walking on two feet with huge snarling teeth. It was coming straight for him. He got to his feet and turned to run, bursting through the doors of the restaurant and reaching for his weapon. But his gun wasn't there.

"Shit! Where is my gun?"

He was on the street, running, and blinded to what was around him. he could hear the roaring of the beast and . . .

hissing. *Hissing*, that was the sound in the restaurant. Thunderous hissing.

He fell as soon as he hit the beach, and they came for him. Hundreds of them. There was no way he would get away.

Freely's eyes flew open, his body drenched in sweat. He could see the light of the motel sign flashing through the curtains in his room. He sat up, swinging his legs over the side of the bed. His head was pounding.

"A damn dream. I was having a dream."

He felt a huge sense of relief. He got up to splash some water on his face and cool off. He grabbed the extra set of sheets in the room to change his bed. He had done a number on the bedclothes. Sweating and thrashing had created havoc.

Face washed and sheets changed, he grabbed a bottle of water and clicked on the TV. He checked his cell phone. Still no return call from his boss. The clock in his room glowed *3:11 a.m.* It was hard to shake the memory of his dream. He didn't know how or why, but Apollos Drake and the dream felt connected. Staring at the TV he heard the news anchor talking about another mass shooting. His stomach turned in knots with each word.

What stupid, sick bastard would do something like that?

The camera scanned over a crowd of people holding candles and praying.

"Hmm. Praying. For what? To who? The God who let this happen?"

He was disgusted with the world. There was no way there could be a God letting all the horrible things happen in this country and across the world. Freely had stopped believing in God years ago, when he was a teenager. Becoming a foster child sealed his faith to the tomb.

What kind of God lets a thirteen-year-old boy lose both his parents within a year? He stood, answering his own thought. "A God who doesn't exist, that's who!"

He walked to the window, parting the curtains with his hand. The parking lot was dark and deserted. Something caught his attention, and he squinted to get a better look. Someone was standing out there smoking. It was a man dressed in dark clothes, and Freely could see the smoke swirling above his head. He felt an intense feeling to close the curtain but couldn't pull himself away. The man began moving closer. He must have seen him staring. Freely was frozen. Whoever this was, he was aware of Freely, staring back, walking slowly, moving closer. The man stopped under a lamp post, leaning against it and continuing to stare back. He was dressed in what appeared to be a nice suit, and he was smiling. A sinister smile. Freely knew immediately who it was.

"What the hell do you want?"

The man slightly nodded in response, and Freely quickly shut the curtain. He grabbed a shirt and slipped his shoes on. His gun was in his hand. He had enough of Mr. Drake. It was time for them to meet. His heart pounded as he yanked open the door and saw nothing, Drake was gone. He ran into the parking lot to see if he could see anything, the smell of Drake's cigarette still hanging in the air.

How does someone disappear into thin air? And what did this guy want?

Freely didn't know why, but he spoke aloud. "I'm right here, Drake." He outstretched his arms. "What do you want with me?"

The air felt heavy, and there was only silence. Freely was ready for daybreak.

Chapter Eighteen

Who will protect me from the wicked? Who will stand up for me against evildoers? – Psalm 94:16

Amy tossed and turned, finally concluding she was not going to sleep. Her room was dark, and the noise of the city buzzed outside. But inside her apartment, she could feel *them*. Master had made sure she was not left alone. He was suspicious of her.

It had been two weeks since she met Farrel in the restaurant, and she had heard nothing from him. Farrel had said he would find her, but how when she was being watched all the time? Fear and worry consumed her every moment.

"God, if you hear me, if you care, please save me. I'm sorry for whatever I have done. I need you."

A tear rolled down the corner of her eye and fell onto the pillow. She felt a warm shiver run over her body. The demons clamored in the other room. Her praying made them frantic. Amy smiled. She knew she wasn't alone. God heard her. She would be strong—for Syene.

****

Kefira watched Master pace the cold stone floor. His stooge, Menti, glared at her from a corner in the room. She glared back.

"What are you staring at, you little cockroach?"

Menti hissed at her but did not reply. He turned his gaze to Master.

"Kefira, I thought you would have made more progress with Enzril. What is the problem?" Master was not happy, and a twinge of fear ran through her.

"Master, please give me more time. He is tougher to break than I thought."

Lucifer was inches away from her, she could feel his breath on her neck.

"I didn't task you to think, did I? I tasked you to seduce Enzril and ensure his loyalty to me."

She closed her eyes and swallowed hard. "I won't fail you, Master, I promise."

He ran his hand over the length of her body and pressed her back against himself. Kefira couldn't stop shaking. She knew Master could and would end her existence without warning. She could see his shadow on the stone floor as he held her to his scarred body. He towered over her, and she watched the outline of his wings expand; the light in the room was darkened. She closed her eyes and waited for the end, but it didn't come.

His serpent tongue lapped at her neck, and he whispered hoarsely, "You have one more chance. Do not blunder, or you will wish you were never created."

Kefira knew without a doubt her Master meant every word. She nodded her head in understanding. Terror had taken her voice.

****

"Girl, what are you doing at night? These dark circles are awful. I'm not a miracle worker."

Amy's makeup artist was talking, but she didn't hear what he said. He snapped his fingers at her.

"Hello? Anyone home?"

Amy focused in. "I'm sorry, Marcus, I'm so tired."

His hand was on his hip looking exasperated. "Clearly! This is what I have been saying. Who or what is keeping you up all night?"

Amy smiled. She knew he wanted some juicy gossip.

He leaned in to whisper, "Is it that sexy manager of yours? You can tell me. Honey, he is as yummy as a brownie topped with ice cream and covered in hot fudge."

Amy's stomach turned every time someone mentioned her Master. If they only knew. If all humans only knew the truth, things would be so different. She did her best to not look disgusted at the thought.

"Marcus, you are so bad. And you know better than that. I never mix business with pleasure."

He went on without skipping a beat. "Well, I guess Patsy Trumane couldn't get enough of him. I hear the pathetic little thing hasn't left him alone since they spent the night together. Not sure what that man has, but it must be something to write home about."

Amy had heard the rumors and felt guilty. Patsy met him at one of her events, the night Amy first met Kefira with Enzril. Apparently, Patsy had been bragging to everyone about her sex-filled night with Apollos and had become obsessed with him. People were saying he wouldn't return her many calls and texts, and now they hadn't seen her in weeks.

Marcus continued dramatically, "poor girl is getting drunk every day. She won't leave her penthouse."

Even though Amy knew Patsy made her own choices just like she had, she felt a sorrowful connection to her. She didn't want to discuss it any longer. She gave Marcus a playful tap on his arm to try to end the conversation.

"She's probably hiding from gossipy divas like you."

Marcus held up his hands with a look of shock and then laughed. "Girl, I know that's right. Gossipy bitches be mean." He looked at Amy in the mirror. "What we really need to talk about is the havoc you are wrecking on your skin."

She shrugged. "Work your magic. You're the best at what you do."

This seemed to satisfy him. Compliments always distracted people. Amy had become a skilled manipulator. She didn't want to talk about her Master, Patsy Trumane, or why she looked so tired. She only needed to get through this photo shoot.

****

The studio lights were glaring and hot as a fan blew her long dark hair. The photographer walked in, and Amy felt her breath catch. It was *him*, he had found her just like he promised. He caught her eye and smiled.

"Amy, this is Farrel Kelly. He is a new photographer for us but comes with amazing credentials, and his work is beautiful." The young editor, Brigitte, madly flirting as she introduced the newcomer to Amy, hadn't taken her hand off Farrel's arm. Amy smiled as well and extended her hand.

"Nice to meet you, Farrel." She felt the same warm shiver she had felt the other night in her room.

"You as well, Ms. Davis."

"Please, call me Amy."

Farrel nodded as he managed to extricate himself from his admirer. Amy was very curious as to how he was going to pull this off. Being a great photographer for a top fashion magazine was not something you just winged.

"Let's get started." He grabbed one of the cameras and worked like a true professional. It was if he had done this his entire life, which Amy knew was not true. She giggled to herself.

Unless God has people taking pictures in Heaven.

"Whatever you are thinking right now, keep it up."

Amy laughed out loud. A genuine laugh, something she hadn't done in a very long time. Farrel renewed her strength and joy.

After the shoot, Amy hurriedly went to change, praying he would still be there. She found the editor leaning in too closely to look at the photos with him. Amy felt a sudden protectiveness toward him. She somehow instinctively knew Farrel belonged to Syene. She nimbly inserted herself between them. Brigitte seemed extremely annoyed until Farrel spoke.

"I typically like to look at the photos with the model without any outside influence, if that is okay with you."

Brigitte looked somewhat crestfallen, which Farrel quickly mollified.

"Only thirty minutes or so, and then you and I can go over everything and make the final picks for editing."

Brigitte smiled. "Okay, I'll be back shortly."

She gave Amy a warning glare. The little idiot was clearly marking Farrel as hers. Amy gave her a look to let her know she really didn't care and then smiled sweetly.

As soon as she was gone, Amy couldn't talk fast enough. "How in the world did you manage this? I thought maybe you had forgotten about me."

"You were never forgotten. Do you not realize how powerful your Creator is? Lucifer is weak in comparison. He was created by Yahweh, and Yahweh has no need to manipulate. He places the path before all of us to follow."

Amy started to tremble at the mere mention of him, she expected Master to walk in at any moment and catch her.

"I will protect you. I promise." Farrel's calm voice eased her fear. She knew he was not going to put her in danger. Amy took a deep breath to help her trembling cease.

"I'm sorry, it's just you have no idea what he will do to me."

Farrel looked at her directly. "Amy, I know exactly what he will do to you. He was once a comrade, and later my entire existence was dedicated to battle him and his forces."

She nodded her head in understanding, barely whispering. "Of course you do. I'm sorry. It is hard to wrap my head around you as a warrior when you look so much like us. I don't see the good side of anything anymore. I only see the bad."

"Then open your eyes, Amy. Good is surrounding you right now. God never left you."

Amy stared in unbelief. "Then why? Why did God let me be taken?"

Farrel shook his head. "Let's talk about freewill. *Did* God let you be taken? Or did you choose the path willingly? Think Amy. Think back to the beginning. Did your friends not warn you about Lantz? Did your mother not beg you to return home? You made choices. I am not trying to hurt you, and I know there are many innocent people in this world who have done nothing to deserve heartache. But all I can tell you is I have been with the Creator when their sorrows are felt. God is there in every moment of pain, and I know something beautiful can always grow from the most horrible situation. Please don't lose hope. God will never give up on those with faith. Allow the Creator to turn your past into a glorious future."

Amy's eyes filled with tears. It was a hard truth to swallow—the knowledge that she was partially responsible for the hell she was in. There was no way she could put herself in the same category of the innocent souls who were subjected to evil unwillingly. She knew Farrel was right.

"I am not saying these things to condemn. Yahweh is not about condemnation. I am only speaking the truth. You stopped seeking your Creator. This does not mean your Creator stopped seeking you. You are the reason I am here. You made the choice to return to the light, whether you realize it or not."

Amy sat on the stool nearby, her head in her hands.

"What have I done? I have completely screwed my life up."

Farrel knelt before her. "Amy, your Creator loves you. It is not the time to have regret. Too much damage is done to the human heart looking back to the past." He gently pulled her hands away from her face. "It is time to fight. You must. We need your help. Syene needs your help."

"But how? What can I do? Master will know I am helping you. He will destroy me and kill my parents."

"He won't know. He can't read your thoughts. He knows Syene will be on the move. And she is moving west to the ocean. Lucifer is going to use you to get to her and Elkan."

"I don't understand."

"You will know what to do when the time comes."

Farrel stood abruptly, and the young editor popped her head in.

"Ms. Davis, your business manager is here. Security is sending him up."

Amy felt the panic constrict her throat. Farrel could see the terror and answered for her.

"We were just finishing up, thank you so much."

The editor gave them both a suspicious look as she left the room.

Amy quickly stood and wailed, "He knows, he knows. What am I going to do?"

Farrel took her by the shoulders and forced her to look at him.

"Amy! He doesn't know. He can feel the presence of his Creator, but he doesn't know. Calm down, or he will suspect. We can't allow that."

Amy took a deep breath to focus in on what Farrel was saying.

"I must go. I will find you, and the angels will be near. You are going to be okay. I give you my promise."

A tear fell down her cheek. She was terrified. She could hear Master's voice outside the door talking to Brigitte. She looked in the mirror, fixing her appearance and wiping the tears away.

Snap out of it Amy, you can do this, you can do this.

When she turned back, Farrel was gone—he had slipped through another door. She grabbed her bag just as the door opened, and Master entered with the newly enamored woman.

"Ms. Davis, you never mentioned how charming your manager was."

Amy gave her best smile. "Well, I figured he didn't require any of my assistance in that department."

Brigitte laughed like a schoolgirl and draped her arm through Master's. She looked around, realizing Farrel had gone.

"Did Mr. Kelly leave already?"

Amy diverted her eyes as she answered, "Oh yeah, he said he had another shoot to get to and would give your office a call, so you can review the photographs with him."

The editor looked disappointed, but thankfully the little idiot was more than willing to hear herself talk, and Amy didn't have to say anymore. She only prayed Brigitte wouldn't use his first name.

"Mr. Kelly is a new and upcoming photographer. His work is brilliant, so don't you worry, he is going to make your model look fabulous."

Lucifer eyed Amy like a piece of candy.

"That isn't too hard to do, now is it?"

The woman clearly did not want to hear about Amy's beauty and untangled herself from him.

He reached for Amy in turn, took her by the arm, and moved her toward the door.

"I wanted to surprise you and take you to dinner, my sweet."

Amy put on her best acting face. "How nice. I would love dinner."

They barely gave a glance back to Brigitte as they made their way out.

Once inside the elevator he pressed her against the wall.

"I smell fear."

Amy turned her head to the side. "Isn't that what you do, instill fear?"

She heard him chuckle as he released her. She faced Master.

"Why the surprise visit?" Amy knew she was in danger. Master was suspicious, and he had been *surprising* her more and more.

"I wanted to see my muse at work."

Amy said nothing. He knew her time working was hers alone. He relished her success, gloated in it, took credit for it. This was the only reason the demons weren't allowed to follow her to her shoots. She had told Master they were too distracting and effecting her ability to work. He moved closer to her again. She knew he found human flesh intoxicating. His obsession repulsed her.

"I thought you would be more excited to see me."

He pressed against her, smelling her neck. Amy cringed inside, thankful when the elevator came to a stop and the doors opened. He reluctantly released her. She knew it was going to be a long night, and her stomach turned. Hope was the only thing keeping her moving. She took his arm extended to her and knew from the outside they must have looked like a beautiful couple. If people only knew the true horror that was before them.

****

Jamille stood alone on the mountainside looking at the valley and house below, their haven for the last six years. She was filled with dread about the imminent move to their new home. She knelt to pray.

"My Lord, hear my prayer of mercy. Please allow me the strength and intelligence to keep Sacred and Elkan safe from the evil plans of Lucifer. I do not want to fail You." A cool breeze blew across her, and she knew she was heard.

"Praying won't stop him." Jamille quickly stood and drew her sword.

"What are you doing here, Enzril?" Her heart beat wildly at the sight of him.

He stepped forward, moving the tip of her sword away from him.

"Is that how you greet an old friend?"

"What do you want?"

She did not put away the sword. Her voice was hard, but inside she was melting. She still loved him, but she knew not to trust him.

Enzril circled her slowly. "I'm only following orders and watching over the move." He paused. "You looked so beautiful kneeling in prayer, I couldn't resist saying hello."

She wasn't going to take the bait. He knew well her weakness for him.

"I will die to protect her and the child, have no doubt about that. I will not hesitate to kill you or anyone else who comes for them."

Enzril leaned against a large boulder and smiled at her,

"I'll be sure and pass your message on to Master."

Jamille spat. "Your Master, not mine. I have a Creator, you are a slave."

Enzril was on her, the sword thrown from her hand. He wrapped his hand gently around her throat.

"Don't battle with me, Jamille. I trained you, I will win."

His touch sent chills running over her body. His lips were so close to hers, she could feel his breath. She closed her eyes waiting for him to press his mouth to hers.

"Am I interrupting?"

The voice startled them, and Enzril released her. Jamille picked up her sword, backing away from the new arrival. Kefira stood staring at the ex-lovers with hatred in her eyes.

"What are you doing here?" Enzril's voice was filled with anger at the interruption.

Kefira stood her ground.

"Master sent me to find you. He needs to see you."

Jamille could see the jealousy raging in the female's eyes. She wanted Enzril for herself, that was easy to see. She felt the twinge of envy for this person who had time with her Enzril. But she quickly knew where those emotions would find her, and she stood tall as she thought of her Creator. She would not become a slave again because of her love for Enzril. He betrayed her once, and she would not allow it again. She gave them both a nod.

"Your Master summons you, slaves."

And with that she was gone, flying high and away from him once more.

Chapter Nineteen

For we live by faith, not by sight. – 2 Corinthians 5:7

Syene stood in the middle of the living room, packed boxes everywhere. Elkan was reading quietly on the floor, his head propped up on Wesley as his pillow. A few more days and they would be gone . . . most likely forever. Elkan was much more excited about their impending plane ride than she. Everyone had gone to town for last-minute travel supplies except Dr. Kaufman. He walked quietly into the room. Syene gave him a warm smile of welcoming.

"You don't need to be quiet. Once he goes into the reading zone, a live marching band couldn't disturb him."

Kaufman watched Elkan. "His intelligence level is fascinating. I hope to get much more time with him."

"Sometimes too smart."

Kaufman looked around at all the boxes. "Is there anything I can help you with?"

Sy shook her head. "I don't think so, we are pretty much done. Time to start loading everything in the moving truck. I can't thank Laura and Thomas enough for volunteering to drive there. I hope they know how much I appreciate it."

"I'm certain they are fully aware. And truth be told, I think they both are a little relieved I chose to fly with you instead of make the drive with them." He chuckled as he sat on the chair ottoman and took off his glasses to clean them. "I can't say I blame them. They already traveled halfway across the globe with this grouchy old man."

Syene sat across from him on the couch, her feet and back aching from all the packing. She really liked Dr. Kaufman. He had a beautiful spirit, and she doubted either Laura or Thomas ever were tired of being with him, he was so charming and engaging.

"Dr. Kaufman, do you mind if I ask you a personal question?"

"Of course not. Please, ask away."

"Do you have a family? I haven't heard you mention a wife or children."

The old man sighed. "I did, many years ago. She was the only love I have ever known."

Syene immediately felt sorry she had asked. She could see the pain of the memory.

"I'm sorry, you don't have to tell me anything. It was rude of me to pry."

"You, my dear, are the furthest thing from being rude. And I don't mind speaking of her. She helped make me who I am today."

He stared out the window and took a deep breath as his memories flowed backward in time.

"Her name was Martha. She was an angel on earth. I swear just as beautiful as the angels you see surrounding you."

Sy couldn't help but smile at the obvious adoration he had for this Martha.

"We met while I was in college. She was working at a local diner, and I instantly fell in love. We got married after I graduated. I found a teaching job in a small town close to the diner and her parents, and life was so perfect. It became even more perfect when she announced she was pregnant. I couldn't have been happier than I was in that moment."

He paused at the memory.

"I thought my heart might explode, I was so happy."

Syene smiled. She was a sucker for a beautiful love story. When she was little she would make her mom tell her over and over how she and her dad had fallen in love.

"She was planning on quitting her job at the diner when she got further along in the pregnancy, but she loved people. She wasn't the type of person to sit at home. She was my social butterfly. Martha was kind to every single person she met."

He placed his glasses back on and let out another deep sigh.

"One evening I had parent meetings at the school and another waitress had called in sick, so Martha had to work later than normal. I told her to have her dad come get her. It was cold outside and got dark early, but she insisted she would be okay walking home."

Syene could hear his voice cracking, and she waited patiently for him to finish.

"I arrived home around nine o'clock that night and knew instantly something was wrong. The house was dark, and she hadn't made it home. I immediately drove to the diner, but it was dark and shut down. I drove to her parents praying and hoping she had ended up there, but they hadn't seen or heard from her. We were in a panic. The police were called, and we all began searching that night."

Syene felt that familiar pain of death penetrate her chest as she listened to Dr. Kaufman relive his nightmare.

"It was the longest night of my life. I walked all the streets, alleys, knocked on doors. No one had seen her. The police finally sent me home and promised they would contact me as soon as they found anything. That moment came to soon. An officer showed up early the next morning with the worse news of my life. Two kids outside of town, walking to school, saw something lying in a ditch."

Kaufman looked at Syene. Tears streaming down his aged cheeks.

"It was my Martha, my beautiful Martha, tossed into a ditch like she was nothing. The monster had raped and strangled her to death, then put her out on the road like a sack of garbage."

Kaufman was sobbing. Syene immediately got up to wrap her arms around him. She was all too familiar with this type of misery and hurt.

"I'm so sorry."

He wiped his eyes and smiled through his tears.

"Silly right? To hurt this much after all these years. Almost forty-five years, and I still miss her."

Syene had tears on her cheeks now too. "Not silly. Human." She didn't want to ask the question, but she had to.

"Did they find who did it?"

"Yes, he almost got another young girl, but he was stopped this time by a passerby. He bragged in jail about murdering Martha and then confessed to the crime to the police."

Kaufman stood.

"He was sent to prison for life, but I could never find happiness in this. I wanted him dead from the beginning, I wanted to hurt him with my bare hands like he had hurt my beautiful Martha. He took everything from me. My wife, my unborn child. I was filled with hatred and rage. Ironically hatred that led me to Cassius and now Elkan. I often think Martha has been behind it. Urging me to forgive and love again."

"And did you? Did you forgive him?"

Syene knew all too well how hard forgiveness could be.

"Yes, finally, I released all the anger after years of wrestling my hatred." He glanced over at Elkan. "And now finding you and Elkan has completed my journey."

"Journey?"

"Yes, my journey to find God. To prove to myself there was a reason for all my pain. All the pain in the world that we see. Senseless violence, hatred, and racism. I had to prove there was more than that. And you, my dear, have given me that proof. Elkan will help change the world. He will bring back the love of God, and of Christ. The love this world has so obviously disconnected from. A child from God to remind us He is here, to remind us of the sacrifice of His son. What an honor for me to be part of this."

Syene couldn't help herself and gave the sweet doctor a warm hug.

"Thank you for reminding me the task ahead. I easily get wrapped up in my own concerns and fears. I needed to hear this, so thank you."

Kaufman hugged her tightly back.

"Don't ever forget if God is using an old Jewish man like me to bring you some hope, I can only imagine the greatness He has planned for Elkan."

Syene felt some of the weight lift off her. All these amazing people brought into her life were handpicked by the Creator. She would never understand the pain that had to go along with the beauty, but it was time to let God's will be done.

****

Freely picked up his vibrating cell phone. Chief Harris had been kind enough to set them up in a small office, and Rebekah had seemed to become part of the investigation team.

"Freely." His voice was gruff.

He didn't recognize the number, and Rebekah looked at him across the desk with a questioning stare. He shrugged his shoulders.

"Agent Freely, I have information about the young mother and child you might find interesting."

He immediately pulled out his pen and notebook. "And to whom I am speaking with?"

He heard a slight chuckle. "You wouldn't believe me if I told you."

An odd feeling came over Freely. "Excuse me?"

And then another chuckle.

"Apollos Drake is the name, if it really matters. I thought you might like to know the little family is moving from the mountains to the ocean, and they are leaving very quickly."

Freely's head began pounding. The man who had been following him was on the phone. His mind felt foggy.

"Why the hell have you been following me? What do you want?"

Only silence on the other end.

"Are you the informant for the FBI? Who are you really?"

"You know who I am, John Freely. I've known you for a while now."

Freely could feel beads of sweat on his forehead forming.

"What the hell are you talking about? I don't know you."

The phone went dead.

He could see the look of concern on Rebekah's face.

"What was that about?"

He wasn't even sure if he could speak. He felt like a dark cloak was covering him, smothering him. He stood abruptly.

"I need some fresh air."

Freely stood, bumping into the doorframe on his way out of the small room, gasping for air as soon as he pushed the front door open. He bent over, hands on his knees trying to clear his head.

Rebekah followed, touching him on the back.

"John, are you okay? Who was that on the phone?"

She looked worried, and for some reason he liked the fact she used his first name. He stood up straight and made his way to a nearby bench. Rebekah followed. He sat down, his head was finally clearing. She waited patiently. John Freely looked around at the main street where the police station was located.

"This place is really quaint." He paused. "Quaint, is that the correct word?"

Rebekah smiled at him.

"Yes, quaint is the right word." She looked at him, her brow raised. "Are you okay? What happened in there."

Freely shrugged. "I'm not sure. Maybe I just needed some fresh air."

"John, come on, what happened?"

There it was again, his name. He liked it.

"I don't know who he really is, but I am pretty sure he has been following me."

"Following you? What do you mean?"

Freely rubbed his head. "I saw him before I ever came to Spring Oak, and then again at the hotel."

Rebekah looked as baffled as he felt. "What! Who is he?"

"His name is Apollos Drake, and all I really know is he's very wealthy and very involved in this case somehow."

"Apollos Drake? He's the famous movie producer and entrepreneur. Did you try to confront him at the hotel? I'm so confused right now."

"Yes, but as soon as I got outside he was gone. Totally vanished. I have to be honest with you. I am as confused as you are, and my supervisor is not providing any information to me. It is all very strange."

"I'm scared, John. Why would Apollos Drake have any interest in what you are doing and be following you? What did he say on the phone?"

"He told me they are leaving the mountain house soon. And it was just the way he said it. I can't explain it. The voice felt evil. Same as when I have seen him . . . evil."

"Are you ever going to tell me why you are really here?"

"Our office was sent information. Copies of very old manuscripts along with an anonymous letter. But now I believe it was Mr. Drake who sent all of it, and for whatever reason my own organization is keeping everything about him classified, even from me."

"Manuscripts and a letter? What are you talking about?"

He shook his head. "Prophesy stuff, it's ridiculous. I can't believe they sent me here to investigate this?"

"But what about what happened to Mr. Reese? What about what you saw on the surveillance video? What about Karen? And now Apollos Drake being involved. This is becoming more than an incident at a grocery store with a drug addict."

It was obvious to him her reporter's mind was going crazy.

"I really felt I could trust you. Please don't make me sorry for sharing this with you."

"I have to come with you to see them again. This changes everything."

Freely shook his head. "It changes nothing. But I would like for you to come."

"Really?" He recognized the surprise in her voice.

He did mean it. He wanted her with him, something about her brought him comfort

"I would really like for you to come."

"Then I will." Her smile was vibrant.

****

The next morning John relished seeing Rebekah smile at him as he walked across the hotel parking lot. She was a sight for sore eyes. He cautiously looked around for Drake or anyone else who might be watching them. He gave her his best attempt at a smile as he got closer.

"Wow, what happened to you? You look like hell."

He laughed. "Well, good morning to you too."

"Sorry. But really, what happened? You look like you didn't sleep at all last night."

"I didn't. I guess I haven't slept much since I realized my own department is screwing me." He was grateful she didn't push the subject.

"How about I drive then? We don't need you driving on a winding mountain road with sleep deprivation."

"That's probably a good idea. I am definitely going to need some coffee before we get there."

Rebekah gave him another dazzling smile.

"Coffee I can easily do."

He couldn't keep himself from thinking how damn pretty she was. He was glad he asked her to join him.

****

The car ride was quiet. He needed quiet. Freely was trying to get his thoughts together. The coffee helped some to clear his head, but everything about the last few days left him with a feeling of dread. His cop instincts were on high alert. Rebekah's voice broke his thoughts as they got closer to the house.

"What exactly are you going to say? You can't make them stay, right? I mean if they really are leaving."

"No, I can't make them stay, not without filing any charges, and I don't have any proof they did anything wrong. But I know without a doubt they have something to do with what happened in the grocery store and what is going on right now."

"So, what are you going to do when we get there?"

"See if I can find out where they are going. They will be required to give me that information because of the ongoing investigation. And then I am going to follow them to their new destination. I'm not letting this go."

She glanced at him. "You really think they were responsible for Phil Reese's death?" Freely could hear the doubt in her voice.

He shrugged. "Do I think they set out to murder him? No. But I know she is hiding something, and that is what I need to find out."

He could see she wanted to say more but was holding back. "What? Say it."

She kept her eyes on the road. "I really don't understand why you refuse to believe there is something really special about them." She quickly glanced at him.

"I mean Karen being healed after he touched her, and then the video. You said yourself there was something there you couldn't explain. What if Elkan really is of something divine?"

Freely couldn't help but laugh out loud.

"Divine? Are you seriously talking about something from God?" He laughed again. "Do you have any idea all the horrible things I have seen in my life, and you expect me to believe this little boy has been sent from Heaven above? You've lost your mind."

"You don't have to be so rude about it! Not everyone has to be a cynical ass like you."

"I may be a cynic, but at least I'm not living in a make-believe world of unicorns, rainbows, and God. There is not a God, nor is there any proof of Heaven. Whatever is going on with Drake and his involvement is not about God, and what I saw in the video was only a trick of the light or a flaw in the recording. It was nothing. And certainly not angels or anything divine."

She gave him a noncommittal shrug. "Whatever you say, Special Agent. Whatever you say."

Chapter Twenty

Jesus immediately reached out and grabbed him. "You have so little faith," Jesus said. "Why did you doubt me?"
– Matthew 14:31

Syene looked around the house. The furniture was covered with sheets, and everything was shut off. It was eerily quiet. She looked out the back windows and felt the aching pull in her chest. She was leaving the last connection to her mom. It wasn't easy, but she knew it was time. Syene fingered the cross hanging from the rosary Father Cervini insisted she keep with her.

Only Dr. Kaufman, Laura, and Thomas remained with them. Dave and Susan had to return home to their home and congregation. Syene had no idea when she would see them. James and Julie hopefully would be joining them after she and Ariel found a permanent residence. Father Cervini was already on his way to their new location, and her grandma and Lizzy would be there waiting for them when they arrived. Syene smiled at the thought of her lifelong best friend. She had missed Lizzy more and more and couldn't wait to see her.

Elkan was ecstatic about flying on the plane, but Syene could not enjoy his enthusiasm. Her hands began to sweat at the thought of it. She was glad to have Ariel and Dr. Kaufman with her on the flight, but her anxiety was on high alert. Laura and Thomas would be leaving tonight in the moving truck and taking Wesley with them. Syene said a silent prayer for their safety and strength. She hoped they made the right decision by having them make the drive with only the two of them, but she knew God's warriors would be with them.

She managed a smile when she looked out the back windows. Thomas, Laura, Ariel, and Elkan were lying on the grass looking up at the clouds, obviously in animated conversation about what shapes they could see. She fondly remembered a simpler time when she and Ariel had done the same thing. Wesley was sunning peacefully next to Elkan, and Dr. Kaufman sat on the back deck, papers and books scattered across the table. He had been working nonstop, documenting everything he was witnessing.

"Well, God, you definitely know how to put a motley crew together."

Jamille appeared behind her laughing. "Motley is a fair analogy. And this isn't even the whole crew." She wrapped her arm around Syene's shoulder. "Everything is going to be okay, Sy. I won't let anything happen to any of you. Michael and I will be flying with the plane, and Gabriel will be with Laura and Thomas."

Syene leaned into her, sighing deeply. "I know you will be with us. It is the unknown that is so terrifying. I keep waiting for Lucifer to pop up at any moment."

Jamille turned her and looked directly into her eyes.

"Lucifer is a coward. He hides in the shadows, waiting and prowling. We watch him just as he watches us." She hugged Syene tightly. "Stop worrying. I will take care of the bad guys. Worry was never meant for the soul."

Syene drank in the smell of her. Jamille was her place of comfort. She pulled away at the sound of a car coming up the long driveway.

Jamille looked toward the front door. "It is John Freely and the reporter, Rebekah."

Syene groaned. "What is this guy's deal? I need him to leave us alone."

Jamille gave her a reassuring smile and directed her toward the door.

"He doesn't believe in the Creator; therefore, he doesn't believe anything he has witnessed. He's only searching for truth and understanding."

Sy rolled her eyes. "Can't we just zap him with some angel dust, so he can see you."

Jamille swatted her behind and pointed to the front door.

"Go be courteous to your guests."

Syene grudgingly walked to the door and opened it, calling for Wesley, who was going crazy barking at the car. He spotted Syene and bounded happily to the house. She immediately directed him through the house and out the back door to join Elkan again. Syene walked back to the front and watched as the pair stepped out of their car.

"Hello, Agent Freely, what brings you out?"

She waited as he made his way to the porch. He was very handsome for an older man. She figured he was in his early forties, he was physically fit, and it was clear his female sidekick was hooked. Sy got a good vibe from her. She liked Rebekah.

She was going to do her best to be nice this time. The less attention on her and Elkan, the better.

"Hello, Ms. Harper." He motioned toward the moving van. "Going somewhere?"

Syene knew if she lied, and he found out after they were gone, it was only going to make things worse.

"Yes, we are moving temporarily." She decided the nicer she was the better. "I can give you our new address if you like.

He nodded. "I would."

"Would you like to come in while I write it down for you?" She opened the front door, and the pair followed her in.

"I guess it's a good thing we showed up when we did. Looks like you are heading out pretty quickly." She saw him scanning the living room.

Syene nodded. "Yes, we are. Tonight actually. Our flight leaves tomorrow.
We are staying in a hotel close to the airport."

She walked to the kitchen. "Let me grab a pen and paper really quick." Syene knew she needed to decide one way or another. She was going to have to share the truth with them or be plagued by him and his digging into their lives.

****

Without Syene watching him with what he considered put-on friendliness, John walked to the back windows, checking on the people outside. He could see the child laughing with Ariel and two other young adults. An elderly gentleman sat on the deck, flipping through papers and writing in a notebook. Their dog was lounging lazily in the sunshine.

"Friends of yours?" He nodded toward the back as Syene stepped back into the living room.

"Yes, they are new friends." She and Rebekah joined Freely at the windows.

Rebekah spoke quietly, "I hope you don't mind me saying, but Elkan is such a beautiful child. He has a real presence to him."

"I don't mind at all, he's my everything."
Freely could hear in her voice she meant it. He could feel Syene's stare upon him and turned.

"May I ask you a question, Agent Freely?"

"Go ahead."

"Do you believe in God?"

Rebekah also turned to look at him, waiting for his response.

He gave her a shrug. "Not sure why it matters, but no, Ms. Harper, I do not."

"Would you mind telling me why?"

Freely wasn't sure why he was compelled to give her an explanation, but he did.

"Why would anyone believe in God? If you have seen the things I have and dealt with the kind of people I have, you wouldn't believe either. So, to answer your question, I find it appalling anyone could believe in a God who allows horrible things to happen all the time."

"I know there are many who feel this way. That is what makes it so hard." Syene sighed heavily. "What if I told you I know God is real?"

He faced her and looked directly in her eyes.

"I would say, prove it." Freely watched her hesitate for a moment.

She began whispering. "Michael, I need you."

Freely leaned closer to her. "Michael? Who is Michael?"

Syene began to pray quietly, and Freely's hair stood up on the back of his neck. Something in the air changed immediately. It was like a vacuum had sucked out all sound from the house and he was standing in another dimension. The surroundings began to cloud. Freely strained to hear what Syene was saying. He turned to look at Rebekah and could only see the look of shock on her face at whatever was behind him.

He wasn't sure if he wanted to turn around. His hand instinctively drew his gun as he turned around.

"What the hell is this?! WHO ARE YOU?" He backed up slowly putting himself in front of Rebekah, with his gun pointed at the winged creatures standing in front of him. The gun was shaking.

Syene raised her hands and began to move toward the two *things* in the living room.

"Mr. Freely, please don't panic."

"No. No. This can't be real." He could hear the quiver in his voice. What he was seeing was impossible. Things like this did not exist.

The massive male stepped forward. Freely raised his gun higher as a warning to the giant.

"John Freely. I know you well. I have protected you many times during your lifetime and career."

John's hands and voice were still shaking. "Protected me? What are you talking about? I don't even know what the hell you are!"

The laugh was loud and genuine. "I am Michael, General and warrior for Yahweh, and protector of all."

Freely could feel the sweat beading up on his forehead. This couldn't possibly be real. None of this could be real. The female creature put herself between him and Syene. He heard Rebekah's voice behind him and watched as she placed her hand on his arm.

"John, please, put the gun down."

Her voice was the only thing real in this moment. And honestly, he knew the gun would do him no good against what was standing before him. He lowered the gun and suddenly felt extremely dizzy and began swaying. He stumbled forward to the sheet-covered couch and sat down. Rebekah sat with him. All sound was muffled, and his head was pounding. He held tightly to Rebekah's hand.

"This can't be real, this can't be real."

"Agent Freely?" He looked up. Syene was holding a glass of water in front of him. The two huge creatures were still in the room. He thought he might throw up. He looked at Rebekah and could hardly believe she looked so calm. She obviously couldn't see what he was seeing.

"Do you see them?" He motioned his head toward the winged giants. Rebekah nodded.

"Then how the hell are you looking so calm?" He wiped the sweat from his forehead with the paper towel Syene handed to him. "I'm freaking out."

Syene sat down next to him. "I know how you feel. I couldn't breathe when I first saw them." She was doing her best to reassure him, but nothing was going to make him feel better about anything he was seeing.

He shook his head in denial. "None of this can be real."

Syene placed her hand on his arm.

"They are more real than the couch we are sitting on."

Freely took a huge gulp of the water. His mouth felt dry as the desert. He tried to stay focused on she and Rebekah and ignore the winged figures lurking in the room.

"What are you and your son running from? I'm assuming you are running from someone?"

"You must understand the full story of who my son is, but we are looking for a place to keep him safe."

"Safe from what?"

"From people like you, working for the government. I mean no disrespect by saying that. And from Lucifer."

Freely couldn't believe what he was hearing. "Lucifer? As in *the devil*?" He laughed, but it sounded a little more like hysteria. "Lady, you have lost your mind, and somehow have sucked us into the hallucination."

He stood, still feeling a little shaky. Rebekah quickly followed, urging him to sit down again.

"John, I don't think this is a hallucination."

He could hear the fear in her voice, but he wasn't going to sit down. He approached the two angels and waved his hand toward them.

"Really, Rebekah? You think these two, whatever they are, are real? You think those wings are real?" His hysteria was mounting. "This is one big hoax! None of this is real."

He was standing next to the angels and couldn't help but notice their size. The male was a good two feet taller than him, and the female was only a foot below that. They were both impressive in stature, but angels? He wasn't buying it. Hollywood-quality costumes and makeup were what this was. He stood directly in front of the one calling himself Michael.

"May I look at those wings?" The skepticism dripping from his voice couldn't be missed. He watched as the enormous male turned slowly. Freely noted the scars across his massive muscular body. This man was a fighter. Those scars didn't come from riding a bicycle.

Michael spoke to him. "Would you like the wings down or spread open?"

Freely didn't try to mask his sarcasm. "Opened, by all means. I would love to see how these are attached."

The massive wings expanded, and he heard Rebekah gasp behind him. They were spectacular. The light coming from the windows glistened across their pure white color. Freely moved closer examining the wings closely. They were not falsely attached to the man's torso. He felt dizzy again. Nothing in his world made sense right now.

"I don't understand how this is possible."

He could hear the sniffles from Rebekah. She was crying.

Syene stepped in the middle of them. She took Rebekah's hand and then his. "I would really like for you to officially meet Elkan."

Freely could only nod. He felt numb. If his senses could be overloaded, then this was certainly what it must feel like.

The angel lowered his wings and faced them.

"Again, I am Michael, General and warrior for Yahweh, and protector of all."

John and Rebekah both sat down again and watched Syene walk out the back door calling for her son. His heart racing, John Freely instinctively knew his life would never be the same. He had been wrong about everything he ever believed.

****

Syene walked out to the back deck. The mountain air filled her lungs. Dr. Kaufman looked up and smiled.

"We have guests. I was going to have everyone come in and meet them."

"New believers?"

She nodded yes.

"How wonderful!" Syene loved Dr. Kaufman's joy for everything. She needed some of him to rub off on her.

She called out and waved for the group to come up to the house and watched as they made their way up the hill. Wesley barked, and Elkan laughed as the loyal Doberman chased him playfully to the house. He and Elkan both stopped at the stairs waiting impatiently for everyone else.

Syene took her son's hand. "I have some people anxious to meet you, is that okay with you?"

He nodded. "I knew they were coming."

She ruffled his hair gently. "Of course you did."

Everyone trickled up the stairs and into the house, one by one. Wesley refused to come in and sat at the back door staring toward the tree line and mountain rage. His ears were straight up, and a low growl rumbled from him. Danger was watching.

Syene gave him a pat. "Let's go inside, boy, I know they are out there." Wesley reluctantly followed her in. He took his place inside at the windows standing guard. The familiar feeling of dread coursed through her body. Elkan gently took her hand, feeling her thoughts. She smiled at her sweet boy, not wanting to worry him. She introduced everybody when they walked inside and explained the events leading to Special Agent Freely and Rebekah Fabinski being there today.

Freely stood to greet the doctor. "Dr. Kaufman, I recognize your name and face from the reports. You discovered the Cassius writings."

Syene didn't conceal her interest. "So, you do know about the writings?"

Freely nodded. "Of course, they are part of the reason I am here."

Now things she had suspected were beginning to make sense. Including the return sudden interest in the grocery store and what had happened to Mr. Reese. But she thought Dr. Kaufman had told her the writings were kept confidential.

Syene turned her attention to the doctor. "I thought no one knew about the writings except a very select few?"

Kaufman looked very confused.

"This is true. I trust those people with my life." He looked at Freely "How is it possible you found out about them?"

Freely shrugged. "I can't tell you because I don't know. But it sounds like you have misplaced your trust." He wasn't ready to divulge anything about Apollos Drake, still uncertain himself who could be trusted. Freely directed his attention to Syene. "But I can tell you whatever all of this is has made the government want to know more. Elkan is not going to be able to remain hidden. They are fully aware of him and of you."

Syene knew this time would come, she just didn't think it would be so soon. She looked to Michael and Jamille for guidance.

"What do we do?"

Jamille moved closer to her. "Sacred, you know we have no control over events set in motion, but we are here to protect you and Elkan at all costs."

Syene looked at the FBI agent. "What are you going to do? Are you going to tell them where we are going?"

She could see his hesitation. "I won't do anything for now. But they will find you with or without me."

Syene couldn't help herself and she hugged him tightly. "Thank you."

"Please don't thank me yet, I'm only buying you some time. I still have a job to do." She nodded her understanding. "But I do have to ask you, what really happened in that grocery store and to Phil Reese?"

Before Syene could respond, Michael intervened. "Phil Reese was possessed with multiple demons. Elkan knew it and tried to help. The demons destroyed him, not Elkan. Phil Reese did not want the help, he wanted the evil with him."

The room was silent. Syene knew her son didn't hurt him that day, but it was a relief to hear the truth. She had always been afraid to ask. Afraid of Elkan's abilities.

She could still see the doubt on the agent's face as he nodded. "And Karen Caldwell's story? The story about the dog?"

Syene smiled. "All true." She took Elkan's hand. "Perhaps it is time for Elkan to show you everything." She proudly walked him over to John and Rebekah.

"I would like for you to properly meet my son, Elkan."

Elkan didn't waste any time and immediately walked over to the new couple, sitting between them on the couch, placing his hands on both their hands. Syene knew the vision had begun. She instantly saw the change on their faces. The look of awe and amazement of first sight never got old. She smiled as she watched John's body relax and his color return. Her Elkan was such a wonderful gift to all. Rebekah had tears rolling down her cheeks. He stayed with them waiting patiently for them to absorb everything they were shown.

Dr. Kaufman broke the silence. "It is amazing, isn't it?!"

Syene laughed, again thinking to herself how much she needed some of his exuberance.

John nodded his agreement but also instantly looked worried. He finally understood the gravity of their situation. "They won't stop coming for him, you know this right?"

Syene did know. She also knew John Freely didn't grasp the whole picture. He was only worried about the human side of it. He hadn't been introduced to the monster he would soon come to know. It was the one thing she hated about sharing the truth. The evil had to come with the beauty.

It didn't take long for the newest believers to decide there was no way they couldn't follow Elkan to his new home. Rebekah was fully engaged in conversation and questions with everyone. Her excitement was contagious with all, except for John. Syene watched the agent walk to the windows where Wesley was still on guard. He stared into the distance.

Syene approached and stood beside him. "Is something wrong?"

"I wasn't sent here by accident, Ms. Harper. The FBI was called and sent information about your son. Information Dr. Kaufman says very few people had. They sent me here because they believe there is something they can gain from

Elkan's gifts. And I believe the man who led me here has been following me. I can't explain it, but I know he is evil. I am scared for the first time in my life."

Syene touched the rosary around her neck and took the agent's hand into hers as they both stared at the mountains.

"'The Lord will preserve him and keep him alive, and he will be blessed on the earth; You will not deliver him to the will of his enemies.'" She smiled at him. "I say that Scripture over and over to myself."

John chuckled. "I definitely have some Biblical reading to do. I have been an atheist most of my life." Syene squeezed his hand tightly.

"Ms. Harper, I owe you an apology. It is a humbling moment when you are awakened for the first time. I have never felt such joy and fear all at the same time, and I can't thank you enough for allowing me to be a part of this." He looked back toward the mountains. "I do know Elkan is in danger, and it's not only from the unseen. The government will see him as a weapon they can use. I consider them as dangerous as Lucifer."

Syene finally understood. It was all God's will, no matter how hard she pushed back. She had been acting like a foolish child. Elkan would do what he was sent to do, no matter how much she resisted, and God was placing the people in their lives to keep him protected.

She stared out the window and shivered. Evil was waiting for them. She had to be strong. It was time to step out on to the water.

****

Lucifer stood at the edge of the forest, watching them. The cloak was discarded, his grotesque figure blended with the trees. Lustful evil coursed through his body watching her.

"Hurry and come to me, my sweet. I've been patiently waiting on you."

He spread his wings and was gone.

Chapter Twenty-One

With flattery he will corrupt those who have violated the covenant, but the people who know their God will firmly resist him. – Daniel 11:32

Kefira moved closer to Enzril. She had been staying a few feet away on top of the building he had chosen to keep an eye on Amy. She loved looking at him. Her obsession was becoming insatiable. His intense green eyes, his muscles, his darkness. She wanted to soak all of him up. His refusal to acknowledge her only made her want him more. When she finally caught him looking at her a few times recently, it gave her the motivation to stay after him. Enzril would be hers, and Jamille would be forgotten.

She stood directly behind him, her body brushing against him slightly.

"Enzril, should we go pay Amy a visit?"

He turned when she was less than an inch away. He stepped back, but she moved again, pressing her body closer.

"Why do you avoid being next to me?"

Enzril didn't move away this time. His eyes burned into hers, and she could feel her pulse quickening.

His voice was deep with desire. "You are a child who wants to play with fire."

Kefira had never wanted anything more than she wanted him right now. He was inches away, and she seized her moment. She wrapped her arms around his neck, pressing her body into his lustfully. His full lips upon hers felt magical, and her body was on fire as his arms wrapped around her. And as suddenly as it started it stopped. Enzril pushed her away.

She was angry and frustrated. "You want me, I know you do. Why are you resisting me?"

He smiled at her. "Your outburst only proves what a juvenile you are. I do not have time for childish games. I am your superior."

Kefira tried to move closer again, but Enzril raised his hand.

"Kefira, I cannot give you what you are looking for. My heart was taken from me long ago. I have no interest in what you have to offer."

Anger, fired by the humiliation of his rejection, coursed through her body as she glared at him. Kefira soared off into the night away from Enzril, vehemently hissing the name she hated most.

"Jamille."

The only solution was to get rid of the problem. An evil smile spread across her face.

****

Amy pulled the cross out of its hiding place and clasped it around her neck. She knew she couldn't wear it for any length of time, but for the few moments it was on she felt comforted.

"Interesting piece of jewelry."

His voice startled her, and she gasped. Amy glared at Enzril in the mirror's reflection.

"But I can tell you now, Master won't appreciate its beauty. I suggest you take it off."

She turned and faced the dark angel

"Where's your little sidekick? Out learning to fly without training wheels?" Amy couldn't stand his new female companion and was happy she wasn't with him.

Enzril chuckled. "I'll miss your wit, Amy."

She crossed her arms across her chest giving him the dirtiest look she could muster.

"And what exactly is that supposed to mean?"

Enzril slowly circled the room, running his hand over the box where she kept the cross necklace and the phone she had secretly purchased. Amy foolishly left the box out. She watched his fingers tap the lid.

"Exactly what it sounds like. As soon as Master finds out about your little treasure chest he won't be happy."

"I seriously doubt a piece of jewelry will affect Master like it does you." But she knew Enzril was right, had it been Lucifer catching her off-guard she would have paid for it. She had to be more careful, and she hoped by blowing it off Enzril would keep his mouth shut.

Enzril pulled the cross up, looking at it in his hand and then letting it drop against her skin.

"You're probably right, but when he finds out about the phone, and you meeting with Farrel, you will be a distant memory."

Amy's heart was pounding wildly. He knew. How did he know?

"I-I don't know what you are talking about."

"Oh, come on Amy, you can do better than that."

"Enzril, please. Please." Amy pleaded, not knowing what else to say. For a moment she saw his eyes soften at her tears, and then it was gone. He stood staring at her for what seemed like an eternity, and finally he spoke. His voice was void of any emotion.

"Get rid of the phone and necklace if you know what is good for you, and tell Farrel I will talk to him soon."

Amy could only nod and whispered a barely audible, "Thank you."

But he was gone before she got the words out. She stumbled over to the box, pulling the phone out. Her hands were trembling as she took off the necklace and placed it back in its hiding place. She sent the short text to Farrel.

ENZRIL KNOWS. I NEED YOU.

****

Amy sat in the small dressing room in front of her makeup mirror. It was the only place she knew she wouldn't be followed. Work was her safe zone. Her hands were sweaty, and her heart was racing. It had been two days since she had sent the text to Farrel, and only yesterday she saw the horrible headlines splattered over social media.

SOCIALTE PATSY TRUMANE FOUND DEAD

The news reported she committed suicide, but Amy knew there was more to it. She had no doubt Master was behind all of it. A deep sadness for Patsy made her chest ache. Her head was pounding, and she jumped at every little sound. She was going to have to leave the safety of her dressing room soon and head home or Master would become suspicious. Today was clearly not the day Farrel would come. Or maybe he just had given up on her. She wouldn't blame him. Why would anyone want to help her? She had surrendered to Satan.

"You're an idiot," she told her reflection. "God isn't going to save you. You're not worth saving."

The soft knock on the door was to let her know the photographer was done with her and she was free to go. She felt the familiar swelling in her throat as tears filled her eyes.

"Thank you, I'll be out in ten minutes."

As she gathered her things, the door opened and there he stood.

"Farrel!" Amy jumped from her chair and threw herself into his arms, sobbing.

"I didn't think you were coming. I thought I was alone again."

Farrel gently pulled himself from her arms.

"I told you I would not abandon you. I meant it. Now quickly tell me what happened."

Amy told him everything about Enzril showing up, seeing her with the cross necklace, and what he said. Farrel was quiet in thought.

"And you are certain he touched the cross?"

"I'm positive. Why?"

Farrel seemed baffled. "Because darkness would not be able to touch the cross without causing extreme pain . . . unless." He didn't continue.

"Unless what, Farrel?"

"It's nothing, and all that matters is you are still alive. I promise if Lucifer knew about this, you would not be." His forehead creased in confusion. "I just need to figure a few things out."

He looked at Amy, who did not seem any calmer.

"And he told you he would find me?"

"Yes, he warned me about the necklace and the phone and told me to tell you he would talk to you soon."

"I don't like it, Amy, but I know he isn't reporting to Lucifer. Not yet, anyway. When can you meet me again?

"My next job is in three days." She wrote down the address and time and felt her immense sadness quickly returning.

Farrel knelt so she could meet his eyes.

"I won't let anything happen to you. I promise. I will be close by."

Amy shook her head. "Please don't leave for long, I'm terrified."

"I understand."

Chapter Twenty-Two

Say to those with fearful hearts, "Be strong, do not fear; your God will come, he will come with vengeance; with divine retribution he will come to save you." – Isaiah 35:4

It was dark on the road as they drove away from their sleepy mountain home toward the city and the airport. Elkan slept in the backseat, and Ariel sat quietly in the passenger seat as Syene drove. They all followed closely together for now. Syene watched the angels glide near the cars as they drove. Jamille was in the lead.

Ariel broke the silence. "You ready for this?"

Syene sighed deeply. "I'll never be ready, but I hope everyone else who wasn't with us in the first battle is taking this to heart. And now a big city? The demons will be everywhere. Is everyone ready to see them in masses?"

Ariel glanced at her. "Gabriel will be with them as they drive."

"Yes, but you and I know what is ahead for them."

Ariel reached over and took Syene's hand. "I have a feeling they can handle it, and just like before we will fight together."

The thought of Ariel having to go through another battle with the dark warriors caused Syene's chest to tighten with worry. She couldn't lose her like she had their mom.

"I often wonder what in the world God was thinking, putting all of us together. I'm so unsure of myself and my ability to guide Elkan on his purpose."

Ariel released her sister's hand. "Isn't that always our problem? Humans try to take the lead when God is the guide, not us. I believe it is Elkan's purpose to remind all of us of that very thing."

Syene sighed deeply and turned to look at her sleeping son in the backseat.

"You're right. Giving up control is the hardest part."

The darkness outside was ominous, and she swore she caught glimpses of the monsters following them. She shivered and said a silent prayer.

****

Syene wasn't wrong. The demons raced through the trees, watching the caravan move over the winding roads. Their screeching could be heard for miles if the humans were aware enough to hear them. Enzril and Kefira flew higher to escape their sound. It was time to report to Master.

Kefira glared at the silhouette flying below her. *Jamille.* The name pounded in her head, and pure hatred coursed through her veins. Soon, very soon, her problem would be exterminated. A smile spread across her face as she followed Enzril away from the cars. Nothing would keep him from becoming hers.

****

Elkan awoke just as they arrived at the hotel they would be staying at for the night. Dr. Kaufman would be the only one joining the Harpers on their flight, while everyone else would be driving on through the night. They decided to grab a bite to eat before they went their separate ways.

Syene spotted a restaurant with outdoor seating, which was perfect for Wesley. He was going to need some roaming time before driving on with John and Rebekah. Ten more hours and they would all be back together, and she and Ariel would finally be reunited with their grandma and Lizzy. She couldn't wait to see them. It had been too long, and she missed them desperately. They found a large table on the open patio where Wesley happily made himself comfortable at Elkan's feet.

Everyone remained oddly quiet, and Syene quickly realized this was the first time all the new believers were in an uncontained environment. She gave all of them a reassuring smile, trying to ease the fear she could see in their eyes.

Dr. Kaufman broke the silence. "Syene, if I may speak freely?"

"Of course."

"You and I have spent many hours now discussing my journey and yours, and I have been trying to come up with different ideas on Elkan's purpose. Please don't get me wrong. I am most certainly not trying to guess the Creator's plan, but I would like to understand how people will react to him when they learn of his existence. I am a scientist after all, and preparation is part of who I am."

She was interested, since she respected the doctor, and knew, other than Father Cervini, he had the deepest knowledge of Biblical history.

"Please share."

"Well, it's only a theory, and I have several, but this is the one on my heart. I feel it is important we understand why Elkan is here based on the writings by Cassius, so we can do our best to explain to new believers and followers when the time comes. We don't want any confusion in what is sure to become a hysteria."

He peered at his notebook through his glasses and began to speak quietly as not to draw attention to their table.

"I have made a list of all the things we know about Syene and Elkan and what Cassius told us." Kaufman had the table's attention. "When the time comes I feel it will be extremely important that Elkan is not perceived as the second coming. We all know he has a very different purpose, but we also know there will be people insisting that this is who he is. In today's world of instant communication, Elkan's existence will be known everywhere. Hatred will be inevitable. We all must arm ourselves with as much truth as possible to disperse the false negatives. To do this, we should examine the similarities and differences of Christ and Elkan."

Syene listened intently, to hear her life laid out in such a scientific way was fascinating. He even seemed to have captured Elkan's attention, who stopped playing with his toy and stared curiously at the doctor. Kaufman held up his notebook for everyone to see his lists laid out in three columns.

"For Syene and the Blessed Mother: both virgins, both young, both from humble and ordinary backgrounds, both given visions. Except, Syene, you have told me, unlike Mary, you were not aware of any warnings or requests before the conception. Is that correct?"

Syene nodded her head. "Except Farrel did tell me the angels were in constant contact. I apparently was not being receptive. And I was having very strange dreams. I just thought it was lack of sleep and studying for school."

Kaufman made some notes. "I wish more had been written about Mother Mary in the Bible, but I digress, so let us continue." He adjusted his eyeglasses once more.

"We know so little about Jesus when He was Elkan's age, so it is hard to compare them, but we know they both have great communication powers, very charismatic personalities, and an undeniable, obvious connection to God. Elkan has the ability to heal, so we can only assume the Messiah possessed this ability not only as an adult, but also at a young age as well."

These are the things Syene feared the most. She knew the miraculous would cause fear in people. She had done her best to contain this in Elkan. The familiar anxiety in her chest pulled.

Jamille crouched next to Syene. "Fear is from the enemy, Sacred. Believe in your Creator's plan and purpose. Dr. Kaufman is knowledgeable, even more than he understands. His connection with the Creator is strong."

Dr. Kaufman continued. "This is why we are going to do our best to be armed with information to deflect the fear of humans. You cannot let your own fear or the fear from others consume you. This is where we always go so wrong as people. Fear is what causes hatred and violence. I believe this is part of Elkan's purpose—to stop fear. We must be reminded of what God has done for us, what Jesus has done for us, before it is too late. Elkan is going to give us one last chance to hear from our Savior and the Creator."

Jamille smiled at Kaufman, giving the doctor strength in his next words.

"What a wonderful God we have, to give us another blessing at the urging of his Son. The message of Christ is so powerful, and I think much of humankind has failed to understand the true meaning of His presence here on earth. Your beautiful Elkan is going to help lead us there. He will lead us back to understanding the one true God. It is our job to help guide and protect him. This was commanded by Christ to Cassius."

****

Everyone had said their goodbyes last night. Syene, Ariel, Elkan, and Dr. Kaufman were taking a flight to California, and the others were continuing the drive. Hopefully they would all make it to their new destination around the same time.

Elkan's excitement was contagious, charming the flight crew who treated him royally. He had the ability to entrance anyone with his beautiful charisma. He proudly showed off his wings he received from the pilot after touring the cockpit. The first-class seats Syene had splurged on were worth it.

He whispered to her when they went to their seats, "Look, Mom! I have wings too!"

Elkan was now sitting next to Dr. Kaufman, asking the doctor question after question about the plane mechanics and how things worked. Syene felt guilty for being relieved she could sleep on the flight next to Ariel, instead of answering her sweet boy's constant questions. She leaned across the aisle to the doctor.

"Are you sorry you volunteered to sit with him?"

Kaufman laughed. "Not at all, he is a joy to my heart."

She smiled as she settled in watching the passengers filter to their seats. Ariel already had her earbuds in and her eyes shut. They both were ready to be with their grandma and friends again.

Syene saw a handsome, well-dressed man coming on the plane. He was maybe a little older than she was and smiled as they made eye contact, but Sy instantly felt something off with him. She saw him looking at Elkan as he stopped at the row in front of them, taking his seat. He sat directly in front of Dr. Kaufman, turning to look at Elkan through the space between the seats. He didn't take his eyes off him.

Distinctly uncomfortable, she was about to lean across the aisle to ask him what his problem was when the young flight attendant began her preflight routine, forcing them all to settle in their seats. Syene didn't take her eyes off the back of his head as the plane began to move down the runway. Before they were off the ground, he leaned up and turned around to look back at her, an evil smile on his face. His eyes were black. She knew immediately he was part of the darkness. Syene touched the rosary she wore around her neck, pulling it loose from underneath her shirt. The cross dangled from her fingers, and she saw him flinch. He slowly broke the eye contact and faced forward once again. She immediately heard Elkan's voice in her head.

"The angels are with us, Mom, it will be okay."
Sy looked out the small window and could see Michael and Jamille soaring with the plane. She took Ariel's hand and gently squeezed it. Ariel opened her eyes and looked at her. Syene motioned toward the man. She knew Ariel had no clue what was going on, but their keen sister-bond clicked in recognition that something was wrong. Ariel removed her earbuds and sat up straighter.

Syene watched the man carefully as the flight continued and felt deep fear for the young female sitting next to him. The woman was clearly oblivious to what he was, by the flirting and laughter Syene could hear. It made her skin crawl. She couldn't believe how clueless people were sometimes. The evil surrounded him like a deep fog—how could the woman not feel it?

Her mind and heart were racing with fear. Who was he? And how was she going to protect Elkan if this stranger decided to do something? Syene reached across the aisle and gently touched Dr. Kaufman's arm.

"Do you mind if I sit by Elkan for just a little bit?"

Kaufman must have sensed something was wrong and immediately released his seatbelt, so they could trade positions. She felt a little better being close to her son. They held hands tightly.

Sy watched in disgust as the pair in front of her continued their flirtatious exchange. He pulled the female's hand up to his lips and kissed it gently. Syene wanted to throw up. Then she heard it. His name as he introduced himself to his unknowing victim. *Lantz*!

Syene was out of her seat and standing beside him before she knew what was happening. White, hot rage coursed through her body.

She yelled loudly, "What did you do to Amy, you bastard?" Syene could see the flight attendant approaching her.

He smiled, "beautiful Sacred, don't worry about our sweet Amy. She is in very good hands."

Syene lunged for him, and the plane nosedived. She and the flight attendant were thrown to the floor. The oxygen masks dropped, and passengers began screaming in terror. She struggled to get up, but the gravity of the plane was pinning her to her spot. Lantz leered at her as she stared up at him, helpless and unable to move. He was joyous and laughed hysterically.

She watched as her son appeared, and she yelled for him to sit down. Instead Elkan raised his hands, speaking prayer over the plane and passengers. Syene watched as the dark angel covered his ears and winced in pain at the words her son was speaking. He stood quickly, stumbling into the seat across the aisle. The flight attendant screamed at Lantz and Elkan to sit down. He shoved his way past Elkan, crying out in anguish when his hand brushed her son's arm. Syene watched as Lantz made his way to the back of the plane until she lost sight of him.

Elkan's voice became louder and louder in her head, commanding the plane to recover in God's name. The flight attendant managed to crawl to Syene, trying to help her up to her seat. They both were able to sit up, still on the floor but clinging to each other. Sy tried to calm the attendant, knowing they would be protected. "It will be okay, I promise."

The woman's eyes never left Elkan. She watched in shock as he continued his prayers in a language she undoubtedly did not understand. The plane pulled out of the nosedive and began flying normally. The terrified passengers quieted, Elkan sat quickly in his seat, and Syene and the attendant helped one another to their feet. Tears were streaming down the woman's face, and Sy could see she wanted to say something. Before she could the Captain's voice came on, asking the attendants to check on the passengers, and announcing they would be diverting the flight to the nearest airport.

Everyone on the plane sat quietly in shocked silence. Syene could hear some crying and praying, thanking God for their safety. She and Elkan sat, saying nothing and holding hands. Dr. Kaufman and Ariel were doing the same. They all knew larger issues were ahead if Elkan had been seen and heard saving the plane.

Syene could see through the windows the plane was surrounded by angels as they headed to their new destination. Not only Elkan's warriors but the guardians for all the passengers aboard the plane were near. She quietly listened for anyone talking about her son and what happened, but she heard nothing. There was no doubt the flight attendant saw all of it, though, and Syene remained hopeful she was the only one. Sy looked toward the back of the plane for the evil warrior, but Lantz had vanished, and no one seemed to notice or care except for her. The female attendant approached her and crouched next to Syene.

"Are you okay?"

Syene gave her the best smile she could. "Maybe just a little banged up, but I'm good. How about you? Are you okay?"

"I think so, I believe I am just in shock." She paused. "Do you mind if I ask you something about your son? I am assuming this is your son?" Syene nodded her head yes but felt frozen inside. She had no idea what she was going to say. "When he stood up, he was speaking something I have never heard, and he changed." Syene could see the woman was struggling to explain what she saw. "Almost like a light was around him. And then the plane was fine suddenly?"

Dr. Kaufman intervened. "Isn't my grandson wonderful? He was praying in Hebrew. I can't tell you how proud this old Jewish grandpa feels right now."

There was instant relief on the woman's face. "Is that what it was? Hebrew? Well, it was amazing. I am so grateful we are all okay." She stood seemingly satisfied with this response. "Please let me know if there is anything you need. We should be landing shortly." She gave Elkan a sweet smile and returned to her jump seat.

Syene gave the doctor a grateful nod and could not believe how easily a witnessed miracle could be explained away and discarded. She shook her head and wept in relief. She glanced around one more time for Lantz but only saw the faces of the many people God had saved. She understood Elkan was only an extension of the miracle.

Chapter Twenty-Three

"Do not be afraid," Samuel replied. "You have done all this evil; yet do not turn away from the Lord, but serve the Lord with all your heart." – 1 Samuel 12:20

Enzril was disgusted at having to take human form. Master, in his opinion, was becoming obsessed with his new identity as Apollos Drake. Lucifer assumed this human role on a regular basis, and it was draining Enzril physically and mentally. He could not fathom what was so fascinating about the humans. They were self-indulgent, mindless idiots, completely unaware of their true surroundings. Humans were not worthy of his time.

He entered the restaurant with Kefira on his arm, both breathtakingly beautiful and mysterious in appearance. The hostess led them to a dark corner booth where their Master waited. Menti, his servant, lurked near the table, ready for any orders Master should give. Kefira clearly enjoyed the stares and admiration from the patrons in the restaurants. Enzril felt nothing but disgust and untangled himself from her arm. The kiss was a mistake, and he regretted it the moment it happened. She was clingy, and he wanted no part of her. Enzril stood back so she could enter the booth and slid in behind her.

"Master." He gave a nod and remained quiet.

Kefira leaned forward, exposing most of her breast to Master, and kissed him on his cheek.

Lucifer lustfully smiled. "Human form becomes you, Kefira, you look ravishing."

Enzril waited patiently while the disgusting exchange was over. He wanted to be out of there.

Lucifer directed his attention to him. "Why so surly, Enzril?"

Enzril could not keep the contempt from his voice. "You know why. I want nothing to do with the humans, and I believe there was a time you also detested their presence."

Master raised the glass of wine to his lips with a vicious look on his face.

"But they are so much fun to toy with, so easy to manipulate. What wicked fun I am able to have."

Enzril remained stone-faced. "I find nothing amusing."

"You are missing tantalizing torment, my loyal General, but this shall remain your loss."

The waitress returned to the table for their order. She was clearly mesmerized by Master and stayed too long flirting and talking. The idiot played right into his hands. Enzril couldn't handle any more of it and cut the conversation short.

"Thank you, that will be all." The young server shot him a dirty look and left them.

Lucifer laughed. "One of the reasons you are my top General. All business."

He raised his wine glass in a toast to Enzril. Menti glared at Enzril, snarling, not happy with any compliment directed from Master to the dark angel.

Enzril impatiently continued. "Master, I do not understand the reasoning behind the plane malfunction. The plane and passengers were saved. It was an opportunity missed to destroy the child. I am unclear on your plans and the direction for my forces. We have been watching with no orders. What are we waiting on?"

Master smiled. "Enzril, you do not see the big picture. The more I expose the child, the easier it will become to access him. A perfect plan must not be rushed." He sipped the wine savoring its flavor. "Now let us enjoy our dinner and tell me how your training with Kefira is coming."

Lucifer took Kefira's hand and raised it to his lips. She smiled seductively at Master. Enzril looked away in disgust. She was smart, too smart for her own good. He was done here and ready to leave.

He stood. "Master, I did not come here to socialize, nor will I be staying for dinner. When you are ready to discuss the battle inevitably ahead of us, you can send your cockroach Menti to fetch me. Until then I will be with my warriors."

Menti hissed, and Enzril gave the demonic creature a look causing him to shrink into the shadows. Kefira began to move toward Enzril to leave with him. Lucifer placed his hand on her arm.

"You'll be staying, my sweet." She stopped and moved back into the booth.

Lucifer calmly looked at his General. "Careful, Enzril, your tone is beginning to sound a little rebellious." The meaning of the look was not missed, and for a moment Master's face distorted to its true form. "Let us not forget what happens to those who rebel."

Enzril nodded; his allegiance was fading. Without speaking a word, he turned and left the restaurant.

Lucifer quietly spoke to Menti. "Follow him."

****

Farrel watched Enzril leave the restaurant and followed at a distance. It was a warm California evening, and the locals and tourists were heavily out and about. Enzril quickly wove through the crowd. Farrel knew Enzril was looking for a safe place to transform and didn't want to lose sight of the dark warrior. This could possibly be his only opportunity to find Enzril alone. Enzril ducked into a side street, and Farrel rushed to catch up. He turned the corner onto the street and was slammed into a wall, Enzril's hand on his throat.

"What do you want, Farrel?

Farrel pried Enzril's hand from his throat. "To talk." He coughed, rubbing his neck after being released. Enzril's strength was intact.

Enzril stepped back. "I said I would find you. I have already told you I am not interested in what Yahweh has to say to me."

"I am not here on behalf of Yahweh. I need your help."

Enzril laughed. "My help? Human form has caused you to lose your senses, old friend."

Farrel knew this would be his reaction, but he wasn't going to give up.

"Please just give me a few minutes. There was a time we fought side by side—at least honor our past."

Enzril was silent for a moment.

"Not here, I'll come to you." He turned and walked down the dark alley until he was gone from Farrel's sight.

Farrel knew he was playing a dangerous game with the dark angel, but he also knew he was right.

****

In the shadows from across the street, Menti watched the exchange. Finally, the great Enzril was making mistakes, and it would be Menti's job and duty to report everything to Master. He couldn't have felt more delighted.

****

The following day, Amy waited patiently for Farrel in the small café, as she was told. The late morning sun shone brightly through the large storefront windows. A young girl approached and asked if she was the model on the front of the magazine clutched in her hands. Amy smiled sweetly and nodded. The little girl asked if Amy would sign the magazine. Farrel walked in as the girl's mother was snapping a picture of the two of them with her phone. The girl gave Amy a hug and waved goodbye.

Farrel slid in the seat across the table. "Fame must be nice for you."

Amy shrugged. "At what price? And is it really because of me? My Master has manipulated everything. I am not even sure what is real anymore."

He could see the immense remorse and sorrow she was feeling.

"Amy, you are forgiven. Trust in that." Forgiveness was something she was not ready to accept.

"Did you find Enzril?"

Farrel nodded. "Yes, briefly last night."

"And?"

"I think my suspicions are right, but I can't be sure. I don't want to jump too fast and be wrong. For now, I believe your secrets are safe with him."

She sighed heavily. "I don't even care about me anymore. Tell me about Syene and her son again. I want to know everything. Hearing about them makes me happy."

Farrel began from the beginning, telling Amy all the details of his time with Syene.

"Unfortunately, I left before Elkan was born. I have only seen him from afar, but I have been told to meet him is a soul-shaking experience."

"You're in love with her." She laughed. "You're in love with Syene."

He slightly shrugged. "Is it that obvious?"

"Very obvious." She paused, looking confused. "Is that allowed? I'm not trying to sound naive, but you are an angel still, right?"

"I am, but I have requested to remain human for now."

"I guess I don't understand. If you love her, what in the world are you doing away from her?"

Farrel raised his glass to his lips. "It's complicated."

"Try me."

"Angels can love in the way you are questioning, but most don't. When we are in the presence of Yahweh it is a consuming and wonderous feeling. But love is not denied to us. We have freewill just as the humans do. But as an angel, when you take human form, you disengage from your constant connection with Yahweh, just like any soul. It is the risk of doing it, a risk I was aware of. Any temptations humans are subject to, so am I. I wasn't planning on falling in love with her, but I did. I fell in love with every part of her soul. And now I am tortured by it. I feel disgusted with myself for my disloyalty to Yahweh and disgusted I could put Syene in danger by loving her."

Amy felt sad and almost wish she hadn't pushed the issue.

"Is God mad at you?"

"Of course not. Yahweh created love. The Creator is perfect love and understands everything I struggle with. The kindness I have been shown makes me more ashamed."

Amy nodded her understanding. "I guess I can see how that would make it worse." She thought about the memories of Syene before she became part of the darkness.

"You know she talked about you. It was around the time Lantz came into my life. When everything changed for me. I remember thinking then she was falling in love with you. Her voice would change when she talked about you. She was definitely in love."

Farrel spoke quietly. "It is a crossroad for my soul, and I do not want to make the wrong decision. My love for both is immeasurable."

Amy looked down, her soul heavy with regret. "I would give anything to go back to the days with my friends and family. I wonder at least a hundred times a day if God could ever love me again."

Farrel reached across the table and took her hand.

"Please don't. That is Lucifer's biggest control over the human soul. Regret and fear. Your Creator never looks back at your mistakes once you have asked for real forgiveness. You cannot hide your true heart from Yahweh. There is no past for the Trinity. If humans could only understand this, they would defeat all their demons. Yahweh never stops loving."

"If it were only that easy."

"I believe it is the very reason Elkan has come. Elkan will be the new fire to ignite all souls. Yahweh is available to all who seek. The answers are right in front of anyone who wants to understand."

Amy stared out the windows, watching the people pass by, knowing so many of them were tormented by the darkness.

"I can't wait to meet him and to see Syene and Lizzy again." She paused. "And maybe even my mom and dad. I miss them terribly. It is amazing what lack of love does to the soul."

"Amy, this saddens me deeply. You should never feel without love. Your angels are always near. Yahweh never leaves you, and you are always loved more than you will ever know."

****

Neither Farrel nor Amy saw him, standing only a few feet away, staring through the glass. Lucifer watched as his human prize betrayed him. The passing crowd put distance between him and themselves as if they could feel the evil radiating and seeping. Amy would pay for her deceit. They both would. A smile curled on his lips thinking of what was ahead for her. But first he had a meeting with his newly reinstated General. Lantz was waiting.

Chapter Twenty-Four

Praise be to the Lord, for he showed me the wonders of
his love when I was in a city under siege. – Psalm 31:21

After the unexpected flight diversion, they opted to rent
a car and drive the remaining four hours to their new
destination on the coast.

They finally arrived at their temporary home, seeing the
moving truck and John Freely's car parked in front of the
house. She already knew they had made it safely but seeing it
for herself made it real. The neighborhood and area were
breathtaking. The homeowners, Darla and Charles, lived on the
beach, and Syene was excited to finally meet them. They were
all more than ready to get out of the car. It had been an
exhausting trip, both physically and mentally.

Their grandmother was waiting out front for them as
they pulled into the driveway. Elkan was already unbuckled,
ready to sprint from the car. As soon as they stopped, he swung
the door open running to her welcoming arms.

She kissed him on both cheeks, returning his exuberant
hug.

"Oh, my goodness, I have missed you. I have missed all
of you." She opened her arms as Ariel and Syene joined the
group hug. "My beautiful babies, I'm so glad you are finally
here, safe and sound. You will have to tell me everything that
happened on the plane. We have been watching the news.

Thankfully there was only a short story saying a plane had to make an emergency landing and everyone was safe."

Syene still couldn't believe the ease of explaining away the miracle of what happened. "We have Dr. Kaufman to thank for that. Like a professional, he distracted the flight attendant who witnessed Elkan." Syene waved him over to meet her grandmother.

"Grandma, this is Dr. Kaufman. Dr. Kaufman, this is my grandmother, Lois McKinney."

He pulled her grandmother's hand to his lips like a true gentleman. "Please call me Robert."

Syene saw her grandma blush and couldn't blame her. Dr. Kaufman was charming, the type of person you were instantly drawn to.

Before Syene could say anything else, Wesley came bounding out the front door. He headed straight for Elkan, barking and licking all over his face. Elkan laughed loudly, returning the dog's love.

And then the famous squeal came. Syene was certain anyone in a mile radius heard her. Lizzy came running out of the house, her beautiful red curls a blur as she met them like a whirlwind. She and Lizzy were in tears of joy as they hugged, neither wanting to let go and neither needing to say a word. Syene had missed her best friend more than she realized. The separation had been hard on all of them. Lizzy grabbed Ariel and brought her into the hug. She tried to grab Elkan, but he escaped her grasp, laughing as Lizzy chased him for a kiss, a familiar game the two of them played.

Father Cervini, John, Rebekah, Laura, and Thomas all filtered outside, greeting and hugging them. Syene felt so much joy they were all together. She was going to miss Dave and Susan and James and Julie so much, but she knew their purposes had called them away. For now, she would be grateful for the people who remained.

Father Cervini ushered everyone toward the house. "The owners of this beautiful house are anxiously waiting to meet all of you. They have some delicious food and refreshments waiting. They are a wonderful couple, Sy. You are going to adore them."

"Do they know anything about Elkan?"

The priest nodded. "I told them, but they were already aware of the situation from Dave and Susan. They have been very open and accepting of all of it. Faith without seeing is something wonderful to witness. They are both so excited to finally meet you."

The house was even more amazing on the inside, and as if on cue, a stunning black woman approached her with a bright and welcoming smile.

"You must be Syene." She extended her hand, and as Syene took the extended hand, Darla wrapped her in a hug. Syene immediately felt at ease. "I'm Darla. Charles and I are so happy you are here."

"It is so nice to meet you, thank you so much for your generosity."

Darla laughed, warm and genuine. "You are most welcome. You are as sweet as Susan and Dave described. And of course, your grandma hasn't stopped bragging on all of you."

"Well, I hope we can live up to the expectations."

Darla waved a man over. "Charles, come meet Syene."

He had to be one of the best-looking men Syene had ever seen. She could feel herself blushing and felt a little embarrassed. His face was dark and elegant with the most beautiful green eyes.

Darla put her hand on Syene's arm. "Don't worry, he has this effect on all women. Doesn't matter how old or young they are, they all adore him."

Syene felt her face heat up even more, but all she could do was laugh.

"He is very handsome."

"And you better believe he knows it. But I can honestly say the best part is his soul is just as beautiful, and I am the lucky woman he gave his heart to."

Charles kissed his wife's cheek and introduced himself to Syene. He skipped the handshake and gave her a hug.

"We are so glad you are here. You are welcome to stay as long as necessary." His voice was deep and soothing.

Syene was so touched by the couple and knew immediately why Dave and Susan had put so much trust in them.

"I can't thank you both enough. There are no words to tell you how grateful we are."
Sy watched as Charles wrapped his arm around his wife's waist. It couldn't have been more obvious how much he loved her, and Syene strangely felt a little sad. Maybe a realization this kind of love would never be in her future.

Syene knew this was going to be a safe place for them, and she felt immensely relieved.

"Let me find Elkan, so you can properly meet him. I think the excitement of seeing the ocean has caused him to forget any manners he has."

Charles chuckled. "Well, I saw a little guy dash past me with his dog as they ran out to the beach. I believe it was your sister, Ariel, in pursuit of them."

"Oh wow, I'm sorry. I guess a six-year-old seeing the ocean for the first time is going to be hard to contain."

Darla touched her arm. "Don't apologize for exuberance. Let me show you the view. We can go check on him."

The view was spectacular, and Syene couldn't blame Elkan for one moment. Ariel and her grandma were watching him closely as he and Wesley ran from the waves rolling in at their feet. She and Darla stood quietly watching him laugh and play.

Darla smiled. "Seeing a child's reaction to the ocean for the first time seems to be a gift from God. A small glimpse of how life is really supposed to be. You know what I mean?"

"I absolutely know what you mean. I'm pretty sure most of us miss how wonderful life can really be. Always looking ahead or in the past instead of in the moment."

"You couldn't be more correct. In the moment is where beautiful happens." Darla stepped back. "I'll leave you to enjoy this. Come in when you are ready, and don't hesitate to let me know if you need anything. Our home is your home."

The sun was beginning its descent, and the brilliant colors bounced off the ocean. Syene could smell the sea air and taste the salt on the wind. Watching her son play and laugh gave her joy she didn't know was possible. Her heart was overwhelmed with love, and she felt happy they were here. Father Cervini stepped out on the deck with her and wrapped his arm around her shoulder. Sy put her head on his shoulder. He had been a replacement dad for her through all of this, and she had missed him during their brief separation.

"I have missed you, Priest."

"And I you."

She pulled the rosary beads from her pocket and dangled them in front of her.

"I used them on the plane. A dark angel was there—the one responsible for Amy disconnecting from us. I'm certain he had something to do with the plane nosediving. And the way he looked at Elkan and me." She shivered at the memory. "I'll never forget it."

Father Cervini's brow creased. "I just don't understand what the purpose was of a stunt like that? They knew God would not allow the plane to crash." He paused. "To test Elkan's powers perhaps?"

"Or to expose his powers."

They quietly watched the sun setting slowly on the horizon. Ariel and her grandma were heading back to the house with Elkan and Wesley. Syene stared out across the water and saw Elkan stop and look up at her. He turned to look at the ocean. She tried to not speak to him very often with her mind, but she felt a sudden foreboding and saw him point to the water.

"What is it, baby?"

"Dragon."

Sy looked at Father Cervini, only she and the priest knew about the dreams of the dragon coming out of the ocean water and devouring everything in its path. Terror filled her heart.

"What is it, Syene?"

"Elkan sees the dragon."

Cervini looked at her son standing on the beach and called for him to come quickly, his jawline tightened as Ariel ushered Elkan back to the house.

He calmly whispered, "'Do not fear, for I am with you; Do not anxiously look about you, for I am your God, I will strengthen you, surely I will help you, Surely I will uphold you with My righteous right hand.'"

Syene reached for his hand, holding it tightly.

Chapter Twenty-Five

I will give them a heart to know Me, for I am the LORD;
and they will be My people, and I will be their God, for
they will return to Me with their whole heart.
– Jeremiah 24:7

Menti led Enzril into Master's chamber. The light from the fireplace bounced off the stone walls, Master's mood hanging in the air. Enzril was leery and not looking forward to this meeting.

Menti made his exit quickly, shutting the door on his way out with a knowing grimace. Enzril prepared himself for a confrontation.

"Enzril, come, it is always good to see you."

Enzril slowly moved into the room. Master was seated, his face cloaked by darkness, but Enzril could see he was in his true form. The fire light outlined the shadow of the massive disfigurement.

Enzril bowed his head. "What may I do for you, Master?"

Lucifer's voice was low and calm, eerily calm. "I would like your updates on our sweet delight, Amy."

Enzril had a choice to make in this moment, to decide his loyalty. Would he remain a reprobate soul or would he seek forgiveness from the Creator? There would be no survival without making a choice. He had been by Lucifer's side since the beginning of the rebellion—they had once been inseparable comrades. Enzril had been Lucifer's confidant before the fall. But those days were long gone, and he had watched his friend lose sight of why they had once stood together. Lucifer had become twisted with his own power, desires, and hatred. Master was a source of pure evil spread throughout the world. Enzril's consort was now his enemy. The decision was made.

"No unusual activity, Master. She is behaving."

"Really? I find this very surprising. I was certain she was up to something."

Enzril's heart pounded in his chest, the beat thundering in his ears. He would be lucky to survive. He was certain Master knew. The silence in the room was resounding. He waited for the explosion, but instead Master remained quiet, almost willing Enzril to speak the truth. But Enzril would not break. This was his moment. There was no turning back. When Master stood, his mind screamed at him to bow down and beg Lucifer for forgiveness. He stood, eye to eye, his jaw clenched tight. He would not be a slave any longer.

To his surprise, Master broke the stare and walked back to his chair.

"Menti, bring in my guest."

Enzril turned toward the chamber door as it opened. His disbelief was not disguised.

"Lantz?"

Lantz smiled. "Enzril, how nice to see."

Enzril could see the madness in his eyes. He thought Lantz had perished. There is no way a soul could last that long being tortured in the pit.

"I can't believe it."

Lantz's laugh was hysterical. The laugh of a lunatic.

"Well, believe it. Here I stand." He spread his arms and gave Enzril a bow.

Enzril stared in astonishment. Master had created an unhinged servant. He could only imagine the horrific torture Lantz had endured.

Master's voice broke into his thoughts. "So nice to see my two Generals back together."

Enzril felt a cold chill run through his body. Master had completely lost all rationality, and whatever he was planning was going to terrorize many.

"Enzril, I have decided to relieve you of your *Amy-duties*. Lantz will be replacing you."

Enzril had to keep his emotions concealed. Any signs of discord, and he would be no more. He had walked into an intricate trap. There was no doubt Master was aware of his deceit.

He bowed his head. "As you wish, Master. And Kefira? Will she remain with me?"

Although his heart would always be with Jamille, he now greatly feared for the angel he had been training.

Master smiled. "I think not. She has proven to be a very delicious and loyal warrior. She will remain under my command. But I do thank you for a job well done with her."

Enzril nodded. "And my new orders?"

Master was silent for a few moments. "I think you will best serve me returning to your warriors and waiting. I will call for you when the carnage is to begin."

He lowered his head. "Yes, Master."

Enzril's mind raced. To get out of here was going to be a miracle. Lantz was pacing, a caged wild animal ready to attack. Enzril had to get to Amy before he did. He turned to go, calmly walking to the door, despite his mind screaming to run. He opened the door.

"Enzril." Master spoke telepathically for only Enzril to hear. He stopped momentarily, not turning around, and remained silent. The searing fury of Lucifer was clear.

"Give Yahweh my best regards."

Enzril kept walking.

****

He flew furiously, the demons screeching loudly at his departure. He waited for the attack, but it didn't come. Lucifer was masterfully planning an onslaught, and Enzril knew without a doubt he would be used as part of the plan. He had no time to think about what he had just done, his heart thundered. He must find Farrel and Amy before it was too late.

****

Enzril entered the condo slowly, his sword was drawn. He quickly searched her home; Amy was not there. He saw the wooden box on her dresser and opened it. Some papers, pictures of her parents and the cross were inside. He grabbed the items, shoving them in his leather belt.

"Hello, Enzril." Kefira stood in the doorway.

"Kefira." He was ready to fight, to kill if necessary.

"You're not going to find her. Surely you are aware Master expected you to come find her?"

"Out of my way, Kefira. I don't have time for this, and I don't want to have to kill you."

Kefira smiled seductively. "I hope quite the opposite." She walked to him running her hands up his muscular arms and wrapping her arms around his neck.

"Can you at least put the sword away. I'm not here to fight."

Enzril did not sheath his weapon. Her body pressed against his.

"Maybe now that you aren't my commander, we can get to know one another better."

Her lips pressed against his neck. Enzril's body stirred, having not desired anyone since Jamille. He grabbed her by the hair with his free hand and kissed her, feeling her tongue enter his mouth. She pressed even closer. Enzril pulled his head back, Kefira's face was flushed with desire.

"As much as I would enjoy taking you up on your offer, I have already told you my heart belongs to another." He pushed her away.

Kefira's face turned red with anger. "You fool, she is never going to love you back. You are giving up everything to chase after something that doesn't exist. How could she ever forgive you after what you did? You left her to die in the pit." She looked at him with the disgust. "Master was right, you are weak."

Enzril smiled and gave her a nod. "Goodbye, Kefira." He was gone before she could respond.

****

The photoshoot was over, and Amy was exhausted and relieved. She gave the photographer a kiss on the cheek as he packed up his equipment.

"You were fabulous, Amy, always a pleasure."

She laughed. "Well, I wish I could say the same about you! You work me like a plow mule!"

He waved and blew her a kiss as he left. "Can't wait until next time, love. Make sure you lock up the door on your way out."

She waved goodbye and headed to the changing room. All she wanted to do was get home, take a hot bath, and go to bed. She walked into the makeshift room, untying her top. Her muscles ached. This had been an extremely hard shoot.

"Hello, my sweet little vixen."

Her heart skipped in her chest, and she squeezed her eyes shut.

No, it can't be! Lantz had been destroyed by Master for betrayal. This couldn't be possible.

Amy slowly opened her eyes. She couldn't believe it. Lantz was sitting in the room, a sadistic leer on his face. He was in human form, just as he had been when she met him for the first time. Amy couldn't breathe. Lantz, the reason she had become a slave to Master, the one who destroyed her life and her innocence. She darted her eyes around the room trying to figure out how she was going to get away. She turned to run. Lantz was upon her within seconds, grabbing her from behind, one hand around her throat, choking her screams. His breath was in her ear.

"Shh, my beautiful, Amy. I've missed you." He pressed his lips to her neck.

She was trapped and alone. Her mind couldn't process how this was happening. She thought he had been destroyed by Lucifer. Lantz slowly turned her around and held her tightly, pinning both arms behind her back with one hand. She whimpered as he wiped the tears off her face.

The sound of his voice was nauseating. "That's no way to greet an old lover." He forcefully pressed his lips against her mouth as she struggled to get free. He pushed her toward the couch in the room, and Amy knew there was nothing she could do to stop him. The back of her legs hit the couch, and she fell backward, Lantz was on top of her, groping her body as she sobbed.

"I think that will be enough, Lantz."

Amy's heart leapt at the sound of Enzril's voice. She scrambled to her feet when Lantz released her and rushed to stand behind the dark warrior who was now her ally. She had no idea she would ever feel so joyful to see the angel she so recently viewed as her enemy, but she knew he was there to help her.

Lantz faced the dark angel, laughing with a hysteria Amy had never heard before. Chills ran through her body.

"Enzril, this little toy no longer concerns you. If I'm correct, Master explained this to you."

Enzril smiled. "Unfortunately for you, Lantz, I no longer have a Master, and Amy is leaving with me."

The look on Lantz's face was sadistic hatred for the angel standing before him. Amy knew Lantz could not beat Enzril while he was in human form, and clearly Lantz realized the same.

His tone changed, and he glared at the two of them. Amy hid her face behind Enzril, unable to look at Lantz.

"This won't be the last time you see me, my sweet Amy. I'll find you."

Enzril unsheathed his sword. "Not if I have anything to do with it."

"I adore this side of you, Enzril, so romantic. I look forward to my next meeting with you. I assure you I will be more prepared." With that Lantz was gone.

Amy collapsed into Enzril's arms, sobbing and thanking him. She was overwhelmed with gratitude.

"Get your things, we don't have much time. And you won't be able to go back to your condo, not without protection. They will be waiting for you."

Amy hurriedly changed and grabbed her bag. She had no clue what he was talking about or what she was going to do, but she knew they both were in extreme danger. Enzril scooped her in his arms, and they were gone. Soaring within seconds above the clouds. Amy could hardly catch her breath. She clung tightly to her new protector. They descended within moments on top of a grassy hill above the city. Enzril gently placed her on her feet, and she immediately saw Farrel waiting. She ran to him, hugging him hard. It was like seeing a loving big brother, and she couldn't have been happier. He squeezed her tightly as she cried and recounted what happened. When she finished her story, both looked at Enzril who was standing nearby. He stared out at the horizon.

His voice was commanding, and there was no doubt he was a fierce leader.

"Find her protection, Farrel. She is going to need it."

"And you? You are going to need protection as well. You can't fight Lucifer alone, Enzril, you must ask for help."

Enzril nodded. "I need some time. I will have to face my Creator soon enough. My soul is not ready."

"You know how to find me."

They watched the dark angel fly off.

Farrel pulled out the items from his pocket Enzril had given him earlier. Enzril had saved the only possessions she cared about. She was overwhelmed with emotion. "How did you know Enzril would turn against Lucifer?"

"A hunch when you told me he touched the cross and didn't react. A truly dark soul cannot be near the cross, let alone touch it."

Amy now held the necklace tightly in her hand, more grateful than ever.

Chapter Twenty-Six

Those who cling to worthless idols turn away from God's love for them. – Jonah 2:8

Syene and Lizzy sat on the couch during Elkan's nap. Liz was watching the news while Syene flipped through a magazine. She stopped on an article and couldn't believe what she saw.

"Oh my gosh!" She held the magazine in front of Lizzy's face. "It's Amy!" There standing with her back to the camera looking over her shoulder, dark hair cascading down her waist was her beautiful friend Amy. The caption read, FROM SMALL TOWN TO BIG CITY.

Lizzy laughed. "Where have you been, under a rock?"

"What are you talking about?"

Liz rolled her eyes. "Sy! Amy is a big-time fashion model. Her pictures are everywhere! She's even done some acting." She sat up and gave Syene a look of exasperation. "Are you seriously telling me this is the first time you have seen her? How is it that we have spent so much time together, and you had no clue? I know I have talked about it."

"I swear, I had no idea. I can't believe how beautiful she looks." She stared at the picture of their friend. "Have you talked to her, Liz? Where is she?"

"I've tried to call and sent a few texts, but not with much response. She's always noncommittal when I ask about seeing her. I have no clue why she won't see us."

"Where is she?"

"She's here in California, she has been for a couple of years. I even reached out to her business manager and got nada."

Sy shook her head. "Well, I'm going to see her, I don't care what she says."

"You know you can count me in. I'm all about stalking and invading someone's personal life."

Sy giggled. Lizzy always had a wonderful way of pointing out how creepy their plans really were.

"Well, I might be a stalker, but I want to see my friend."

Lizzy picked her phone up. "I'll text her right now and let her know she has no more excuses. We are here, and we are going to see her."

Sy watched the puzzled look on Liz's face after she sent the text.

"What's wrong?"

"The text came back undeliverable."

"Try to call her then."

Liz dialed the number. They both heard the message signifying the phone had been disconnected. Liz had a look of disbelief on her face.

"I can't believe she changed her number and didn't let me know."

Syene wasn't giving up that easy. "Didn't you just say you had the number to her business manager's office?"

Lizzy nodded.

"Then we call it and set up a meeting through him or her, right? We can't give up on her."

Liz agreed. "It's a him. I'll have to search the name again and give it a try."

Sy waited while Liz did some research and listened to her calls. Lizzy hung up the phone in less than five minutes.

"Well, what did they say?"

"We have an appointment tomorrow with her manager. I actually can't believe how easy that was this time." She gave Sy a wink. "You must be good luck, last time I couldn't even get a call back from anyone."

Sy blew on her fingernails and rubbed them on her shirt. "When you've got it, you've got it."

Lizzy shoved her shoulder. "Eww, stop! That look is not good on you."

They both laughed and excitedly talked about the possibility of getting to see Amy soon.

****

Lizzy and Sy walked into the impressive glass building. They both looked out of place and couldn't help acting like tourists gawking at everything they saw. This was the first time since Elkan had been born Syene had been away from him. She hated it but knew he was safe with his protectors, both human and angelic.

Ariel practically shoved her out the door. "Go! We are fine, he is surrounded by all of us and at least five angels. I'm certain there are more of them lurking around. Go have some fun. You need it!"

Syene gave her sister a hug and told Jamille to get the worried look off her face when Jamille tried to go with her and Lizzy.

"Jamille, please stay. I would feel better knowing you are here with Elkan. I'll be fine. My other guardians will be nearby."

"I feel uneasy, Sacred."

Syene genuinely laughed. "Probably because I have never stepped more than twenty feet away from Elkan. I feel uneasy too." She paused. "But I know I want to see Amy, and I know I need to start giving him his independence." She stepped on her tiptoes urging Jamille to lean forward, giving her a kiss on the cheek.

"I'll be okay."

Now as she looked around the intimidating building and décor she hoped she had made the right choice. Sy nervously looked at Lizzy.

"We are definitely fish out of water."

Liz snorted. "Obviously." She squeezed Sy's hand. "But who cares, let's go rescue our friend from the world of the rich and famous."

Sy laughed, her heart was beating with excitement. They exited the elevator on the top floor and walked into a lavish reception area where water trickled over a beautiful rock creation. The area smelled of lavender and vanilla. Very calming and welcoming.

"May I help you?"

The receptionist was stunningly beautiful and spoke with a bit of a haughty tone. It had to be obvious they were way out of their element.

Lizzy gave her a toothy smile and spoke in her best aristocratic voice.

"Elizabeth Richardson and Syene Harper here to see Mr. Drake."

The receptionist was not impressed.

"Have a seat. I will let him know you are here."

They watched the leggy young woman walk down a hallway.

Syene giggled as Lizzy looked at her and crossed her eyes, imitating the woman in a nasally voice. "Have a seat. I will let him know you are here."

Sy swatted at her. "Stop it. You promised to behave."

Liz rolled her eyes. "Whatever. Life is too short to be acting that way. She needs to get over herself."

Syene held her finger up to her lips telling Liz to hush. The blonde ice queen was coming back down the hallway.

"Mr. Drake will be with you in a few moments."

She said it without even looking at them and began working on her computer like they weren't even there. They giggled. Liz was right, the young receptionist needed to get over herself. Syene prayed Amy hadn't turned into one of those high society snobs.

They waited quietly. Liz picked up a magazine, and Syene got up to look at the view. It seemed as if the entire city was in front of her, and in the distance a small view of the ocean. She looked down and watched all the cars, they looked like small toys from up here. Sy saw several angelic warriors atop the nearby buildings. It gave her some peace knowing they were close. She thought of Elkan and wandered what he was doing. Her heart ached for him. She hated being away.

"Mr. Drake will see you now. Follow me."

They walked the long hallway in silence. The ice queen opened the door, allowing them to enter, and then quietly shut it behind them. The atmosphere in the room had changed. It was no longer a feeling of lavender and vanilla. Mr. Drake had his back turned to them, and the phone pressed to his ear. His view of the city was even better than the one Sy had just seen. Lizzy and Sy awkwardly looked at each other, and Liz shrugged her shoulders like *what the heck?* Sy shrugged back, acknowledging her confusion. Amy's world was way different than theirs.

After five minutes he finally was done with his phone call. He stood and turned. He was gorgeous. Sy was pretty sure she heard Lizzy gasp, and she felt own her face getting hot, which also meant red.

He walked around the desk.

"Ladies, my apologies for keeping you waiting."

Syene didn't think she had ever seen a man better dressed than him. His custom suit fit his body perfectly, and even though he looked old enough to be her father, he was hands down sexy.

He walked toward them, offering his hand. They both tried to stand.

"Please, stay seated. Allow me to introduce myself." His smile was mesmerizing. "Apollos Drake."

Lizzy's face was bright red as she fumbled over her own name. He kissed her hand and gave it a pat. He took Syene's hand, and she felt a shockwave. She felt dizzy as he lifted her hand to his lips. What was happening? Everything felt off, and she couldn't clear her head. As soon as he released her hand, she felt normal again. He walked back to his desk and sat down.

"So, you ladies are friends of my Amy?"

Syene felt a knot in her stomach at the way he said *my Amy*. Something wasn't right with him. She was grateful Lizzy was doing the talking. She noticed the warriors outside on top of the buildings. There were more. Something in her must have triggered their presence. She was not comfortable.

Lizzy happily took charge. "Yes, we were hoping you could tell us how to reach her. The number I had for her has been disconnected."

His voice was like silk. "Unfortunately, Amy was receiving some threatening phone calls, and we had to change her number. Sometimes the fans can get a little crazy." He laughed. "The perils of her job."

He flashed another smile.

"But I am more than happy to give her your phone numbers and tell her you are looking for her."

Syene didn't like him at all. He seemed hauntingly familiar. Something was wrong. She could feel his eyes on her.

"How is your son, Syene?"

Sy knew she looked shocked. "My son? How did you know about my son?"

His lips slightly curled up. "Amy has spoken of you both often. She always mentioned she wanted to meet your son."

Syene's voice was cold. "He's fine."

She doubted Amy even knew she had a son or anything else about her life. This man had done some research, and Syene didn't like it or him.

Lizzy excitedly wrote down both of their phone numbers, oblivious to the look of distrust on Syene's face and the tone of her voice. He folded the piece of paper and slipped it into his pocket. He stood, clearly signaling this meeting was over.

"Is there anything else I can do for either of you?"

Lizzy said no, but Sy wasn't done with him.

"How is Amy? It's odd she hasn't returned any of our texts or calls, so I am surprised she would even know I had a son."

She saw him falter, only for a second, but she saw it.

"She's doing wonderfully well. She has been very busy. I am sure she will call as soon as she can."

Syene stood looking at him. There was something so familiar about his eyes, and she was doing her best to try to place where she knew him. He smiled at her, but his eyes were dead. He ushered them to the door, opening it politely.

"I will tell her you stopped by and give her your numbers."

He patted his pocket where he placed the paper. Lizzy thanked him graciously for seeing them and walked out first. Syene slowly followed, then she turned as she stepped into the hallway.

"Mr. Drake, have we met before? I feel like I have seen you before today?"

He stared, his face was void of emotion. His eyes full of contempt for her.

"Perhaps in a dream, my love."

Syene stared back. This man was not good. She was now even more worried about Amy. Her voice was stone. "I don't think I would call that a dream, Mr. Drake, but maybe it will come to me."

She could feel his eyes boring into her back as she walked away.

****

As soon as the elevator door shut, Liz screeched at her.

"What the hell was that? What were you doing?"

"Something was wrong with that guy, Lizzy."

Liz gave her a *whatever* look.

"Like what? Being too handsome?" She shook her head. "I can't believe how rude you were. We are going to be lucky if he actually tells Amy we came by."

Sy lashed out at her friend. "I'm serious. He didn't have a clue how Amy was doing? And you seriously think Amy knows anything about me or Elkan? I doubt she has been mentioning us frequently."

Lizzy rolled her eyes. "I don't get you, Sy, I didn't see, hear, or feel any of those things. And I've mentioned you and Elkan in my texts to her. Just because she didn't respond doesn't mean she stopped caring about us."

Syene could see she had hurt her friend's feelings, and she felt bad. It wasn't Lizzy's fault she was a paranoid freak. She reached out and touched her arm.

"I'm sorry, Liz. I shouldn't have snapped at you. I'm sure I'm being overly suspicious."

Liz softened. "It's okay. I know you're worried about Amy, and I am too. I need to be more understanding."

Syene shook her head. "I just can't shake the feeling I had. Something wasn't right."

"I'm sure you are feeling anxious about being away from Elkan also, and Amy is living a life you and I aren't used to."

Syene knew it had nothing to do with her missing Elkan or Amy's lifestyle, but she didn't feel like having a debate with her friend.

****

Lucifer stood at the windows staring at the Creator's angels on the surrounding buildings. Hatred boiled inside him. He called for his own warriors and watched as they arrived in numbers. The Creator's warriors dispersed.

"That's right, run away. I'm coming for your precious Sacred and her son. Nothing will stop me."

Chapter Twenty-Seven

...but God has surely listened and has heard my prayer.
Praise be to God, who has not rejected my prayer or
withheld his love from me! – Psalms 66:19-20

Amy closed his apartment door quietly behind her, so she didn't wake Farrel. She knew she should have told him she was going back to her place to get some of her things, but he had done so much already, and she didn't want to put him in any more danger. She worked so hard for her career and her belongings, she wasn't going to let Master take everything from her. All she needed were some of her clothes and the items in her safe. She couldn't calm the voice inside her head screaming, *what are you doing!? Don't do this.*

She whispered, "In and out, it will be fine. God, please let it be fine."

She reached for her cross necklace and immediately realized she had forgotten it.

"Dang it!"

She couldn't go back and risk waking Farrel. She would for sure not have another chance if he knew what she was planning.

You can do this, Master has no power over you. You can do this.

Amy weaved in and out of the people on the sidewalk. She thought walking would be the best way to get there. The more people around, the better. Twenty minutes later she stood at her building. Joey, the sweet doorman, greeted her with a smile.

"Good morning, Ms. Davis."

She did her best to calm her voice

"Morning, Joey."

He opened the door for her as he always did. *Well, at least he thought she still lived here. Master hadn't done anything to keep her out of the building.* She hurried through the entrance and rode the elevator to the penthouse. Her heart was pounding in her chest.

"In and out, in and out. You can do this."

The elevator doors opened, and Amy stepped into the place she had called her home. Nothing felt like home right now, and she began questioning why she had even returned. She moved slowly, cautiously looking around. No sign of Master or his little monsters. She rushed down the hall toward her bedroom. Amy grabbed a small suitcase from the massive closet and began throwing her clothes into it. She walked to the wall safe tucked away at the back of the closet, her hand was shaking as she entered the code to open it. It beeped loudly, causing her to jump.

She laughed nervously at herself. "Stop shaking, idiot. Get your stuff and get out."

She grabbed the stack of cash, documents, and the jewelry. She knew if necessary the jewelry could be sold. She shoved all of it into the suitcase, zipping it shut.

"Time to go."

Amy glanced around her bedroom one last time. This place never felt like her home. She had always been his slave, but now she would finally be free.

"I hate to admit it, but Enzril is correct. Humans really are stupid."

Amy froze, not wanting to turn around to face him. Why had she come back?

She slowly turned. "Hello, Lantz."

He was in his true form, and she did everything to keep the fear out of her voice. He filled the doorway, blocking the only way out, and stepped closer.

"You don't seem very happy to see me, my pet?"

Amy couldn't find her voice. Her mind was spinning. *How am I going to get out of here?*

He reached out stroking her face with the back of his hand. She recoiled in disgust, backing further into the bedroom.

"Don't touch me!"

Lantz laughed. "My, my, how times have changed. There was a day when you begged for my touch." He stepped closer. "No matter, I'm going to kill you anyway."

"Lantz, please. I only want to leave."

"I'm afraid I can't allow that. And you were stupid enough to come back for your things." He chuckled. "Humans are predictable, greedy, mindless imbeciles."

Amy began begging. "Please, let me talk to Master. I will stay. I won't leave. You don't have to do this."

His laugh was soaked with evil. "You think Master negotiates? You little fool. Your duties are done, and now so is your worthless life."

Amy saw him before Lantz did, the sound of his sword whirring through the air. Lantz winced in pain, hurling forward and knocking Amy down. She crashed against the wall, and her head hit the nightstand as she fell to the floor. She could feel the blood trickling down the side of her face. She felt nauseated and disoriented as she tried to focus on what was happening. She couldn't remember how she ended up on the floor, but her hand touched the warm blood. She struggled to keep her eyes open. The two figures fighting were a blur, and the clank of the swords faded as her eyes closed.

****

"Amy?" She could hear the voice, but she didn't want to open her eyes. Her head was throbbing with an excruciating pain.

She managed to pry her eyes open with what felt like tremendous effort, and Farrel came into focus.

She moaned. "What happened?"

"You took a pretty nasty fall and hit your head."

Amy began remembering and tried to sit up. The wave of nausea hit her immediately, and she fell back on the pillow. Farrel put a cold towel across her forehead.

"Lantz was there, Farrel. He was going to kill me."

"Shh, I know. Enzril brought you to me."

"Is he okay? I saw him behind Lantz, and they started fighting."

Farrel touched her arm to calm her. "He's fine. He's here."

Amy struggled again to open her eyes and focus. She turned her head to look around the small studio apartment. The pain was unexplainable when she tried to move. She could see Enzril move closer.

"Enzril, I'm so glad you are okay! Thank you. I seem to be making a habit of becoming the damsel in distress. You saved me, again. Two for two." She couldn't help but laugh a little, cringing at her pounding head. "Who would have ever thought I would be saying those words to you."

She heard him chuckle.

"Farrel, can I please have some water, I want to try to sit up."

He returned with a bottle of water and slowly lifted her to a sitting position.

"What were you thinking, Amy? Why would you go back there?"

Amy shrugged, because at this moment she had no idea why she went.

"Because I am an idiot. I was so mad, thinking of all the things I worked for, and I was losing all of them. He has already taken so much from me, my soul, my mom and dad, my friends." She began crying. "I just thought I could at least hang on to some of the things I worked for."

Farrel sat next to her and wrapped his arm around her shoulders.

"It was stupid. Possessions are meaningless. And Lucifer has taken nothing from you. Your Creator has won you back."

Amy sat with her head in her hands. She knew Farrel was right, it had been very stupid, but she also didn't understand how God could ever forgive her.

She covered her face at the sudden flash of light in the room. It was blinding, causing her head to hammer even more. Farrel immediately stood and then went to a knee. Standing in the room were two of the most beautiful creatures she had ever seen. One of them touched Farrel on the shoulder,

"Stand, my comrade." Farrel stood and embraced him with a genuine love. The other angel approached him with the same affection.

Farrel looked at Amy with a smile on his face she had never seen.

"Amy I would like to introduce you to two of my very old and dear friends and fellow warriors, Michael and Gabriel."

Amy was stunned and speechless. She had never seen anything more incredible than the two angels who stood in front of her. Enzril was beautiful but in a dark way. He looked dull compared to the radiance of the angels standing before her. She looked at Enzril, who stood quietly away from the scene and noticed his wings were no longer a deep black but had turned to a dark grey. The words came out without thinking as she looked at Enzril.

"Is this what you used to look like?"

Enzril nodded. She looked at Farrel.

"And you too?"

He laughed. "Yes, me too."

She smiled. "No wonder Sy fell in love with you."

Farrel laughed even harder.

"Well, she actually met me in human form, so I'm not sure if I should be offended or not."

Michael stepped closer to her. "May I?" He reached his hand out toward her head, and Amy nodded. The instant he touched her she felt everything wonderful in the world all at once. The feeling was unspeakable. It was love. God's love. Her head no longer pounding, she reached up and found the gash was gone. Tears filled her eyes. The sudden knowledge of the deep darkness she had been living in overwhelmed her.

She whispered, "Thank you."

Michael's voice was gentle and reassuring.

"You are welcome, Amy Davis. Do not fear any longer."

Both angels turned toward Enzril. He bowed his head, and it was Gabriel who spoke.

"It is time, Enzril. You must face your Creator."

Enzril looked up, and Amy could see the fear in his eyes. It was the only time she could remember seeing him this way. He seemed so weak, and it pulled at her heart. Michael and Gabriel stepped forward on each side of him and with the same brilliant flash of light, all three were gone. Amy turned to Farrel with a million questions in her head, but instantly decided not to speak when she saw the sadness and tears on his face. She said a silent prayer for Enzril, whom she now considered a friend.

****

Enzril stood before his council, thousands of angels were gathered, but the silence was deafening. Michael and Gabriel stood only a few feet in front of him. Once they had been the closest of comrades, and now he was here to face justice. His Creator's justice. His apprehension was greater than anything he had ever felt with Master. He looked around and immediately saw Jamille. Their eyes locked, and her fear for him was visible. He had betrayed his Creator, and now he would pay the consequences. Gabriel and Michael both stepped aside as Enzril watched Jesus approach. He willingly and immediately went to his knee, his head bowed. Ashamed for every moment he had been gone.

"My Lord." He felt Jesus's hand on his shoulder.

"Stand, Enzril, and look at me."

Enzril shook his head. "I cannot, my Lord. I am consumed with sorrow and shame. I stood by and watched as You sacrificed Yourself and did nothing to stop it."

Jesus spoke again. "Enzril, look at me."

Enzril raised his head and looked into the eyes of Christ.

"I was not to be saved. I was there to be the One saving. Your sin is great, but I was sacrificed for all souls. You cannot hide your heart from the Father, and you must reap the punishment for your betrayal. I have pleaded your case to my Father, and now you must do the same."

He touched Enzril's arm, and the familiar feeling of everything good overwhelmed him. Enzril stood and wept.

Jesus wrapped the warrior in his arms. "It is time, the Father awaits."

Michael and Gabriel led Enzril forward, all three went to their knees as the Creator's presence filled the area. Enzril pressed his head forward to the ground not daring to look up. He was shaking the moment the Creator's voice boomed.

"Enzril, come forth."

Enzril slowly stood and stepped closer. The light shot through his body bringing him to his knees once more. The pain was searing as any residue of darkness was washed away. Every thought and feeling he ever had was revealed to his Creator. He knew it was his past sins causing his misery.

He cried out, "Father forgive me!"

As fast as it began it was over. He lay before his Creator, weeping.

"Stand, Enzril, and hear my words."

He stood exhausted and vulnerable.

"Your sins will not go unpunished, but you will be punished with mercy. You have selflessly rescued a human soul, and our warrior Jamille, on more than one occasion. These acts have been inscribed, and I have considered everything; my decision has been made. You will be stripped of your wings and you will return as a protector of the Sacred and Elkan. You will do this as a human."

Enzril dared not move or look up. He heard the murmurs of the surrounding angels.

"Enzril, you will feel everything a human soul feels, and you will learn all the reasons for their creation. You will learn love, humility, and sacrifice as a human. When you have true understanding of My love for all creations, then you may return home as the warrior you were created to be, but not before. My presence will be with you as it always has been."

The Creator had spoken, and the punishment was delivered. Enzril stood, his soul crushed. Michael and Gabriel both appeared by his side.

"Michael will take you immediately. Learn the lessons I have asked of you."

There were no words needed. He had been given a second chance. Enzril was to do this or not return.

Chapter Twenty-Eight

And if I go and prepare a place for you, I will come back and take you to be with me that you also may be where I am.– John 14:3

Syene stood and stretched. She was tired of listening to the debate among Dr. Kaufman, John Freely, and Darla. The entire group had been in deep conversations, and the current topic was the necessity of keeping the Cassius writings a secret. Dr. Kaufman did not divulge to anyone where the original writings were being kept, but they did all learn Apollos Drake, Amy's manager, was also the man who had both supplied the FBI with valuable information about Elkan and also followed John.

Everyone was in shock when they were told the true identity of Apollos Drake. Lizzy couldn't stop apologizing to Syene for her stupidity and for not listening to Sy when they were in his office. She seemed to be the most freaked out of all of them. Syene did her best to reassure her friend it was okay and that neither of them knew.

Sy excused herself from the table after growing tired of the conversational banter. Today she wanted some peace. She walked out to the back deck and smiled as she watched Elkan run up and down the beach with Wesley and Ariel. Wesley ran in and out of the water barking and splashing Elkan with water. She could hear his laughter bouncing off the waves.

She noticed several people stopping to enjoy the sight of Elkan and Wesley at play. There was something about her son that attracted people. They were drawn to his presence and had to be watched carefully. He managed to mesmerize every single person he met. They wanted to only be near him, although they didn't know why. Syene knew it was the presence of God shining through him. She sighed deeply. It was selfish, and she knew it, but this is exactly what scared her. People wanting too much of him. How would he survive being pulled all the time?

"He's quite the charmer." Syene turned to find Charles standing behind her.

"Yes, he is, and he knows it." She shrugged. "I would, however, like to do my best to keep him a little humble."

"You have done a wonderful job, Syene."

"Thank you, but it was a group effort. I have had plenty of help."

"Well, I would like to thank you for trusting Darla and me and for sharing him with us."

Syene looked at him with sincerity. "Of course, I knew immediately how wonderful you both were."

"Can I tell you a little secret?"

She was curious. "Of course."

He let out a heavy sigh. "I spent a chunk of my life as an atheist. I never believed in anything nor did I care to. I believed the Bible was a jumbled mess of fictional stories."

Syene was surprised but not shocked.

"I think our friends Thomas and John would really enjoy speaking with you. I know they see all of it, but I also know they struggle because of their past beliefs."

Charles nodded. "Yes, we spoke briefly. I think Thomas is struggling the most because he doesn't understand why God doesn't just reveal Himself to the world. Why the secrecy, why the bad in the world, when all of it could be changed with a wave of His power? Thomas now sees the mighty power of God, and it is almost making it harder for him to understand. But John seems to have embraced it with great joy."

Syene remembered these very same questions she once had.

"I had a dear friend named Farrel, in the beginning of all this. He was a warrior for God and had chosen to take human form to protect me and Elkan before he was born. He once told me if not for freewill we would be nothing but slaves to our Creator. I believe with all my heart God wants us, desires us, and loves us, but is allowing us to figure it out without enforcing His will upon us." She stopped speaking for a moment, lost in her own thoughts. "I have often thought what love Farrel must have felt for his Creator to be willing to separate from that love for a human existence."

"Aww, the true mystery of the Bible. Why is it Christ would sacrifice His own life to save ours?"

"Exactly. It had to be something extreme and amazing, and humankind has managed to mangle it, dissect it, and disregard it. Why is it so hard for us to give and accept love? Why is it so hard for us to believe the unbelievable? Why do we refuse to realize all of us are here for a higher purpose, God's purpose? Why is there so much animosity for one another when we have all been loved so much. We are all loved by the same God. I think this is exactly why Elkan is here."

Charles gave her a warm smile. "In the words of the great Dr. Martin Luther King, Jr., 'I have decided to stick with love. Hate is too great a burden to bear.' And I believe it to be the ultimate truth. Hate is a burden no person should carry. We were never meant to be filled with hatred. You are exactly right, Syene, all of us are guilty of judging each other. We have lost touch with who we really are meant to be."

Syene looked out at the beach where Elkan was still playing. She prayed he would grow into a strong teacher with the ability to show as many people as possible how to love one another. It had never been about us but always about the Creator. She knew without a doubt love was the heart and desire of God.

****

Syene could see her mother in the distance. She was with another woman, and they were talking quietly while they picked the vibrant, colorful flowers surrounding them in the meadow. She walked slowly toward them, afraid her mom would disappear if she rushed over to her. Her mom turned to look at her and smiled. The same beautiful smile Syene remembered. Sy raised her hand and waved and began to walk more quickly. She couldn't let her get away. Syene couldn't see who the other woman was, her head was covered with a gold veil, and she was in a flowing blue dress. They began walking away, and Syene called, "Mom, don't go! I'm coming!"

Her mom held up her hand for Sy to stop and shook her head *no*. She could see she was saying something, but Syene couldn't hear her.

She cried out. "I can't hear you, Mom! Why can't I come to you?" Her mom only stood there smiling. She turned and began walking away again.

"MOM! Wait!"

Suddenly there was a creek in front of Syene separating her even more from her mom. Sy frantically looked for a way to cross it. The young woman with her mom waved for Syene to follow her. The woman left her mother's side and began walking down the opposite side of the creek. Her gold veil blew in the breeze, covering her face from view.

Her mom fell back, and Sy rushed to keep the other woman in her sight. She spotted a wooden bridge up ahead and ran to get to it. She crossed to the other side of the creek and hurriedly raced to catch up with the woman, who now had vanished as well. Then she saw her sitting under a huge tree with white blossoms covering it. Syene slowed and walked up the hill to the waiting female. As she got closer she knew immediately who it was, and she stopped a few feet away staring in amazement. She had no clue how she knew, but she just did.

The woman smiled. "Come. Sit."

Sy slowly approached and sat down. She watched as Mary unwrapped her golden veil, and her dark hair cascaded past her waist. Syene wanted nothing more than to be as close as she possibly could to the Holy Mother. Her words wouldn't come, and she could only stare at how breathtaking beautiful she was. More beautiful than Syene could have ever imagined.

"Syene, you are struggling, yes?"

Sy nodded, and Mary smiled, taking her hand.

"Your mom and I watch over you. She is very proud of the mother you have become."

Syene bowed her head.

"I miss her."

Mary squeezed her hand tightly. "I know. Death is painful for those left behind."

They both sat quietly looking at the spectacular view of the flowers in the meadow and creek running briskly in the distance. Syene felt so safe. The way she would feel as a child when she had a bad dream and her mom would come lie with her in bed.

"What is this place?"

The look of peace and happiness on Mary's face was something Syene longed for.

"This is where I first welcomed the news I was going to have a Son." She paused at the memory. "I was so young and terrified."

"Really? You were terrified?" Sy was shocked.

"Of course! I thought maybe for a moment I was losing my mind. An angel appearing and telling me God needs me? Not something easily believed, even for me. I had so many doubts and could not understand why I had been chosen."

"I kind of know the feeling."

"Yes, you do."

She patted Sy's hand. She stood and pulled Syene to her feet. "Come, let's walk." She wrapped the veil around her head as they stood and began to walk.

They came to a structure built of partial stone in the side of a hill. Syene watched as a young boy, ran in and out of the house, and a young woman laughed and chased him. She realized it was Mary and Jesus she was seeing. Jesus as a boy, maybe a little older than Elkan. A man and woman appeared crying and pleading with Mary for help. She watched as Mary and the child hurried along a path following the man and woman. A young girl was on the ground, surrounded by a small crowd of people. Her head was bleeding, and a large stone was near her body. Possibly the stone had fallen from above, striking the girl. The girl wasn't moving. A woman was draped over the girl's body, crying out to God.

She watched as Jesus tried to walk over to the girl, Mary holding Him back. She could see the fear in Mary's eyes. Jesus broke free from her grasp and ran to the young girl and the woman. He placed His hand on the girl and His other hand on the mother. Syene could hear Him praying. Praying well beyond His years. The young girl opened her eyes and smiled. The crowd gasped and began yelling.

"שד, שד" Demon! Demon!"

Syene watched horrified as Mary grabbed her son, rushing Him back down the path, away from the angry crowd. She couldn't believe they were acting this way after He had saved the young girl. Her heart ached for Mary.

The surrounding scenery began to disappear, and they were walking on a different road. Mary took Syene's hand.

"This is where I followed my Son through many towns. I would sit in the crowds and listen to Him teach. I was so proud of Him, but I also knew the adversity He was facing. He was loved and hated, and I could no longer protect Him."

Syene could see the sadness of the memory on her face.

"Did you know? I mean did you know what was going to happen?"

Mary spoke carefully. "I suppose a mother's heart always knows. And I always knew He was not mine to keep. When I would hear Him as a child, teaching the teachers. I knew I would never have Him to myself again. I prayed He would remain safe, but the more He spoke, and the more He loved, the angrier the crowds became."

"I thought the people came to hear Him and wanted Him to perform miracles?"

The dirt around their feet began to swirl and suddenly they were surrounded by thousands of people. They were everywhere. Men, women, children, and animals scattered over the landscape. Syene could see Jesus in the distance on a hill, His voice boomed down into the valley where they stood. Sy heard loud angry yelling behind her as a fight broke out, and then people began shoving and pushing, the little children were crying, and hundreds of men began rushing up the hill, screaming.

"Blasphemy!" They were yelling it, over and over.

Syene watched as a small group pulled Jesus away and out of her sight. The crowd disappeared, and she and Mary were back in the flower-filled meadow. Syene's heart was racing, and she could only imagine the fear Mary must have felt. Guilt overwhelmed Sy's soul.

"I'm sorry. I'm sorry we couldn't understand why He was here. Here for us. It is so shameful."

Mary touched her face. "Sweet Syene, I only show you this so you know you are not alone on your journey. Although I prayed fervently for the outcome to be different, I never forgot He didn't belong to me. He was here to fulfill His purpose as

He always knew. Just as Elkan knows. But what you need to remember is the purposes are different. You spend hours angry and worrying. Comparing the two very different reasons. You must stop. Your lesson is to trust your Creator. It will be the lesson for many. My Son paid the price for all, and now He has mercifully asked for mankind to have one more chance at redemption. The Father has granted the request. Worrying will not stop Elkan's purpose. Let him be a reminder of my Son's sacrifice. Let him be a reminder of my Son's love."

Syene sighed deeply. She didn't know how to let go of the worry.

"Prayer is how."

Sy smiled. Of course, Mother Mary could hear her thoughts.

"Fear and worry are of the enemy. Trust your Savior. Use the rosary Father Cervini gave to you. Use it as armor, use it as a sword, and use it as a lullaby when you need to feel closer to my Son; it is His story within the beads. I will pray on your behalf when asked."

Syene reached into her back pocket and pulled the rosary out. Mary wrapped both her hands around Syene's hand, holding the rosary together. She watched in amazement as they turned from simple wood to a sparkling blue and gold.

"When you feel hopeless, Syene, when you feel disconnected from the Holy Trinity, the rosary will be the conduit to revive you. You can always find peace there. Pray."

Mary embraced Syene in a warm hug, and Sy closed her eyes breathing in deeply, taking in her wonderful scent as the scenery faded away.

Syene's eyes opened to the walls of the room in their temporary home. Elkan was lying peacefully next to her. He must have snuck in with her during the night. The sound of the ocean waves could be heard through the open window. Clenched in her hand was the rosary, now glistening gold and blue, and Mary's scent lingered. Syene smiled, immediately knowing God had allowed this moment and feeling overwhelmed with gratitude. She gently stroked Elkan's curls while he slept.

She whispered, "Thank you." A warm shiver ran through her body. She felt true peace.

Chapter Twenty-Nine

Do you think I cannot call on my Father, and he will at once put at my disposal more than twelve legions of angels? – Matthew 26:53

Lucifer stood in the dark staring out the glass windows at the skyline. Buildings glistening with night lights. The hurriedness of life could be seen far below. He typically thrived on these nights, thinking how much he controlled the humans below, but tonight was different. Lantz and Kefira waited quietly behind him. Neither of them dared to say a word. Enzril's treachery was confirmed. He had returned to Yahweh.

"Can you explain to me, once again, how it is Enzril and my Amy both escaped your grasp?"

Lantz did not raise his head when he spoke. "Master, I have no excuses. I failed you. Enzril's strength was greater than I had anticipated. I will do whatever you ask of me to redeem myself."

"I know you will, or this time there will be no return for you."

Lantz nodded and went to his knees. "I am your servant, Master."

Lucifer looked at him in disgust. "Get up! Groveling will not fix all that has gone wrong."

He turned his attention briefly to Kefira, standing only inches away from her. She submissively stared at the floor.

"And you, what a disappointment you have been. In constant companionship with Enzril and unable to seduce him. Useless."

She began to speak and immediately was silenced when Master held up his hand.

"I want to hear nothing from you."

He turned to look at the night sky.

"I find myself in a moment I was not expecting. I have lost one of my fiercest warriors in a time when he is needed most. Yahweh is sending out another messenger to destroy all the hard work I have accomplished. The great Creator believes these simpletons can still be saved, that they will turn their hearts from all the pleasures I provide." He laughed, shaking his head. "Fool."

He slowly faced the two angels. "You both will take human form. You will infiltrate the network our beautiful Sacred is building around herself. And you will make sure you are not recognized by our old friends. I want the mother, and with the mother I will get the child. I will seek my revenge on Enzril. I am not to be betrayed."

Lantz looked up. "Master, they are constantly being guarded. How do you expect us to accomplish such a task? And without alerting them of who we are? I don't understand."

Lucifer transformed before them into his true form. "Do you doubt me, Lantz?"

Lantz fumbled, shaking his head. "No, Master."

Master walked circles around them, "It sounds like doubt. I AM the King of Mankind. I rule every uncontrollable impulse and desire of the human heart. I will get what I seek and you will not fail me." His anger radiated throughout the room.

"Understood?"

The dark warriors answered in unison. "Yes, Master."

****

Ariel took Elkan's hand from Syene's. He was dressed and ready for the beach. Sam had arrived for a short visit, and she could see Ariel's happiness. She was glowing. Syene had no doubt this would be the young man Ariel would marry someday. Sam picked up Elkan and swung him in a horizontal position, carrying him underneath his arm. Elkan laughed and struggled to get away from his pretend captor.

Syene called after them, "You know the rules, Ariel. Life jacket, sunscreen, shade as much as possible."

Ariel tickled Elkan's tummy while he was trapped under Sam's arm.

"Your mom is cray-cray, Elkan. Did you know that?" He belly-laughed.

Syene folded her arms across her chest. "Ariel!"

Ariel looked at her, exasperated. "What? You are!" She rolled her eyes at Syene. "Let us go have some fun. You can see us from the deck."

Their grandmother walked up behind her as she watched the threesome run toward the water. Wesley was barking and chasing after them.

She hugged Syene from behind. "What a wonderful thing to be young."

Syene looked at her lovingly.

"Grandma, you are so young still."

She kissed Syene's cheek and laughed. "Well, my bones and wrinkles tell me different." She glanced at her watch. "And now the time. It's only ten in the morning, and I have been up since four, so I'm ready for my midday nap."

Syene giggled. "If that's what it's like to get old, then sign me up."

Her grandmother released her. "Well, instead of a nap, I think I'll grab my hat, a good book, and join the younger generation on the beach." She nodded toward the kitchen. "You should join the intellects in the kitchen, they are having quite a debate with the great Michael."

Syene laughed out loud. "Oh, this I have got to see."

She gave her grandma a quick kiss and made her way to the kitchen.

Everyone had gathered around the large kitchen island, mesmerized by the very animated conversation happening between Michael, Dr. Kaufman, and John Freely. Thomas was the only one staying back, leaning against a wall. She thought he was the safer place to be. He smiled as she walked up.

"Thought I would stay in the safe zone."

He laughed at her statement. "You got that right."

"This all must be pretty overwhelming for you." He glanced quickly at her and then turned away, his cheeks beginning to flush. "You have no idea."

Syene realized how unbelievable all of this really had to seem to a complete outsider.

She touched his arm. "I understand. We all went through this at first. You don't have to be embarrassed by it."

"I just can't wrap my head around it. I mean I see it. I see it with my own eyes, but I just can't believe it. It's like I keep waiting to wake up." He gave her a sheepish look. "Does that make sense?"

She could see he was struggling. "Perfectly."

He almost looked stunned. "Really? I mean, you're Elkan's mom?"

Sy laughed. "Yes, but also very human. I've struggled many times with all of it."

Thomas still looked at her in disbelief. "When we were in Egypt and Dr. Kaufman told me what he had found and then what he was searching for, I just thought he was an eccentric, very possibly crazy, old man. I had no idea all of this really existed. I feel as if my whole life has been a lie. I feel like an idiot."

"Thomas, we all question what is real!"

"But I've lived my life never believing. None of this should be happening. Everything I have ever believed is based on science and facts. And now, nothing I thought to be true is . . ." he paused, "well, true."

He waved toward the scene before them. "I mean, that is Michael. Michael the Archangel. I see him standing there: wings, sword, flesh, blood. And I still can't believe what I'm seeing. I actually want to start dissecting everything about him, so I can understand how he is even standing there."

Syene couldn't help but laugh. "I would actually enjoy a good Michael-dissection."

Thomas smiled. "I'm being ridiculous, huh?"

She immediately softened. "Not at all. I had faith when I found out I was pregnant with Elkan, and I still struggled every day with the knowledge. I can't imagine what it must feel like to have never believed and to have your world turned upside down."

They stood listening to the continuous debate.

"Let me ask you something, Thomas, and I want you to give me an honest answer."

He looked at her very seriously. "Of course."

"How do you think people like you in the world are going to react to Elkan?"

He grew quiet for a moment. "I'm assuming not everyone will have the privilege of seeing the proof of angels, such as I and the others have been given?"

"I have no idea, but I am going to assume no."

Thomas gave her a very serious look. "Then I would be terrified if I were you. People like me will rip everything about this to shreds. They will accuse you of a hoax and using your son to trick people."

"Is that what you would have thought without seeing for yourself?"

He shook his head. "Yes, without a doubt."

Syene nodded her understanding.

"I'm sorry if I have upset you, Syene."

She gave him a reassuring smile. "You haven't upset me, Thomas. You only confirmed what I already knew, what everyone else has been afraid to tell me."

He reached for her hand and squeezed it tightly. "I promise for what it's worth I will do everything in my power to convince anyone I meet Elkan is real. Your son has changed my life forever."

"I'm counting on it."

Chapter Thirty

But the Lord is faithful, and he will strengthen you and protect you from the evil one. – 2 Thessalonians 3:3

Jamille and Michael were talking to someone outside close to the water. Syene did her best to peer around them but couldn't see who it was. The conversation looked serious. Father Cervini and Dr. Kaufman walked through the room, and Syene asked them both.

"What's going on out there?" Nodding toward the two angels.

The priest answered, "Michael brought him here earlier this morning."

Syene turned back to the threesome outside. "Michael brought him? Is it an angel? I can't see who it is."

Cervini walked up behind her. "No, he is human. I'm not sure why they are huddled together like that."

Syene opened the back door and stepped onto the wooden deck. The smell of the ocean filled her senses, and the sun instantly warmed her skin. She took the stairs to the beach and walked toward the trio. Jamille turned, and Syene finally got a look at the stranger. Her mind instantly raced back to the beginning over six years ago. She was in college walking on campus, and there he was standing across the pond staring at her with contempt and hatred. The man with the green eyes.

She stopped in her tracks, and Jamille immediately began walking toward her.

"Syene, it's okay. He is not an enemy."

Syene looked at her in shock. "Are you kidding me? I remember him! He was there in the beginning. And I saw him during the battle when my mom was still alive. He is evil!"

She turned to rush back inside, her head pounding as she ran. She was not going to let that man anywhere near Elkan. Jamille had lost her mind. Syene ignored her calling, unable to believe Michael had brought him here. Elkan was quietly playing with Sam in the living room and smiled when she walked in.

Elkan, in a matter of fact way, told her, "Enzril is here."

Syene looked at her son with confusion. "What?"

He pointed and said the name again. "Enzril. God sent him." She followed her son's finger and saw the dark stranger standing on the back deck.

Syene's voice was shaking. "Sam, will you please take Elkan to the back bedroom."

Sam could certainly see she was upset. He ruffled Elkan's hair.

"Come on, buddy, let's go play in the other room."

Elkan looked back as he left the room and waved to Enzril. Sy watched the man awkwardly raise his hand at an attempt to wave back. She had to admit he didn't seem nearly as menacing as she remembered. In her heart, she knew

Michael and Jamille would never bring harm to Elkan, but she couldn't trust this situation.

Enzril walked slowly into the room, Jamille and Michael close behind. He looked small and defeated standing between the two warriors. Syene couldn't see at all the dark, menacing person she remembered. Curiosity had caught the attention of everyone, and Sy felt her people standing with her. It gave her comfort and confidence. Ariel's hand slipped into hers. Everyone could sense something was happening.

Her grandmother must have sensed Syene's initial fear and spoke up.

"Do we have a new guest?"

Michael stepped forward. "Yes, allow me to introduce Enzril." Enzril looked out of his element and completely uncomfortable. He stood staring at the group without saying a word and only nodded his head. His eyes were the intense green Syene remembered so vividly. Wesley stood closely, feeling her tension, and let out a low growl. Syene patted his head to let him know it was okay and found her voice.

"I don't understand. Why is he here?"

Jamille spoke this time. "Sacred, I know this is all very confusing, but you have to trust us."

Father Cervini stepped closer. "What is going on? It's obvious Syene is afraid. The entire atmosphere in this house changed as soon as he stepped in here."

Michael started to speak, but Enzril raised his hand. "I will answer."

He stepped forward to face the group of spectators but locked his gaze with Syene. His voice commanded attention. He bowed his head slightly to Syene.

"I am Enzril, former warrior for Yahweh. I was with the Creator in the beginning and followed Lucifer during his rebellion. I have been a General in Hell's army and a servant to my Master. I betrayed Lucifer to return home, and now my sins of the heart and soul will be punished as required by the Creator. I will be hunted, as will you and your son, by Lucifer. I am here to serve you and protect you."

The room was in stunned silence.

Cervini broke the silence. "I didn't even know this was possible."

Sy watched as the priest wrapped his hand around the cross dangling from his neck. He looked as shocked as she did. Thomas sank on the couch with his head in his hands.

"This is too much."

John sat next to him. "You aren't kidding. I'm not sure how much more I can take. What's next? Is Satan about to show up with horns and a tail?"

Syene could hear Dr. Kaufman and Laura talking with great animation. They apparently already had a ton of questions for the new arrival. Ariel still clung to her hand tightly. And Sy watched as Enzril stepped back from the chaos. He was not doing well in his new human form. Anyone could see that.

She caught the look of concern on Jamille's face for the dark stranger and sudden recognition hit her. This was him. This is the one who betrayed Jamille. Her great lost love. Something immediately softened in Syene as she watched her beautiful protector look at the former dark warrior. A longing for Farrel tugged at her own heart. If Jamille could trust him, then she knew she could. She released Ariel's hand and approached Enzril. The room grew quiet.

Enzril watched her cautiously as she came closer.

"I'm glad you are here with us, Enzril." He nodded his head in acceptance.

Sy turned to Thomas and Freely and cheerfully announced, "And by the way, Lucifer does not have a tail and horns."

The mood was lifted, and everyone laughed. Enzril remained uncomfortable in this environment, but she watched as he patiently answered the onslaught of questions he was receiving.

Syene suddenly realized Lizzy was missing from the group and asked the question to no one in particular, "Where is Lizzy?"

Susan answered, "She said she had something to do to make something right for you and Amy."

Immediately Syene's heart started pounding, and her phone began to vibrate in her back pocket. It was a text from Lizzy. Her hands were shaking as she read the message.

COMING

Her eyes immediately locked with Enzril from across the room. They both knew.

Lucifer had Lizzy.

****

Lucifer sat at the desk, his back turned to the young woman sniffling behind him. He had grown weary of her crying and her unstoppable mumbling of how stupid she was. He already knew exactly how stupid she was, and the constant reminder was beginning to drive him mad.

"Kefira, please take Ms. Richardson to some other room, I cannot take one more moment of her whining."

He turned and watched as she yanked the young woman from her chair. Lizzy let out a yell in pain. Kefira hissed at her. "Shut up, you sniveling idiot. You're lucky you are still alive." She shoved her toward the door.

"Lizzy, my dear."

Kefira forced Liz to face Lucifer as he spoke to her and squeezed her arm tightly to make sure he had her full attention. Liz looked at him. Tears of fear and pain streamed down her face, the wound across her cheek from Lantz, bloody and raw.

"Be grateful I wasn't in my true form and appreciate I have spared you of seeing the real horror of evil. Your little friends will be here shortly, and it will all be over soon enough."

Lizzy spat on the floor and glared. Kefira wrenched her head back by the hair, and Lizzy cried out.

Lucifer laughed. "Such spunk in the face of the Master of Hell. We will see how long that lasts once I have you back in my lair, sweet Elizabeth."

Lantz stood, ready to provide her another lesson, but was stopped. Lizzy closed her eyes, bracing for what was next.

"Stand down, Lantz. She will succumb. It is only a matter of time. Save it for our guests, who will be arriving soon."

Kefira hauled her out of the office. Lucifer stood, touching a button on his desk, and the windows in his office were darkened. He stretched, letting out a vicious growl as he transformed into his true self. He ran his hands over his muscular, disfigured body.

"Aww, much better. As much as I love toying with the humans, I do hate how weak they are." He spread his wings with ecstasy.

Menti, his loyal demonic servant, immediately approached with Master's cloak in hand. He took it from the demon and wrapped it around his body. Lucifer turned, facing Lantz.

"Now we wait for the tradeoff. They will do whatever it takes to save her. Sacrifice is always what the Creator does best, no matter the price."

The stench of evil was palpable, and Master could see the lust and excitement exuding from Lantz. His warriors were ready for battle, as was he.

****

Syene lunged in a rage for Enzril. "If you had anything to do with this, I will kill you! I just welcomed you into this home." She felt an arm from behind wrap around her waist, holding her back. Enzril didn't budge, and this enraged her even more. She clawed at the arm holding her, struggling to be released.

"Let me go!"

"Stop, Sy! He had nothing to do with it." She spun around at the sound of the voice. Farrel was standing inches away from her, his hand still resting on her waistline.

"Farrel?"

She couldn't believe he was standing there. She didn't believe it was real.

He gently released her. "Hello, Syene."

The last several years of pain and anger from missing him came spilling out, and tears sprang to her eyes immediately. She couldn't find the words. She was furious and elated all at once. Syene could only stare in shock. Thankfully,

Ariel broke the tension as she raced for him, and they embraced in a warm hug.

"Farrel! I'm so happy to see you!"

He laughed as he lifted her off the ground. "Oh, I've missed you, Ariel."

Farrel looked at Syene as he set her little sister back down. "I've missed all of you."

Sy couldn't look at him. It was too painful. He had left her, deserted her when she needed him the most, and as much as she wanted to run into his arms, she couldn't. She turned and left the room without saying a word, walking through the back door, down the stairs and onto the beach. Her tears flowed as she began to sob. The sound of the waves silenced her crying. She had no idea if she was feeling joy or anger. She honestly didn't know what to feel. She sat down in the sand and watched the sun glisten off the water as the birds dove in out of the waves on the hunt for fish.

It was all too much—Enzril arriving here, Lizzy being taken, Farrel showing up. Her senses were on overload. She reached for her back pocket, pulling out the rosary. She squeezed it tightly in her hands and closed her eyes.

"You said I could always find peace with these. Please, bring me peace."

A warm wind blew at her hair, and she felt a calming rest upon her. She sat there for quite a while in silence holding the beads, grateful no one came for her right away. She needed to be alone.

Chapter Thirty-One

For You have girded me with strength for battle; You
have subdued under me those who rose up against me.
– Psalm 18:39

Kefira watched from afar. Sacred sat on the beach alone. She could not see Enzril but knew he was near. He was now in human form, and she couldn't believe it. He had really gone back to the Creator and agreed to be a despicable human.

"What a fool." She snorted in disgust. He had been Master's lead General. He could have had anything he desired, including her. The jealousy still raged in her veins.

"May I help you with something?" Kefira swirled around quickly, drawing her sword. Jamille stood before her. The one who blocked her from having Enzril for herself. Pure hatred was now seeping through her body.

"I need nothing from you, Jamille."

Jamille stepped closer, her sword not even drawn. Kefira could kill an unarmed enemy with ease but still found herself shaking in fear.

"Well, it seems you know my name, and I am left in the dark on who you might be."

"I am Kefira, warrior for the Master and former lover of Enzril." Knowing of course the latter was not true but wanting to do anything to hurt the Creator's angel.

Jamille looked her over, and Kefira hated herself for feeling inferior. The Creator's warrior stepped a little closer to her.

"Well, let me tell you something, Kefira, warrior for *your* Master. If I ever find you anywhere near the people I love and protect, I assure you my sword will be drawn, and you will not have the opportunity to explain your presence." She stepped even closer. "Consider this a warning of mercy, there won't be another."

Kefira knew she didn't stand a chance against her in this environment. She would be attacked and destroyed by the Creator's warriors.

She stepped back, sheathing her sword and spreading her wings She gave Jamille her sweetest smile.

"Tell Enzril I stopped by."

As she soared off, Kefira vowed to make sure Jamille was destroyed.

****

Father Cervini approached quietly sitting next to Syene on the sand. Wesley trailed closely behind and laid his head on Syene's leg. She rubbed his ears gently. Syene finally spoke after several minutes.

"I'm angry he thought he could just show up. I need to be thinking about Liz right now. I don't have time to worry about him and why he is here."

Father Cervini nodded his head. "Fair enough."

She looked at her dear friend. She was a little shocked at how much he had aged. It was like she hadn't been paying attention at all for the last few years. His hair was completely silver now, and the lines around his eyes had deepened. The worry on his face was evident.

"How are we going to get her back, Tony? I've been sitting here going over everything in my head. Where does he have her? How come Michael and Jamille aren't doing something?"

The priest released a heavy sigh. "I'm worried as well. But Michael is working on a plan, and our new member Enzril is helping him."

Syene's eyes flashed with anger. "I don't want his help! He was there in the beginning. Hunting me—he's part of the evil. It's like everyone has gone crazy! I can't believe I told him he was welcome here."

Cervini put his hand on her arm. "Stay calm, Syene. We all understand what you are feeling. But I have been listening to him and what he has to say. He has a beautiful story of God's love to tell, and he is the one thing we have right now to give us an insight into what is ahead. More than anyone here." He paused. "He was sent by God to be here with you, Syene. You cannot ignore it. You do not know better than your Creator."

Sy felt hurt at his reprimand; she only wanted one person to be on her side. She knew everything he was saying was correct, but right now she wanted to feel angry. She stayed quiet for several minutes trying to calm her mind.

She clenched the rosary beads tightly. "What is his plan?" She could see the small smile on the priest's lips. He could always talk her back to sanity.

"Why don't you come back to the house and talk to him? I know there is a young man waiting to talk to you."

He moved his head toward the house. Syene looked back and saw Farrel sitting on the deck.

"He has been there the entire time you have been out here, waiting for you."

Syene shrugged. "Well, that would make him a creepy stalker, wouldn't it?"

Father Cervini laughed as he stood up and held out his hand for her.

"You can be a handful, young lady. If our young Elkan has half your spunk, he is going to be something to see."

Syene stood and on impulse wrapped her arms around her friend.

"I love you, Father. I don't think I have ever told you, but it is true, and I thank God for you. You have been like a dad to Ariel and me."

He squeezed her tightly. "What a gift to hear those words. I chose a life dedicated to our Lord, and He in his infinite love and mercy has still allowed me to experience the joy of fatherhood. You girls and Elkan have brought me a happiness I can never repay. I am blessed beyond belief." He kept his arm around her shoulders as they walked back to the house.

When they approached the stairs, he spoke these words to her. "Be strong, Syene. But also be kind in your forgiveness."

****

Farrel stood up as soon as Sy and the priest walked up the wooden steps. Father Cervini slipped into the house, leaving Syene and Farrel alone on the deck. She could hardly catch her breath and didn't dare look at him. Neither of them moved.

"I am sorry for leaving and hurting you. I can only ask that you forgive me."

Syene could feel her eyes begin to sting with tears, and she quickly wiped them away. She was done with crying and hurting. She looked at him directly and could see the pain in his eyes. Her heart was filled with compassion, but she wasn't ready to talk about this yet.

"Farrel, my heart has been broken since you left. In this moment I feel so much happiness you are here, and in the very same instant I feel so much anger. I need you to understand I can't have this conversation with you right now. Lucifer has Lizzy, and I cannot think of anything else but how to save her and what she must be going through. Anything else has to be put to the side."

343

He nodded. "You owe me nothing. And everything should be focused on her return. I am here to do whatever is needed."

Syene wanted to reach out and touch him, but she remained where she stood.

"Thank you for understanding."

Things had changed for her over the last few years. She was a mother now, and so much had happened. Farrel had missed all of it. He stepped back to allow her more room to go inside.

"I should let you know you have someone here to see you. She is waiting for you inside."

Syene was confused. "She?" She wasn't sure if she could take any more surprises and couldn't imagine who would be waiting to see her that Farrel knew. He opened the glass door, and Syene stepped into the house. She couldn't believe her eyes.

"Amy!"

Amy stood up from sitting on the couch. They both burst into tears as they ran to embrace each other.

****

The two young women spent the next two hours privately talking, laughing, and crying.

"I can't believe I wasn't there for you when your mom died, Sy. And to know I played a part in it. How can you ever forgive me?"

Syene grabbed her friend's hand. "Amy! You had nothing to do with it. Lucifer was responsible for all the lives lost that day. I have peace knowing her spirit is free and with my dad now. She would never want you to carry around the guilt of her death."

Amy looked away, whispering, "Master . . . and now he has Lizzy."

Syene couldn't imagine the horrors her friend had been through over the last few years, and she knew Amy was terrified for Liz. The look on her face told Syene she probably didn't want to know what Amy had endured at the hands of Lucifer.

"When you are ready to talk about it, I'm here."

Amy's smile was weak, and the pain in her eyes could not be hidden.

"We have got to get her back, Sy. She won't survive it. I chose to be with Lantz in the beginning. Liz didn't choose this."

"Father Cervini said Enzril is helping with a plan. I can't believe they have allowed him to be here. And now they are trusting him with saving Lizzy. It doesn't make sense. Why not just send God's warriors to get her?"

Amy squeezed Syene's hand. "It isn't that easy, Sy. It's a very dimensional world. I know you have been living with God's creatures, but for the angels to enter into Master's darkness, I imagine would take enormous numbers and power."

Syene looked at her friend, realizing how frozen in fear she truly was. Syene had fought her Master's warriors. She was fully aware of the danger.

"God's hand can reach into any depth of darkness. God created the one you call Master."

Amy's cheeks burned with embarrassment.

"I'm sorry, Sy. The fear will be a hard habit to break."

She hugged Amy tightly and released her.

"Don't apologize. But he is your Master no longer. God saved you, Amy. He sent Farrel for you. They are going to save Lizzy."

Amy nodded. "You're right, Sy. I don't have the faith you have, but I know there is truth in everything you are saying. And I also know you can trust Enzril. He saved me twice from being destroyed."

Syene couldn't help but think how ironic it was for Amy to believe so easily, when she herself had been struggling with faith this whole time. Thinking of what poor Amy had gone through made her feel both ashamed and empowered. She was not going to let doubt invade her thoughts any longer. She would do whatever she could to save Lizzy.

Farrel walked into the room, "I am sorry to interrupt, but we need both of you to join us."

Just then Syene's phone buzzed with a text.

> **Meet me tomorrow, 8 p.m. My favorite intimate restaurant. Our sweet little Amy can provide the location. Come alone.**

****

Everyone was gathered in the living room. No one spoke, even Elkan remained quiet. She knew everyone was looking at her as if she had lost her mind. Syene stared at all of them defiantly.

"I'm going. No one is going to stop me."

Jamille spoke and the concern in her voice was undeniable. "Sacred, you cannot put yourself in this kind of danger. Do you not remember what it was like to be confronted by him?"

Syene stood and faced her protector.

"You won't stop me. It's a restaurant. He's not going to transform into a monster in front of everyone. I'm going. I will fight my way through all of you if I must. Lizzy is my best friend. She gave up everything to be here with Elkan and me. I will do everything in my power to save her. And I know my Creator will be with me in every moment. I am not afraid."

Her new strength in her faith empowered her in ways she couldn't believe. She knew in life or death she would be okay. Fear would not control her any longer. Fear was what Lucifer wanted, and she would not give in.

Enzril stepped forward. "I will be close by."

Syene glared at him, still not trusting his motive.

"The text said alone. I won't do anything to put Lizzy in more danger."

Enzril stared, his intense green eyes boring into her,

"He will be expecting me. I have a plan to save her."

Syene knew she was not going to win this argument.

Jamille looked defeated and for an instant Syene wanted to tell her she wouldn't go so her beautiful protector would not worry, but she knew she had to do this.

"Fine. Enzril can go." This would be the only thing she would cave on.

****

The rest of the evening was much calmer, and Syene wanted to spend as much time with Elkan as she could before she went to meet Lucifer tomorrow. She walked to an area just off the living room. Darla and Charles had been kind enough to turn a small sitting area into a play space for Elkan. She stopped in surprise and stepped quietly to the side, so they didn't see her but she could see them; Elkan and Enzril were sitting together talking while Elkan colored. She wanted to hear and see their interaction. If this man was part of them now, she needed proof. Elkan was of course full of questions and so smart. She often forgot how intelligent and mature he was for his young age.

His voice was filled with innocence and curiosity. "Why did you leave our Father?"

Enzril seemed surprised by the question. "And how do you know that is what happened?"

"I know who you are. I know you are really an angel, and God is punishing you by making you stay in human form."

Enzril chuckled. "Forgive me. I haven't had much interaction with humans. I didn't realize how smart the little ones were."

Elkan stopped coloring and looked at him. "Not all of us. I'm special, but there are some others who can speak to the angels and Jesus."

"Really? And how do you know this?"

Elkan shrugged. "Jesus tells me in my dreams. But He says they don't tell anyone because people fear Him and the angels. He told me people have forgotten Him and this is why I'm here."

Syene didn't know any of this. She had no idea Jesus came to Elkan in his dreams, and she felt a little sad he hadn't told her and was confessing all of it to a stranger.

"Well, you must indeed be a very special young man."

Elkan shrugged. "I don't feel special."

Syene felt the tears come to her eyes. She was so busy protecting him from the world she forgot how much the world needed him. She watched as Enzril stuck out his hand to touch Elkan's hair, her heart lurching for a moment like a lioness, but she calmed herself. He stroked her son's curls in what seemed to be fascination.

Elkan stood and faced the dark warrior.

"I like you." He wrapped his arms around Enzril's neck in a warm and genuine hug. Enzril clumsily did his best to hug him back.

Syene stepped into the room, and Enzril quickly stood up, apologizing.

"I am sorry, he hugged me and . . ."

She stopped him. "It's okay. He is a pretty good judge on a soul's character, so if he wanted to hug you, well, he knew you needed it."

He looked at Syene with honesty. "This has been very hard for me. I have forgotten what it was like to feel. It has been wonderful and painful at the same time.

Sy softened some, seeing him for the first time as something other than an enemy.

"I would like to hear your answer sometime."

He looked confused. "My answer?"

"Why you left your Father?"

He nodded respectfully. "That will be a story for another time, if I may pass for now."

She nodded. "For now."

"We need to prepare for tomorrow. You have been surrounded by the Creator's warriors for so long you have learned to block the evil. You will be too close to Lucifer in the restaurant for all your defenses to work. You need to be prepared."

Syene nodded and sat down next to him.

"Well, let's get to work. Tell me everything I need to know."

They spent the rest of the night talking and strategizing into the early morning hours. It was past two when she finally stood for bed. Ariel had come and taken Elkan long ago. Enzril stood with her and looked down into her eyes.

"You are a brave soul, Sacred." On impulse, she wrapped her arms around him. She felt him stiffen, and she giggled.

"Elkan is right. You definitely need to be hugged."

She released him, and they walked into the living room. Farrel was asleep on the couch. He had been out here waiting the whole time.

"He loves you." Syene didn't say anything. "He has given up everything to make sure you are safe."

She had a lump in her throat and couldn't find the words.

Before Enzril turned to leave her, he spoke quietly. "I once loved and was loved in this way. You will miss it if it goes away."

Syene watched as he left and then turned to look at Farrel. She never stopped loving him and knew she had to tell him. Now was not the time. Her thoughts had to stay focused on Lizzy. Syene turned to go to bed, when that familiar feeling of foreboding washed over her as she left the living room. She pushed it aside and kept walking. She knew the heart of evil was waiting for her. Focus would be the only thing to get her through.

Chapter Thirty-Two

***They come out at night, snarling like vicious dogs as they
prowl the streets. – Psalm 59:6***

Lucifer stared into the fire, sitting quietly for hours
thinking of what was to come. He stood expanding his wings,
releasing a low growl of pleasure. As much as he enjoyed
toying with the humans, he preferred to be home and in his true
form.

"Menti." His voice was hoarse as he called for his
faithful servant. "Bring me my cloak." Menti appeared quietly,
handing his Master the cloak and keeping his eyes diverted.

"How may I help and please my Master?"

"How is our new guest?"

"She is unresponsive, Master."

Master walked toward the door. "Interesting. Let's go
have a look."

Menti rushed ahead to open the door and followed
Master out. The demons quit their screeching at the sight of
him and bowed low as he passed. The labyrinth halted, and
Menti scrambled forward, making sure to have the door open
and waiting for Master at the bottom of the stone staircase. The
room was dark. With a wave of his hand Lucifer lit the torches
on the stone walls. Huddled in the corner, chained to an unseen
object, was Lizzy. She shielded her face from the light. He
approached slowly and could see her shivering in fear.

He crouched to be near her face. "Sweet Elizabeth. I hear you have become unresponsive, my dear."

She flinched and scooted away as he reached to stroke her hair.

He followed. "Now that is no way to treat your host. What is it, Elizabeth? Is it your accommodations making you so unhappy or is it me making you so uncomfortable?"

The evil and lust dripped heavily from him. She refused to look at him, and he could hear her mumbling. He leaned closer to hear her.

"Praying? Are you praying?" He laughed loudly and grabbed her hair forcing her to look up. "Open your eyes and look at me."

He yanked her head roughly until she cried out in pain. She opened her eyes.

"You pray to nothing, my little Lizzy. Your God does not care about you or your measly stupid prayers. If He cared so much about you then how did you end up here?"

He could see the tears in her eyes, but she still refused to speak.

Lucifer was done playing games.

"Menti!" Menti appeared immediately.

"Show our brave little guest to my chambers. I will deal with her when I return." He pulled her face close to his, lifting her completely off the ground. He inhaled her scent deeply.

"We will see how quickly you break after I'm done with you."

He roughly tossed her back to the ground. As he turned to leave he heard her whispering the prayers again. Fury coursed through his body. She was going to pay dearly.

****

Syene brushed her hair slowly, trying to calm her nerves. Her dress and heels were laid out on the bed. Less than an hour and she would have to leave. She had already given Elkan a kiss and told him goodbye. She knew she wouldn't be able to do it as she was leaving, it would be too painful. She had also made phone calls to James and, of course, to Susan and Dave. James spent most of the call trying to talk her out of doing this, and Susan couldn't stop crying. Syene was determined.

Someone knocked softly on her door.

"Come in."

Ariel poked her head into the room.

"Since when do you knock?" Syene was trying to keep the mood from being so dark. Ariel's face was strained.

Sy put down the brush and patted the bed next to her.

"Come here and sit."

Ariel immediately wrapped her in a tight hug, pressing her face against Syene's chest. Sy held her and let her be as quiet as she needed to be. Finally, her sister found the words. "Please don't go."

Syene gently pushed Ariel away from her. "Look at me, Ariel."

She raised her head slowly, and Sy could see her eyes were red and swollen.

"You and I both know I have to go. He has Lizzy. Have you forgotten that?"

Ariel shook her head. "I haven't forgotten, I just don't understand why we can't just storm where he has her and save her. We've battled those bastards before." She looked at Syene with tears on her cheeks. "Why do you have to go alone?"

Sy brushed her sister's hair from her face. "Have I told you lately how stunning you are?"

"You're avoiding my question, Sy"

Syene sighed. "Yes, I am, but you are beautiful. I see so much of Mom in you. You're the strongest person I know, Ariel."

Her sister stood up. "Then let me go with you. I have my sword. I practice all the time still. I can help protect you."

Sy smiled. "It's not that kind of battle this time Ariel. What are you going to do, carry a huge sword into the restaurant?"

Ariel looked defeated.

"Ariel, it's about the mind now, it's about battling with our dimensions intertwined. He's playing a mind game. And he's already taken someone I love. I would be destroyed if something happened to you too."

Ariel rushed to her, crouching by her legs and looking up at her. "How do you think I feel? What will I do if you are gone?"

Syene hugged her. "You would be there for Elkan, just like I would expect you to be. He needs you as much as he needs me." Syene laughed. "Maybe even a little more."

"I love you, Sy. You've been the best big sister anyone could ever have."

Syene stood and pulled her sister up with her. "Be brave, Ariel. Be bold. You are a warrior for God, and don't forget it. I am so proud of who you have become, and I know Mom is looking out for both of us. I love you so much, sis. You are my real-life hero." They hugged tightly for a moment, until Syene turned her around and swatted her bottom.

"Now get out of here so I can get ready. I'm going to be fine."

Ariel walked slowly to the door and turned to give her one more glance. "I take that as a promise. And you can't break a promise. You have to be okay."

Syene smiled. "I promise."

Ariel walked out and shut the door. Syene's heart sank with dread. She got dressed slowly, her heart pounding. *Was she crazy? Could she trust Enzril?* Syene looked at herself in the mirror. The black dress clung to her body tightly and had her feeling very uncomfortable. Her legs were accentuated by the four-inch ankle-wrap heels. Enzril had told her to dress as seductively as possible. She had protested, but he had promised it would be a necessary distraction for Lucifer.

"Well, this is as good as it gets." She turned to look at her image from behind. "I guess it's not terrible for almost twenty-seven." She could hardly believe so much time had passed since it all began.

Syene grabbed the small clutch purse and looked at the rosary on her vanity. It wouldn't be with her tonight. She left a letter for Ariel with the rosary.

She placed her hand on the beads and note. "Just in case I don't come back."

She was ready no matter what.

****

Syene walked down the stairs. Almost everyone was waiting in the living room, the mood was heavy. Darla and Charles were the only ones missing, since they had agreed to be the ones to keep Elkan occupied as his mom left. The sun was setting, and it cast a beautiful golden light on all of them. She smiled as she reached the stair landing. Everyone had a stunned look.

"You all look so shocked."

Syene looked down at her dress to make sure she hadn't had a wardrobe malfunction.

"What is it?"

Her grandmother spoke up. "Your stunning beauty has left everyone speechless. We are used to seeing you slouch around in jeans, shorts, and T-shirts."

Everyone seemed to all respond in unison their agreement.

Sy laughed and walked up to her Grandma to give her a hug.

"You were always biased."

Her grandma hugged her tighter than Syene had ever remembered.

"Not biased, Syene, only stating a fact." She clung to her. "You have always made me proud, and you are a wonderful mother."

Syene could feel her tears forming and quickly pulled away.

"Please don't act as if this will be the last time you are going to see me."

Her grandma gave her one more squeeze. "I love you."

Syene looked around at all their faces, wanting to say something to each one of them but knew there wasn't time. Enzril was waiting in the car.

"I love all of you, old friends and new friends. I hope each of you know how much your never-ending faith has inspired me. We will celebrate when I return with Lizzy."

Only Dr. Kaufman gave her a small smile. Thomas and Laura couldn't look at her. Father Cervini approached and embraced her.

"God speed, Syene." Tears were in his eyes as he released her. Syene felt the lump in her throat and choked it away.

Ariel rushed at her for another hug, and Syene lovingly embraced her sister and whispered, "Remember what I said. Be the bold warrior you were meant to be. I love you. I'm going to be fine."

Ariel couldn't hide her tears and quickly walked away. Syene gave all of them her best smile and a wave.

"Wish me luck."

Wesley ran up to her, nudging her for her attention before she left. She crouched down to whisper a soft goodbye to him.

"You've been the best and bravest dog ever, Wesley. Take care of our boy if I don't make it back." When he tried to lick her face, she laughed and barely missed the tongue.

Farrel quietly approached and walked with her to the door, and Syene was grateful to have him near. The years he had not been around seemed to have melted away.

"You look breathtaking, Syene." She looked up at him as they reached the door. She could see the worry and sadness etched on his face.

"Farrel, I need to tell you something."

He put his finger to her lips to quiet her and then bent down to kiss her softly. It was the most magical thing she had ever felt.

He whispered, "Tell me when you get back."

Syene smiled up at him. "Thank you."

He opened the door, where Jamille and Michael were waiting for her. She was relieved to see them both, and they enfolded her.

Jamille spoke softly. "You know you don't have to do this."

"Yes, I do. We have to get Lizzy back."

Jamille nodded. "I won't be far."

Syene smiled at her beautiful protector. "I know."

Michael walked with her to the car in silence. She turned to look up at him and was still always amazed at his beauty.

"Wouldn't it be wonderful, Michael, if some day everyone's eyes are open and are able to see how wonderful and beautiful God's angels are?"

"Yes, but with that comes the bad, little one. They see us then they see the evil as well. And I know Enzril has already told you, but you have been living in somewhat of a veil with us around. You still see, but you have been protected. Once you are in Lucifer's presence the veil will be completely removed."

Syene nodded her head in understanding.

"Be brave, Sacred. I will be near."

Syene opened the door and slid into the leather seat of the black luxury car. Enzril looked at her approvingly but did not comment on her choice of clothes.

"You ready?"

Syene nodded. "Ready as I will ever be."

He pulled slowly away from the house, and they began moving through the night. Evil was waiting, and Syene could only pray.

****

They pulled up to the restaurant, where the valet was waiting. Syene looked at Enzril, she could feel her fear and doubt begin to take over. He unexpectedly gripped her hand.

"I will save Lizzy, I promise."

She looked directly at him squeezing his hand tightly for strength.

"I know."

He nodded. "I will go in with you, and then you will be on your own as planned."

Syene slipped out of the car as the valet opened the door for her. Her mind was going crazy. *Deep breaths, Syene, deep breaths.* She looked around for any signs of Jamille and Michael but didn't see them. She knew she wouldn't, they would not be obvious about their presence. She and Enzril walked into the intimate restaurant. The patrons turned to stare,

Syene knew most stares were probably directed at Enzril. The hostess seemed to be stammering as she took his name.

"We are meeting Mr. Drake." His deep voice seemed to be almost too much for the young woman.

She stumbled over her words. "Ye-yes, Mr. Drake is waiting."

Enzril gave her a stone-hard look, and they followed the poor girl to the table. Syene knew immediately the veil of protection had been removed. She could see the demons everywhere clinging to the unknowing people in the restaurant. She felt dizzy.

Enzril must have felt her falter. "You okay?"

Sy nodded. "Yes." Her heart was pounding.

She saw *him*, smiling at her as they approached. He stood. Syene thought she might faint.

He spoke to Enzril as the hostess walked away. "Enzril, what a surprise. You can see I was not expecting you and only have a table for two."

Enzril pulled the chair out for Syene, sensing her need to sit down. He did not say a word to his former Master and leaned closely to Syene's ear.

"Be brave."

He looked at Lucifer but was speaking to Syene.

"I'll be close by."

Lucifer nodded his head. "Nice to see you again, Enzril."

Enzril departed, and Syene was left alone. Alone with the creator of evil. Panic set in.

"I must say, you look incredibly delicious, my beautiful Sacred. Motherhood suits you."

Syene could see the lust in his eyes; she felt sick to her stomach. To be this close to him was too much. She remembered when he had caught her in the bathroom all those years ago. Terror coursed through her body.

He poured a glass of wine for her and lifted it toward her. Syene took it, her hands shaking uncontrollably.

"My sweet, why so nervous?"

He touched her hand, and she felt the evil rush through her veins, her blood running cold. The restaurant seemed to shift, and Syene could see demons surrounding the people inside, wrapping themselves around them. She wanted to yell at all the diners to open their eyes, but she couldn't find her voice. She looked at the table next to them, the man sitting at the table smiled at her, but his face distorted and she could see the evil inside him. Her mind was racing, and she could only hear a Bible verse in her head.

"Simon, Simon, Satan has asked to sift all of you as wheat."

She abruptly pulled her hand away. "Don't touch me!" Her teeth were gritted as she spoke.

Lucifer smiled and sat back in his chair as if he didn't have a care in the world.

"Aww, now there is the fight I like." He looked around the restaurant. "Are you not enjoying the show?"

Syene was doing her best to stay focused, and she began to pray. He laughed, throwing his head back.

"Praying? Your sweet little Lizzy was praying too. We will see how much she prays when I'm done with her." He leered at Syene. "Would you like me to pray with you?"

At sound of Lizzy's name, Syene attacked. "Don't you dare hurt her."

"Or what?"

She was furious she couldn't concentrate.

"Don't you understand, my sweet? This place is mine. All the human race belongs to me. Your precious God has sold you a lie. You were set up for failure and heartbreak. Your son will do nothing to change this, and neither will you."

She was confused and could feel the sweat beading on her head. She tried to call for Jamille but couldn't get the words out. Everything suddenly went black.

Chapter Thirty-Three

He led them from the darkness and deepest gloom; he snapped their chains. – Psalm 107:14

Enzril landed quietly. Permission from the Creator had allowed him a temporary restoration to his wings. They were no longer black but a soft grey as his soul was cleansed. They would be gleaming white one day, just as before. He pressed himself to the stone wall, careful to not disturb the demons. This was his element. He had not become Lucifer's greatest warrior by making mistakes.

He carefully unsheathed his sword, knowing he would no doubt be using it. The cold walls seemed to echo his every move as he made his way up the winding staircase. He stopped at the entrance to his former Master's chambers, listening for anyone inside. He heard nothing and knew he was taking a gamble, but he felt certain this is where Lucifer would have brought her. He opened the door and slipped inside. He hoped Syene was doing okay and silently prayed their plan was working. If Lucifer showed up now, then he most certainly would not make it out.

He couldn't help but realize how ironic it was he was praying for a human soul. Elkan had softened something inside him, and he could feel Syene's love for her son. He began to understand why his Creator loved them so much. They were willing to die for each other, and he found this brave and genuine.

He heard a groan by the lit fireplace and slowly walked to the figure he could see by its glow. When she saw him, she quickly crawled to a nearby corner trying to hide in the darkness. She was chained to the wall.

He softly spoke, "Lizzy?"

She didn't answer.

"I'm here to help you. I'm a friend of Syene and Amy."

Her voice was barely audible. "I've seen you before, and you're not a friend. I don't believe you. Do whatever you've come to do to me. I don't care."

Enzril urged her quietly and moved a little closer.

"Lizzy, I need you to believe me. We don't have much time, and Syene is in danger if I don't make it back to her. I need you to trust me. Please. I promise I am not here to hurt you."

He extended his hand and waited. Finally, she emerged, and he could see her better in the firelight. She was half dressed, and he could see Lantz had paid her a visit, the burn mark was inflamed and clearly visible. Rage flooded his thoughts.

"Turn your head." He raised his sword and slammed it into the chain, breaking her bondage.

Enzril yanked a veil-like curtain from the ceiling and wrapped Lizzy's body with it. He scooped her up gently as she put her arms around his neck tightly.

She whispered, "Thank you."

He turned slowly when he heard the voice behind him.

"How sweet, Enzril, your wings are changing colors."

Enzril was seething. "I should destroy you, Lantz, for touching her. Among all the other sadistic, things you have done. Your soul has become sick. I have no memory of who you once were."

Lizzy buried her face into his chest, and he could feel her trembling.

"Now get out of my way." He did not want to release her but knew a battle was near.

Lantz laughed loudly. "Enzril, you know it won't be that easy. Come, my friend, surely you aren't that stupid."

Six more warriors appeared behind Lantz, including Kefira. She couldn't make eye contact with him. Enzril knew he would not make it out. Not without help.

He raised his sword. "YAHWEH! I need your mighty power now more than ever."

Lantz's laughter was that of hysteria. "Yahweh? You really are a fool!"

The blazing light flashed off Enzril's sword, violently knocking the dark warriors back. The stone ceiling came tumbling in around them as Enzril shielded Lizzy from the debris. He spread his wings, soaring high. The light was blinding, but he followed his Creator's voice to guide them out. Enzril could hear the demons screeching in agony. He flew, swift and furious, knowing Syene didn't have much time. Lizzy sobbed in his arms when she realized she was free. He held her closely until they arrived at the beach house. The angels were waiting to take her from Enzril. Amy and Ariel rushed outside as they arrived.

Enzril was gone as soon as she was delivered. He knew the urgency to get to the Sacred.

****

Syene's eyes slowly opened. She felt like someone had hit her on the head, and she struggled to sit up. She was in the office where she and Lizzy had gone to meet Apollos Drake. She should have known right then who he really was. He was standing by the glass windows the city lights were twinkling behind him. All the lights were off in the room. He turned to look at her when he heard her stir.

"Oh good, you're awake. Let me say how sorry I am about the restaurant. It seems my legions were a little too much for you."

Syene sat up, rubbing her head. "Where is Lizzy?"

He walked to her slowly. "Funny you should ask. It seems our friend Enzril wanted to play hero and rescue her."

Lucifer leaned over her, placing his hands on her wrist.

"But I guess you already knew that." Syene cried out in pain as his hands burned into her flesh.

"Now, my sweet, why don't you and I remove all of our pretenses and talk about what we really want from each other."

His human form melted away, and there standing before her was Satan, more terrifying than any nightmares. Syene found strength in knowing Enzril had saved Lizzy. Their plan had worked. Well, almost worked. It was never planned for her to be here. But some of the fear was disappearing. Lizzy was safe. She knew Elkan would be protected. There was nothing he could take from her that she cared about.

She looked at him defiantly. "I want nothing from you."

He smiled. "We will see about that."

He yanked her violently from the chair, lifting her off the ground with one hand, pressing her against his body. Syene fought but knew she could never overpower him.

"It seems some of your friends have come to join the party. Let's say you and I head to the roof so you can watch as I kill them, one by one."

She was lifted off the ground and the ceiling disintegrated before her eyes. Syene felt the rush of the night air as he flew higher. He circled the top of the building, and she could see Jamille, Michael, and Enzril waiting for them. She wanted to cry with relief when she saw them. Lucifer threw her down on the roof as they approached, and she winced in pain. He kept himself between her and her protectors. She frantically looked for a way out, but the dark angels landed, surrounding her.

Lucifer's voice roared with anger as he spoke.

"Michael! It has been so long. I would love for all of us to have a reunion, but as you can see, I have a mother to kill and a child to find."

Syene could hear his warriors snickering.

"And you, Enzril, this will make the second time you took something that belonged to me. I just can't have that behavior, especially from one of my Generals."

"Former General. I will never serve you again." Enzril sounded strong and brave to her. She heard the swords unsheathe and scrambled to a corner. Michael stepped forward; he looked as powerful as his adversary.

"You know you will never win in the end, Lucifer. There is only one ruler, and you belong to Yahweh."

Lucifer roared with anger and lunged for Michael with his sword. The battle began. She watched as Jamille fought a female dark angel. She was magnificent and powerful. She and Enzril kept close, their backs almost touching, protecting each other, as Enzril used his sword against three others appearing on the roof. Michael and Lucifer battled one-on-one, it seemed Michael was overpowering him. The swords clashed forcefully, when suddenly Michael's saber slashed into Lucifer's side. He exploded in anguish as he fell back. Dark angels swarmed the roof, protecting him as he retreated. He turned, looking at

Syene with fury. He snatched her and lifted her in front of him, his warriors stepping to the side.

"IS THIS WHAT YOU WANT? YOUR PRECIOUS SACRED?"

Syene could hear him gasping with pain. His evil penetrated the air. He thrust her in the air, and she could see Jamille move forward. She and Jamille made eye contact. Syene could see the terror in her beautiful protector's eyes. Syene held out her hand and shook her head *no*. There were too many of the dark warriors. Jamille would be overpowered. Syene saw the recognition on Jamille's face.

Lucifer roared out angrily. "THEN YOU CAN HAVE HER."

Syene closed her eyes as the sword entered her body. She heard Jamille scream as her body fell to the ground. She could hear Lucifer laughing and see him retreating with his warriors. Enzril chased after them. Jamille and Michael rushed to her side.

Jamille screamed, "No, no," over and over.

Syene looked at her and smiled. It was strange to feel her soul leaving her body, but she could feel it separating quickly from her physical form. Farrel appeared, and she was so joyous to see him, but she couldn't speak.

She watched as he pulled Jamille from her body and watched her beautiful protector collapse into his embrace.

Michael spoke softly, "I will take her, Jamille, it is time for her to go home."

****

Syene felt disoriented. She knew she was no longer in her body, and it felt strange, but free. Her soul felt sorrow for Elkan and Ariel, but she was so peaceful. It was confusing to be feeling conflicting emotions. She was grateful Michael was with her.

"How are you?" They were speaking telepathically now.

"I honestly don't know. I feel confused with different emotions."

She watched as they sped through time. Or that's what it seemed to be. It was like they were in a time machine with beautiful colors whizzing past them. And if this was her going to heaven, it was not what she had always imagined. It was dimensional, not ascending into the clouds. But this was better, she decided.

"What about Elkan?" As soon as she asked the question she could feel Elkan's sadness but also the love he was being surrounded with. She knew he would be okay, and she would be able to watch over him, always.

Things stopped as abruptly as they began, and suddenly she was in the most beautiful place she could ever imagine. It was unexplainable, the colors, the smell, but most of all the feelings. It was as if her mind had exploded with knowledge. She could feel everything around her. It was simply spectacular. It looked like places she knew but so much better.

"Oh, Michael. People don't have any idea what is waiting for them. This is unbelievable."

He looked around. "The Creator allows it to be what each soul needs it to be. Quite amazing."

He released her, and she flew. Syene looked around and could see colors spreading and expanding from her own energy. She laughed as she followed Michael across water so blue it couldn't have really been blue. There was white sand in the distance with lush mountains behind the beach. A group of dolphins began jumping out of the water with her as she flew over. She could hear them and feel their joyfulness.

"Incredible." She laughed. There were just no words to explain how she was feeling.

Michael came close, diving in and out of the water with the dolphins, he glistened beautifully. The blue of the water against his wings was breathtaking.

"Come, they are waiting."

Syene followed as he veered toward the land she could see in the distance. In an instant they slowed and were surrounded by a meadow like the one in her dreams. Huge trees and wildflowers were everywhere. The fragrance in the air was wonderous. She could see a group of souls waiting for her and immediately felt the love and welcome. Her angels were the first to greet her. They had been with her always, and they greeted her with elation. Her mom and dad were together, and the joy she felt to be with them again was fantastic. They separated as she passed, and then there it was: perfectness. How else could anyone describe the feeling of everything at once?

She stopped as Jesus stood before her, smiling as He took her forward. She looked back at Michael, who lagged back and smiled, obviously knowing what beauty was ahead for her. Her Creator was here and waiting. The Creator's presence filled every portion of her soul. Suddenly she felt everything, every emotion and thought she had ever had instantly exploded and then disappeared. She was left with no doubts, no fears, nothing but true love. True love. She finally understood and realized how wrong most humans have it. It has always been about love. Pure and simple love. Spending our human existence in constant turmoil was never what it was meant to be.

For a fleeting moment she felt disappointed she had wasted her life judging others, worrying, guessing, and then second-guessing herself. It was so simple, and the human soul made it so complicated.

The Creator was always with us. She had always been loved. ALWAYS. The love she felt surrounding her could never be verbally explained. She now knew throughout the darkest moments she was never alone. It was up to us through freewill to turn the tragedy, mistakes and disappointments into a way closer to God.

Syene felt she had failed, but the feeling was instantly gone, and she understood every soul had to learn their own purpose and lesson. She knew exactly why Jesus had to die for humankind and now understood Elkan's purpose. Love. He was sent to remind everyone to love. It would be the only thing to destroy Lucifer.

Humanity had to learn to love each other and themselves unconditionally—just as Jesus had done. He lived the example of love for everyone to understand, yet it was missed by most. Humankind fought against each other— warring, competing, judging, chasing nothing but false hope, when they were all meant to live in unity. She could feel the Creator's presence pulling away. Not leaving but only fading.

She faced Jesus. He had never left her side.

"So, you understand now? The human soul is to live out life to the fullest, keeping God always at the center. The trials and joy of life only make the experience of heaven even greater. Human creation is never left alone. Freewill is a gift, not a burden. Clinging to the Father in moments of adversity and sadness binds the soul to eternity and to me."

Syene nodded. Her soul was at peace, recognizing why Jesus came in human form. Given the chance she would do all of it again for her Creator.

"I understand. I finally understand."

"Well then, you will have the opportunity to help Elkan understand this as well."

She shook her head in confusion. "What do you mean?"

He embraced her tightly. "It is not your time, Sacred, but now you know your true purpose. It was never only about Elkan. Live your life for the Creator, help your son through his struggles. I will always be near, as I am for anyone who calls for me."

With that he was gone.

****

Syene gasped in pain. She stared up at the night sky and could hear Farrel screaming for someone to call for the ambulance. He was sobbing as he lifted her.

"Don't leave, my Syene, don't leave me." She felt his lips gently press on hers.

She smiled through the burning in her side. "Can't wait to hear how you explain this one away to the paramedics."

He laughed. "I love you, Sy. I have always loved you."

She opened her eyes to look at him. "Ditto."

Farrel held her tightly as she closed her eyes once more. She could hear the sirens in the distance.

Chapter Thirty-Four

You can make many plans, but the Lord's purpose will prevail. – Proverbs 19:21

-Years Later-

Syene sat and watched her son throw the ball on the beach for his loyal Labrador, his laughter could be heard over the ocean, and it was still just as beautiful as when he was a child. Farrel's shadow appeared over her, and she felt his hand on her shoulder.

"He has grown into an amazing young man, Sy. You should be proud."

She gently kissed the hand of the man she loved so much. "We should be proud; I couldn't have done any of this without you; without God. I honestly cannot believe how fast the years have gone by, and now he is done with medical school and ready to start a new life."

Farrel sat down, she knew he could feel her pain. He wrapped his arm around her waist, trying to reassure her. "He is going to be okay. I will be here for him." He was holding back his tears and doing everything he could to be strong for her.

Syene sighed heavily, she was telling Elkan tonight she was not going to allow him to heal her of the cancer. It was her time and she knew it. Now she needed to make her child understand.

"It is not his time to be exposed. And healing me will raise too many questions. His gift and purpose as an adult are not meant to start with his mom." Sy looked over at the man she loved so dearly, and she gently wiped the tears from his cheek.

"You know how much I love you right?"

"Of course I do, Sy. This is between you and God. I can't come between the Creator's bond, no matter how much I would like to change your mind."

She was grateful for Farrel's love and understanding. "It is not only about Elkan, I know it is my time. God has gifted so many years to me I never deserved. This part of the journey is part of His purpose and will for me; I am at peace."

Syene watched as Elkan stopped throwing the ball and stared out across the water. Her eyes roamed over the ocean for what caught his attention. She felt it before she saw it. A feeling of darkness consumed her, and she could see the large wave forming into the shape of a dragon. Instinctively she felt Farrel pull her closer and he called for Elkan as if were a young child still. But Elkan did not budge, he stood staring and seemingly unafraid, looking like a fierce warrior. Syene still had the ability to communicate with her son through the mind when needed and he was not responding. She heard him speak to the lurking evil.

"I'm coming for you. Time for the awakening."

www.ingramcontent.com/pod-product-compliance
Lightning Source LLC
Chambersburg PA
CBHW070907260626
47162CB00007B/2581